'Sums up and reshapes the rural and martial past in common on both sides of the Tasman and does so in a fashion intrepidly original…*Traitor* is brilliant, poignant and provoking…Myths and propaganda are quietly set aside. The moral imperatives to which rare (and in this case reticent) individuals can attend are strikingly set forth. Here is another arresting renovation of what maleness—and decency in anyone—might be.'
Judges' comments, Prime Minister's Literary Award

'One of the finest debut novels I have read. Indeed it's one of the best novels I have read in recent years…I want to add it to the list of great modern novels about war…There are so many breath-catching set-pieces in *Traitor* that it's a difficult pleasure to single out one.' Stephen Romei, *Australian*

'A confident and haunting exploration of the nature of betrayal…Daisley's confident handling of the complex chronology is a major strength, as is his command of narrative…All signal the debut of an important new talent.'
Listener

'Suffused with love, beauty and loneliness. The creation and development of the character of David Monroe is masterful, not least because he is a man of so few words. Also impressive is Daisley's control of structure…A rare pleasure.' *Australian Literary Review*

Stephen Daisley was born in 1955, and grew up in remote parts
of the North Island of New Zealand. He served for five years
in an infantry battalion of the NZ Army, and has worked on
sheep and cattle stations, on oil and gas construction sites and
as a truck driver and bartender, among many other jobs.

He has university degrees in writing and literature and lives
in Western Australia with his wife and five children. *Traitor* is
his first novel.

Reading group notes for *Traitor* are available at
textpublishing.com.au/resources

STEPHEN DAISLEY

TRAITOR

TEXT PUBLISHING MELBOURNE AUSTRALIA

The Text Publishing Company
Swann House
22 William Street
Melbourne Victoria 3000
Australia
textpublishing.com.au

First published by The Text Publishing Company, 2010
This edition 2011, reprinted 2011

Cover design by WH Chong
Page design by Susan Miller
Typeset by J&M Typesetters
Printed in Australia by Griffin Press, an Accredited ISO AS/NZS 14001:2004
Environmental Management System printer

National Library of Australia
Cataloguing-in-Publication data:

Daisley, Stephen

Traitor / Stephen Daisley.

2nd ed.

9781921758379 (pbk.)

World War, 1914-1918--Campaigns--Turkey--Gallipoli Peninsula--Fiction.
Soldiers--New Zealand--Fiction. Soldiers--Turkey--Fiction.

A823.4

This project has been assisted by the Commonwealth
Government through the Australia Council, its arts
funding and advisory body.

The paper this book is printed on is certified against
the Forest Stewardship Council® Standards. Griffin
Press holds FSC chain of custody certification SGS-
COC-005088. FSC promotes environmentally
responsible, socially beneficial and economically viable management of the
world's forests.

Dedicated to the memory of
C. A. Daisley—née Lal Radcliffe
1920–2009

I hate the idea of causes, and if I had to choose between betraying my country and betraying my friend, I hope I should have the guts to betray my country.

E. M. Forster

Lemnos 1915

He moved his leg and the cloud that covered him moved. And then he thought perhaps it wasn't him but the cloud that was moving his leg.

Then he knew he was on a hospital barge, crossing a white sea. A thousand bandages unravelling in its wake.

Seagulls and the shadows of seagulls followed the barge. With wings as sharp as razors they crossed above him calling *come away with us…*
  Children come away with us.

He was being touched by hands from out of the darkness. Rolled over by many hands, cold scissors along the inside of his right leg. Someone asking is that you Julia? And for the rest of his life he would never know what this meant.

The light in the surrounding darkness smelled of kerosene and Condy's crystals.
  A nurse was holding his wrist. He could feel his pulse against her fingers. He looked at her face as she studied the watch in her

other hand. She glanced at him, smiled. Looked back to the watch.

A few moments passed in silence. She put his wrist down, patted the back of his hand. Picked up a clipboard and said as she wrote, hello there Sergeant David Monroe.

She was purple and gold and ivory coloured in the light. He couldn't speak.

She leaned forward and smiled. You are a very lucky young man. A few scars is all you will have now. Make the girls love you even more. She looked at him with grey eyes. Winked and turned away.

He wanted to say, you are Irish. And, can you sing to me?

Then the wind moved the white canvas of the tent walls. They buckled like wet bedsheets on a washing line. The suspended hurricane lamps swayed. Shadows swayed.

Coughing and the creaking of cots. A groan and someone called out in their sleep *muster the Darling Ridge down to the bottom Melodies.* A hushing sound.

David closed his eyes. Clinking noises of metal instruments in enamel bowls. A hissing of lamps.

Somebody was answering a question he didn't remember asking. He is badly wounded but will be all right.

Papanui Station New Zealand 1965
Mr Monroe?

Catherine reached out and held his arm. Tugged at the cloth of his jacket.

Mr Monroe? She shook his arm.

The old man had closed his eyes and his head was tilted back. He opened his eyes and looked at her. His head was still back. He was looking at her from a great height.

Are you all right?

But it was already too late. Yes, he began to say when he felt the spiral screwing sensation come from his ring finger up and into the biceps of his left arm. He could feel the wet swishing of his urgent heart.

A daily heartbreak, he whispered. He smiled as he whispered to himself. Began to fall to his knees.

He felt them, the waves, hissing into his left arm and shoulder. Like the love thoughts of a young man. A daily betrayal of who we are. Almost laughed.

The words of Mahmoud. Always the words of Mahmoud.

He saw both knees fall into the earth.

When we are in love we think our hearts will burst. That we can fly. Our heads on fire.

He tried to say, I loved your mother Catherine more than I can say to you, but as he spoke he was gripped by a pain that doubled him over and made him cry out with no sense except his pain.

He heard her calling to him as he fell forward.

The earth was black and green and it rushed up towards him. There in the middle, far off, a circle of the brightest light.

So it was that he began to die.

Often the beckoning and wailing sound of ten thousand voices. The sound of bees. Everything he has known coming towards him as he rushes through the darkness at unimagined speeds.

And nothing will be as it was. And that which was will echo in us like the whispering of that companion who was always with us and will always be with us.

Exquisite delight, our hands touching once again as if for the first time.

For there are talismans that only we will recognise.

These are the strange and wonderful words that came to him as he fell into the earth with the weight in his chest, like that young horse falling on him in the summer of 1947. And, he thought, why should I the he of this dying and remembering recall that young horse called the Layla, which is *Night of Obscurity*; a small white mare with hairy ears and a fondness for Bartlett pears coming back on him with such clumsiness, cleaving his pelvic bones, that if it wasn't for her sweet eyes and evocative name he would have sold her to Clementine Fabish the man who wore a black raincoat even in summer.

Mahmoud is sitting on a white block of stone in the shadow of the wall. Behind him, in bright sun, there is an arch covered with a grapevine. The leaves turning orange and red in the autumn. The colours in such contrast to the white arch whose keystone mortar is crumbling. One of the stone segments has slipped, giving the arch a slightly skewed look. Small lizards sunbake and dart across the stone. Rosemary bushes and wild thyme grow among the flagstones which form a curving path into the ruin. Jerusalem rock roses, tiny and blood red, flank another low wall.

He is smiling in welcome.

Assalamu alaiküm, brother. Peace be upon you. You are coming home.

He who dies before he dies will never die. Welcome.

David is raising his hand but is unable to speak.

New Zealand 1965

He walked into the small police station at Ruatane with one of the Government Communications Security Bureau men in front of him and the other behind.

Inspector Ogden led the way and said Mr Monroe sit here thank you. Indicated the chair with his hand as he walked and did not look back.

The old man sat and looked through the high window at the passing clouds. There were two iron bars across the window. Painted white.

We have asked you to come here today Mr Monroe to clear up a few matters in relation to your service during the First World War.

The old man nodded and said yessir. He had removed his hat and was holding it in his hands.

As you probably know New Zealand has, in accordance with the ANZUS Defence Treaty, committed combat troops to Vietnam.

No sir, Vietnam?

Yes, Inspector Ogden said. He sat at the desk facing the old man. He reached into his coat pocket. Took out a packet of Camel cigarettes and a Zippo cigarette lighter.

Cigarette? He offered the packet.

No sir thank you.

Inspector Ogden extracted a cigarette from the packet and flicked open the lighter. Lit the Camel and drew the smoke into his lungs. Snapped the lighter shut.

We are, as a precaution and on advice and as a matter of routine national security, examining and questioning all those who have a cross reference to trials by court martial and or with known links to the Communist Party, conscientious objection, pacifism and Islam. You Mr Monroe tick the box, as it were, on at least four counts. Perhaps all. Smoke was trickling from both nostrils. The inspector placed his palm on a pile of yellow files. The top file was open.

I do?

Yes you do, the inspector said quickly; he had continued to stare at the file as he spoke. He looked up at the old man. His lips pressed together. I realise Mr Monroe that this occurred some time ago. Nevertheless let me assure you that what we have here is still of some concern. Considerable concern actually.

The old man nodded. Yes sir.

Very good then. The inspector moved his hand and looked down. Your service record states that in October 1915 you aided a prisoner of war to escape from detention in a camp on the island of Lemnos. That you also deserted with the said prisoner, when you were later recaptured and imprisoned you claimed to have become a conscientious objector and a pacifist. You would not take up arms against the enemy. In that case the Germans. Is this true so far?

The old man looked at his hands. His fingers holding his grey felt hat. Said yes sir. He kept looking down. Thumbs just starting to touch above the brim of the hat. His head beginning to shake, gently, from side to side.

Inspector Ogden drew on his cigarette and looked over his shoulder at Sergeant McMillan who was standing behind him with his hands loosely clasped, fingers intermeshed. Big hands and big fingers. There was black hair on the backs of his fingers and on the side of each hand. Flat broken knuckles. Sergeant McMillan raised his eyebrows and then pulled his lips in to form a thin line across his teeth. Tilted his head slightly. His nose had been broken at least once. There was a scar across the bridge.

Inspector Ogden turned back to the old man with a smile. His own father was about the same age. Said all right then, and picked up the cigarette lighter. He turned the lighter over in his fingers and frowned as he examined the emblem.

Is there anything you would like to tell us Mr Monroe?

The old man stared at the inspector. Shook his head, no sir. There is nothing.

Inspector Ogden stared at him for a moment and then looked down and opened the yellow file again, turned over two sheets of paper.

Sentenced to…The inspector paused as he read. Death. He looked up from his reading. A finger marked his place.

The old man was looking above his head out the small window with the two bars.

You were sentenced to death Mr Monroe. He tapped his finger on the page. To be shot. Is that right?

The old man barely moved his head to nod, blinked, still staring out the window. The brim of the hat moved between his fingers.

The inspector looked down and continued to read. Desertion

and aiding the enemy to escape. Pretty serious stuff. Treason. Traitorous conduct it says. You were a traitor to your country Mr Monroe is that right?

The old man made a noise in his throat like a father would make to a child who asked him a question he couldn't answer. A why is God question.

Is that right Monroe? The inspector smacked his hand down flat on the files. Is it? What do you have to say for yourself?

The old man looked at him. They were both quiet for some time.

Nothing, he said.

Nothing?

No.

They waited. Then the old man said, I have been called that. Traitor. That name. Moved his gaze away then to his left.

Really?

The old man closed his eyes. Nodded.

The inspector smoked and squinted at him. You were almost shot Mr Monroe. Executed.

Yes, the old man said, cleared his throat. His eyes were still closed. They were short of stretcher bearers. There were some other considerations. The Australian boys refused to carry it out. It was a different time. The sentence was commuted to twenty years hard labour and I served out the war as a stretcher bearer. France, then Belgium. Another six months in Germany with the occupation force. I received a full pardon. And I came home then.

The old man spoke as if reciting something rehearsed. Lost all privileges, he said. Pensions or grants. Medals. All that.

Then he opened his eyes and nodded towards the yellow files. Should all be in there.

The inspector paused, looked at him for a while, nodded. Your file, Mr Monroe mentions a probability of you converting to Islam. I suppose you have heard of El Hajj Malik El Shabazz?

The old man sat back in his chair. Who?

El Hajj Malik El Shabazz.

No. No sir.

Also known as Malcolm X.

No sir. I am a shepherd. I am getting older now. I have worked on Papanui Station since I came back from the war. It was forty-five or something years ago. 1920. Sir, I have to get back. At the moment it is lambing, the early ewes are all along the river flats. There are over five hundred head of the earlies.

He was shot to death this year. By his own people, fellow Muslims. They used a sawn-off shotgun and pistols. A mess. But you would know all about those things Mr Monroe. You and your fellow Muslims. Is that your name? David Monroe?

The old man recognised these questions, it had been years but he had been asked such questions before. What was being asked was different. How was the same.

The old man looked out the window. The clouds were building. It would be another wet night. Bad for the lambs. Some blue sky appeared between the cloud mass. Early afternoon sun broke through and shone on the glass.

Inspector Ogden was still speaking.

Malcolm X as you may know was a member of The Nation of Islam. Americans with a hatred of America. Inspector Ogden cleared his throat. We are in a defence treaty with the United States of America. ANZUS. And we are committing to a war with America against the communist threat in South East Asia.

The old man was looking above the inspector's head. He could see the sun coming through the window and illuminating a rectangular piece of wall. Two bar shadows lay across the rectangle.

You must understand Mr Monroe why we would wish to ask you a few questions. Given your service record. Are you also a communist? As well as everything else Mr Monroe?

The old man was silent.

I am speaking to you Mr Monroe or is it Mohammed el something or other I don't want to say what? Do you hate America?

The old man thought about saying it is unusual how wide you open your mouth to speak Inspector. I am sure you could touch the end of your nose with the tip of your tongue. You move it a lot. You have a very mobile tongue.

Instead he said, not yet.

Inspector Ogden stood up.

The atmosphere in the room became still. Sergeant McMillan moved his head around his shoulders as boxers do. Watched.

Inspector Ogden stared at the old man as if taking in what he had just said. He looked down and squeezed his lips together. Then he laughed. You are probably right.

The old man was looking out the window above the inspector's head.

Not yet, the inspector said.

I don't know anything about America.

The inspector came out from behind the desk and was standing in front of the sergeant. He said something quietly.

The sergeant nodded.

We are stepping out for a moment Mr Monroe. They left the interview room.

The old man heard the door lock behind them. He sat there quite still. Looked at the glass of the window. In his small musterer's hut, when the afternoon sun was at a certain angle, he could see himself reflected in the glass.

Do you see the glass, what is beyond the glass or yourself in the glass?

It was Mahmoud who had taught him to ask such questions. Such is the way of learning how to know, he had said. Who is asking such questions? Is this acquired? Or revealed? David, he would say, raising his voice, pointing at him. You David. Is this acquired knowledge or revealed knowledge? I ask you so because I love you so.

The mirror always made him remember the second time he had seen Mahmoud. It was always the second time that came to him first.

He saw his face in the mirror and sometimes his face became Mahmoud's face. It transformed before his eyes. Now isn't that the strangest thing? The words were almost like a song. Or an invocation. The second time. It was on the Island of Lemnos; Mahmoud was sitting on a hospital cot, gently rocking back and forth, reciting verse. He was watching where the sun and shadows came into the tent entrance of the Wounded Turkish Officers Lines. Fifty years ago.

The man's face was pale; the sun touched it, making it paler against the blackness of his beard. His head was bare and shaved; and now he had only one foot. He had removed the bandages from the amputation. A red bony stump bisected by a neat row of black stitches. The strips of cotton crepe lay in a tangle by the remaining foot on which he had put a leather sandal. He was reading from a small book held in his hands.

There was a plate of white cheese blocks and green olives near his hip. A fig. Five or six cigarettes and a box of English matches. The photograph of a smiling woman with a headscarf. A small ink drawing of a mosque, another of unknown calligraphy.

He had looked up at David. He was wearing glasses. Thick lenses with wire frames. When the man moved his head to look at him, David saw a flash of sunlight reflected in the lenses. It blinded him for a moment. He blinked in the blackness. The man on the cot smiled and said, *assalamu alaiküm*; hello thank you Johnny.

Raised a bandaged hand. Only two fingers no thumb. The ring and little. The bandages were ink stained.

The marks under his eyes like bruises.

He took off his glasses. A gesture of courtesy, dipping his head.

His wounds, his smile, the reflected sunlight made David step to one side. He moved his head to the left and then his feet. Blinked. Began to raise a hand.

Then he began to weep. He had no control. The tears came, that was all.

He said nothing. Continued looking down so the man he would know as Mahmoud would not see his tears. Lowered his hand and squeezed the bridge of his nose. He did not understand this reaction in himself. He had never wept like this. Except perhaps when he was sixteen and his mother was drowned. He opened his mouth. Breathed in and then, pursing his lips, out. Cleared his throat.

He looked up, wiped away the tears and said hello to you too Mehmet. Don't thank me. My name is not Johnny. It is David.

Mahmoud smiled, shook his head and said something in a language David did not understand, nodded to him. His hand still raised. He would tell David one day soon he had been so moved by the tears that he said, thank you God. And, God is truly great.

My name is Mahmoud. Spoken in fine, clear English. Not Mehmet. How are your wounds? Cigarette?

David thought, my wounds are nothing, look at you. Missing bits. A foot. A bloody patched-up mess. Said instead, no.

No?

No I don't want a cigarette.

Olive?

No. Cheese either, David said. No cheese. I came here to give you something. Here. He held out a small flat can.

Sardines?

From Scotland.

David put the can of fish down next to the plate of olives.

Thank you, Mahmoud said and smiled.

He would say later the tears are trying to wash away our made selves. When we encounter someone, something, that moves us

15

to weep spontaneously we have somehow encountered the very core of our existence. We have met, come upon, the most sacred part of our being. Our Godliness. It is here we are most terribly vulnerable and most terribly strong.

Then he began to recite a verse in Persian. Stopped and said forgive me. This is from a blessed poet of my country. He speaks to God. My language is the most beautiful to express this love of God. But of course my friend I am a little biased.

David had then no idea what Mahmoud was talking about. He shook his head and wanted to weep again.

Instead he said, my name is David. David Monroe. Pleased to know you Mahmoud. I am from New Zealand. He put out his hand. I am a shepherd. I am a Methodist. A Wesleyan. That is what I have been told I am at least. I don't own land I work for other men. I believe in Jesus and I am not sure what that means either. But I do. I am sorry I could not have done more. For you. Mah, um ma um med.

Mahmoud tilted his head to one side. Looked at his bandaged hand. It was the left.

Said, David. Waited. Said I too believe in the prophet Jesus. Peace be upon Him. And his mother Mary.

Looked up at him. David shook his head.

The silence between them like an enormous question.

Mahmoud spoke, still looking at David. He spoke as if singing, bless you now don't apologise for being who you are do not ever apologise for being who you are I too believe the most blessed saint Jesus was of God. I believe the blessed Jesus, praise His name, peace be upon Him, was an Essene, a prophet who died for love. You are God we are all gods. I also believe He, Jesus, was a secret Sufi.

Some believe this is blasphemy, I do not. I do not. Many of my faith would execute me for such beliefs. I am a fool and a dog. There is no hope for me. Do you hear me?

He reached out and took David's outstretched hand. Held it. There is a hadith from our Prophet that mentions that a man who wears wool lacks an ego. And you are a wool farmer who works for other men. So, there we are. Humility is the first step.

David said nothing. He did not know what to say. He understood very little of what he was hearing. But he knew he had not felt such peace in the presence of another for as long as he could remember. He felt forgiven. And capable of anything. He just smiled and again the tears welled into his eyes.

Mahmoud shook David's hand and then held his undamaged hand up towards David's face as if to touch the tears. Brought that back to his lips. Nodded. Held up his other, bandaged hand. Smiled. But there is no hope.

David frowned. I, he said and then smiled.

Just as well the British navy took most of my left isn't it? Mahmoud said. And what is God telling me? This fool Mahmoud who sits before you now? What do I know?

And they both remembered as they looked at each other how they had been trying to save the life of an Australian boy with a black thumbnail not a week earlier.

By the way David my name is Mahmoud. That is Mah, moud. Not Mahmed and Memmet. Or even Mohammed, Mahmoud said and laughed very gently. Spelled out the letters to his name.

It was the first time David had heard any Turk laugh. His teeth were so white. Thought, he is teasing me, and smiled.

Look at how the sun comes into the tent David. Mahmoud pointed to where the afternoon sun was falling on the ground just outside the tent. Across the ground, he said, like the footsteps of a beautiful woman. Like Layla, the Night of Obscurity, would come if she could to the mad man who loved her more than life itself. His name was Quais but he became a mad man for love and so that is what he was known as, Majnun, mad man, a drunken lion exiled to the wilderness. He would write love poems on slips of paper and cast them to the desert wind.

David said nothing, again he had no idea what Mahmoud was talking about. But then he said yes. And the two names Layla and Majnun but he tried to pronounce it as Mahmoud had Majj-noon.

Mahmoud was laughing again and then he stopped. He bit his bottom lip. And he nodded and said you are beautiful. It means the absorption into a single thought and it also means mad man knowing nothing of good and evil. A disgrace.

That was the second time. It was always the second time that he remembered first.

It came every day. Like the heartbreak in his chest. He had never been called God before.

⁓

The first time he had seen Mahmoud.

The first time made him want to hold his hand up to wave something away. Say *aaaah* and no. *Sssssh*. Be quiet.

He was wearing a red crescent armband, had what appeared to be scissors in his bearded mouth and was bent over the convulsing body of the young Australian man who called out fuck this and *jesus*.

They were in a small hollow on the seaward side of a ridge less than three yards wide. A spur off Ari Burno.

The Australian's hands were big and a thumbnail was black. It was on his left hand. He reached out with that hand, grasping at the air. The other hand was grabbing at the ground. He had vomited. He was badly wounded. In arms and leg and body. The hair on one side of his head was burnt off.

His blood had begun to coagulate into a jellied pool beneath him. He was splashing in it. Crying out in the pain of his wounds *who who who*... His hips were thrusting up and down as if he was trying to get up. Where are you Tom? Tom I am bleeding. It is. Sorry sorry I can't. Who the fuck are you bastard?

Mahmoud was trying to hold him and press down on where the most blood was coming from. It was high on his right thigh, almost in the groin. There was a lot of white powder; a medical pad and a khaki bandage unravelled away to their right that had stopped uselessly against a small rosemary bush.

The old man remembered what Mahmoud had said before the howling British naval shell came over them.

He took the scissors out of his mouth and pointed at David. Please. You. Yes you with the open mouth. Take his feet. Don't point that at me. Just...just bloody help.

Such clear English. Almost no accent. Almost British. Then he said, he doesn't have any bloody hope if we don't. The femoral.

He remembered how huge and sluggish he felt, standing there with a rifle and bayonet. This Turk pointing scissors at him; he pointing a bayonet at the Turk. Not knowing what the femoral was.

The Turk looked up at him and said do you speak English?

19

David still wanted to shoot him. Felt vaguely offended that this Turk had asked him if he spoke English.

Parlez-vous Français?

David said English. New Zealander. Help him…

But even as he said it he felt stupid. It was obvious the Turk was already trying to.

Good, I am a doctor. Of course I am helping him. What do you think? Do you understand? His helmet, lying on its side, was next to the Australian boy.

He could see the exposed webbing and blackened sweat band. There was a small, jewelled book in the helmet, tucked up in the top of it.

The Turk, this doctor, this man who would become Mahmoud, looked up at him. His eyes were a dark blue and he was wearing glasses. He frowned at the dying Australian, nodding to David in urgency. Said come on, are you an idiot? Put that damned thing down and hurry up. Please for God. For Allah. For this one. Wake up. Please, I beg you.

He remembered how white the man's teeth seemed within the black beard. His hands were bloody. Head shaved. The rubber band holding his glasses dug into the skin of his head. Beards were unusual. Most of the Turks had moustaches only.

Thank you.

He had kneeled to hold the boots of the Australian who still was trying to get up and roll away from where he was. He pulled his legs together and down to keep him still and the right leg from just above the knee came away in his hand. He thought I have pulled his leg completely off.

Part of the trousers material was attached. The bone ends

ragged. The femoral artery was like a hose. The Australian was growling now, deep in his throat, convulsing, shivering. David heard the words coming out of the boy's chest: *Who who mum mum mumm.*

Mahmoud said nothing. And looked at him. David remembered he had shining eyes. Dark blue shining eyes. And the dark blood pulsing against his hand as he tried to stop it. He bent over the Australian's body, searching for the artery. Pushing aside tissue, muscle and sinew. He began speaking, chanting in a language David didn't understand.

He was sweating and yet worked frantically, wiping his forehead with his shoulder and bloody biceps as he searched.

Shook his head and began to tie a tourniquet. Said damn it, in English. This will have to do now. Was twisting the scissors around a tourniquet bandage to stop the bleeding.

David couldn't stop staring at him. He still held the two legs of the Australian. One loose in his hand.

They aren't like this he thought. They aren't like this. I am not an idiot.

From away to their left and below them came a series of cheers and hurrahs. Whistles, and the machine guns.

And then they all exploded. The three of them. They went up into the air and over the side of the spur, torn apart.

That was the first time.

He always hated the first time and the memory of the Australian boy's leg in his hand. It no longer belonged. Legs and feet shouldn't be so light. They should belong together.

Mahmoud would say later, on Lemnos, what about his mother?

What comfort for her? Her tears? We must never forget that. Or them. There is a saying, Paradise lies beneath the feet of our mothers.

But not then.

Then they all should have died.

The old man heard the door unlock. The two government men re-entered the room.

The sergeant stood again by the door and again crossed his hands in front of himself while the inspector walked around behind the desk. The inspector sat down and then leaned to one side and took his cigarettes and lighter out of his pocket.

Have you Mr Monroe, for the last time, anything you would like to tell us?

The old man looked at Inspector Ogden, paused and then said, well we all should have died but we didn't.

Immediately regretted saying it.

What? The inspector was lighting another cigarette. Made a *mmm* sound with his mouth as he did it. Snapped the lighter shut.

No. Nothing, sorry sir.

What do you mean nothing? You said something Mr Monroe. He tapped the cigarette in the ashtray.

The old man remembered a prayer rug Mahmoud had posted to him just after the war. It had been waiting for him when he arrived back at the Papango Valley. He still had it on the wall of his small cottage. Woven into the edge was a verse from *Jalal al-Din*. It was written in Persian script; he knew only the translation. He thought of repeating some of the lines to the inspector. Decided against it and whispered to himself *You are the cure hidden in the pain. / Concealed in anger and betrayal / Everywhere on earth*

What is it Monroe? Inspector Ogden was frowning. What are you talking about? Are you not feeling well?

Nothing, the old man said. Nothing sir sorry, he repeated. I was just thinking aloud about my job. I have to get around the early ewes. It is lambing time.

He had learned enough to be careful when addressing men from the government. He shook his head, looked down and made a noise as if shushing himself. *Shhist.*

The inspector stared at him for a moment and then gave a small cough. Puffed on his cigarette, drew on it again as he exhaled the smoke. The smoker's double tap. Gave another short cough and cleared his throat.

He waited and smoked and stared at the old man.

Then the inspector leaned forward and stubbed the cigarette out as he spoke. Well I think I have heard about enough, he said. All pretty harmless now I think. How old are you Mr Monroe?

I was born in 1892. I am seventy-three.

And you have never left New Zealand since you returned from the war in 1920?

No sir.

You have worked as a shepherd on the station. He looked down at the file open on the desk in front of him. On Papanui Station ever since you returned?

I have sir.

Do you send any correspondence overseas? Letters? Parcels?

No sir.

Do you receive any correspondence from overseas?

The last letter I received was from Mahmoud's wife Aisha.

Who?

Aisha. Mahmoud's wife.

Elsa? The inspector mispronounced her name. Imsa? Yes? Wrote something on his pad.

The old man's head was shaking but he made an affirming noise. Cleared his throat. Whispered, Aisha yes.

And she wrote to you in regard to? The inspector said, lit another cigarette and squinted against the smoke.

His death. The old man nodded, yes and looked up at the window with the two white bars across it.

Sorry?

She wrote to tell me Mahmoud had been hanged.

The inspector studied the old man. Made a small cough and then asked, hanged?

Yes. That is what she wrote.

The old man reached down and scratched the inside of his calf. Straightened and sat still.

This Ma ma person the inspector said, how do you say his name? Turning the cigarette lighter end for end as he spoke.

Mahmoud.

He was your friend? The one you helped? The Turk you helped escape and was court martialled for?

Yes sir.

And they hanged him?

Yes sir they did.

Who? Who hanged him?

The Turkish government. And the leader of Turkey at the time. His name was Ataturk I believe. Kemal. His jailors. Aisha said his name meant perfection or something. Father of the Turks, something like that. The chosen one.

And why, the inspector said, did they hang him for Christ's sake?

He was a Sufi, the old man said.

Yes, and that is? The inspector made an encouraging gesture with his hand.

A man who wears wool and believes in God. I can't really say. I am not able…

What's that Monroe? What's wrong with you?

The old man had stopped speaking and then suddenly put his hand to his bearded mouth, his face contorted.

Sorry, he said and then again. Sorry. Sorry. I am so. He was. The old man held up his hand, away from his mouth in apology. He didn't. Mahmoud, he. He would hate me acting like this.

And, he thought, he would nod in forgiveness.

Then there was the moment when they all felt the room become very still. The light changed as cloud crossed the sun and then moved on.

There was still nothing said. Another darker cloud; the light in the room became quite dim. The sergeant standing at the door said shall I? Indicated the light switch.

Inspector Ogden nodded. Continued to stare at the old man. Go on Monroe he said.

The old man sniffed and continued to speak. That was in 1920-something from memory. Forty years ago. I still have the letter. I have never written a letter to overseas. I never knew where they lived. Mahmoud said it is for the best. There was a war with the Greeks.

The sergeant switched on the light.

26

The air in the room was pale blue with cigarette smoke.

Go on, the inspector said again.

No no letters since the 1920s. 1922, 1923 at the latest, the old man said. Sniffed again and wiped his hand across his eyes.

Inspector Ogden watched the old man who sat there again looking down at his hands holding the hat. His finger squeezing the point of the crown between thumb and index and middle fingers. Giving it shape.

I see, the inspector said. He cleared his throat. Said, very good.

They all seemed to be waiting.

The inspector asked 1922?

The old man nodded.

I think it was. 1922 or 23. Yes.

Inspector Ogden leaned forward and stared at him again for what seemed like a long time.

Then he said, it's 1965. Bit of a wild goose chase this one Sergeant. He continued to stare at the old man while speaking to the sergeant. Forty bloody years ago. Long enough I'd warrant. This silly old bugger is pretty bloody harmless. Made a big mistake I would say.

Sir. Sergeant McMillan said and moved his feet.

You can go now, Inspector Ogden said and looked down at the file. Closed it. What on earth were you thinking Monroe?

The old man looked into Inspector Ogden's eyes and said I don't know.

We have no more questions for you. The inspector stood up and put his cigarettes and lighter in his pocket.

Maadi Camp Egypt 1916

After the charges had been read the officers sat down. Their swords and spurs rattled.

The major nodded to the regimental sergeant major.

Escorts and prisoner stand at ease.

What on earth were you thinking Sergeant Monroe? the major asked.

David looked at the three officers seated behind the camp trestle tables. A covering of khaki felt was stretched across the tables on which there were thick books and water jugs beside the officers. On the left there was a Coldstream Guards lieutenant in a scarlet uniform. A New Zealand Army major in the centre and an Australian Army captain on the right. They all wore parade uniforms and ceremonial swords at their sides beneath the table. When they moved their feet or buttocks in their chairs, David could hear the metallic rattle of the scabbards and hilts. Behind them, pinned to the canvas wall of the tent, there was a Union Jack and a New Zealand ensign.

The three officers each had a pen, an inkwell and a notepad in front of him. A Holy Bible and a copy of King's Regulations.

A corporal orderly waited in attendance at one side.

David stood silently at ease, hands behind his back, feet shoulder width apart. He was dressed in a plain cotton field uniform, hatless and beltless. Still with his sergeant's chevrons on the sleeves.

He was flanked by two sergeants, men of equal rank, in full parade uniform and behind them the regimental sergeant major.

A shining brass-topped parade pace stick under his arm.

Well? The Guards lieutenant said. Speak up man.

David looked at the canvas wall behind them between the flags. The air in the tent smelled of sun-hot canvas.

The lieutenant turned to the major. Can he speak sir? Does he understand English?

The major nodded. Yes Lieutenant, until he was wounded off a Sari Bair ridge, Sergeant Monroe had an exemplary record. Mentioned in dispatches and recommended for field promotion by his battalion commander for actions on the Chunuk Bair heights. Unfortunately Colonel Maloney was later killed. The major looked away to his left for a moment. Colonel Maloney had been a friend. Then nodded. Looked up at David again. Very well, he said.

The Australian captain was writing something on his pad.

A large fly buzzed through the tent. They could hear some *Maadi* food vendors outside the tent.

Eggs a cook for you General Colonel?

Fuck off Abdul before I kick you in your arse.

You no want?

The major turned and motioned to the orderly. The corporal bent and listened to the major. Would you Corporal? He pointed in the direction of the tent entrance.

Very good sir.

The corporal marched out of the tent. They could hear him shooing off the food vendors.

As the corporal re-entered the tent, the major raised a hand. Stay out there would you Corporal there's a good fellow? Keep any locals at bay.

Sir.

The major refocused his attention on David.

Sergeant Monroe I ask you now if you have anything to say for yourself?

David blinked. No sir.

The major nodded, looked down at his notes and the charge sheet in front of him. Put an index finger on top of his moustache and read. He was still looking down when he said, it says here you did not want any legal representation. No officer appointed to represent you. Is this the case?

Yes sir.

Do you understand the serious nature of these charges? These are offences which carry capital punishment Sergeant.

Yes sir David said.

The Australian captain looked up from his writing and whispered something to the major. The major nodded.

You do understand the nature of the charges brought before you Sergeant? The Australian captain repeated the major's words and spoke in a more clipped and military manner.

Oh yes sir.

The Australian said, what is your regimental number? Quickly man.

L45918. Sir. David replied automatically.

The captain stared at him and then nodded. Very good. He wrote something on the pad.

The major turned a page. There was silence in the tent. He made an *ah ha* sound. Looked up and addressed David.

Do you suffer from headaches Sergeant? From your head wounds?

No sir.

The medical reports say that you had shrapnel wounds to the

head, face and back. Backside and legs. I can see the wounds from here and the top of that one ear.

Mostly superficial the doctor said sir. Healed now.

Do you believe you are thinking clearly?

The lieutenant put his hand to his mouth and cleared his throat. Blinked and mouthed *for God's sake*.

More than ever sir.

What do you mean?

David shook his head. Doesn't matter sir.

You have freely admitted to the charges brought before you of desertion, aiding an enemy officer to escape, theft of both medical supplies and military ordinance.

David was silent. He continued to stare at the canvas wall and flags behind the officers.

The major lifted a glass and took a drink of water. The tent was silent. The intestines of the sergeant on David's left made a long gastric squeal. The major looked up from the glass at the noise. The sergeant moved his feet and the regimental sergeant major made a slight hissing noise.

The major put the glass down and looked at David.

Sergeant Monroe. The final sentence will be cabled from General HQ in Cairo but I suggest you prepare yourself for very bad news. I must ask you now and for the last time. Do you have anything to say in your defence? Go on now for goodness sake man.

David looked down and then back up at the major. I cannot explain what I did sir. It was like I became I don't know what. I just felt enormous affection even love for this man. He said that his face was the often repeated seven and that his only ascension to Paradise was by the scaffold. He kissed me on the mouth and called me God. Named me, in love, Mohammed which means

31

he who should be praised. He said that to proclaim I am the truth is a death sentence...

A sword rattled in its hilt and one of the officers coughed.

I beg your pardon? Excuse me Sergeant. Sir I...say. The Guards lieutenant turned to the major. This is somewhat irregular. He must be unbalanced, become mad sir.

David ignored the Guards lieutenant, kept speaking.

And he said it was a mirror, that I was seeing the love that I was capable of. That which is in me. In all of us. I don't know what it all means. I just know...

What is all this babble Sergeant? The Guards lieutenant interrupted once again. I have never heard the like.

I felt an overwhelming love for this man sir. The so-called enemy. I don't understand it. But I don't think you have to, do you?

Are you a homosexual? The lieutenant leaned forward, staring at David.

David frowned. Mahmoud said what we see in others is often a mirror of ourselves.

One of the escort sergeants laughed. The RSM hissed, shut up man. He had not moved. He cleared his throat, gaze fixed straight ahead.

The officers were staring at him. The Australian smiling, his eyes wide. The Guards lieutenant standing, hands on hips. The New Zealand major was red faced, embarrassed, furious.

March him out Sar'major he said, pointing. I have heard enough. This is completely out of order. See to him will you.

Sir. The RSM saluted. Hold him escorts, the RSM said. Take his arms. About turn.

They turned awkwardly.

By the front. Quick march. Left right left right left.

They held his arms and marched out of the tent.

Mark time.

The RSM halted and turned at the tent's entrance. Sirs, he said and saluted.

The three officers were standing and returned his salute.

They followed the duckboards across the sand towards the ancient fort that was the prison.

When they reached the interior of the prison the RSM called out: escorts and prisoner halt. He approached David. There was a dried mud and stone wall behind him. Glass shards embedded in the cement. What the devil was that all about Monroe?

I doubt if you…

The RSM stabbed the pace stick into his solar plexus. David doubled over. He could not get his breath. His mouth was open and he closed it and opened it again, like a fish in a boat. A high moaning noise came out of his mouth.

You. The RSM bent over and spoke into his ear. You. And then he drove his knee up into David's face, breaking his nose and mashing both lips against his teeth. One of his front teeth broke off.

David's head snapped back and then he fell to his knees. Spat out his tooth.

Fucking you. The RSM put his foot on David's shoulder and pushed him over. He sprawled off the duckboards onto the sand. He reached up and held his face. Blood was pouring out of his nose and covering his mouth and chin. A coating of yellow sand clung to the blood.

The RSM turned to the escort. Sergeants. I want you two to take this sorry bastard also known as the attempting to escape prisoner to his cell. I want a gag in his stupid stupid mouth; his gear off; a sandbag over his head and I want him handcuffed, standing up. There is to be no water or food in his cell until I say so. Is this clear?

Sar'major, both the sergeants said and nodded.

And then we will see who loves fucking who eh?

David did not know how long it had been. About a day he thought. Perhaps two.

He was naked and gagged, hooded. He had been handcuffed to the wall of the cell. He had been unable to sit or lie down. His feet were grotesquely swollen and he had fainted at least twice. The agony of his hands when he had fallen with his weight on them had awakened him. There was nothing but blackness. His mouth was dried out with the rag that had been pushed into it. The broken tooth throbbed. His throat was raw and with every breath through his nose he felt red needles running beneath his eyes and into his face and larynx and trachea. His throat constricted and seemed to cling to itself. It seemed to become a separation from who he was and begged him for water.

He had begun to speak to himself through the rag ball in his mouth. His words were not words but just sounds; he knew the words he spoke in his mind were spoken to some other entity that the betrayer, his body, had become. Saying *sssh* and no I cannot. Please what do you want?

He had urinated and defecated. There is no other way of it you see. The faeces had run down his legs. His hands were black from the congestion of blood.

He was coming in and out of the agony of consciousness, of being in the horror of here and out into a dream of floating in a lake beneath a sky filled with mare's tails and feeling the cold currents of the deep water coming up beneath his back.

He woke as his hands were unshackled. Someone was saying, you stink, *jesus christ* Monroe, you have shit yourself. Sar'major look at his hands.

Get some water. Take off the sandbag and let's be having him. Outside. Wash him down.

David felt the water splashing over him. He opened his mouth and caught some of the water. His eyes burned with the blinding brightness of the sun. Through the slits that were his eyes he could see pairs of boots and khaki puttees.

Hands helped him to sit. Someone whispered sorry Monroe. Sorry mate. Oh my godfather.

All right then. Give him a drink and then let him rest. Put a blanket on him.

His hands seem to be good enough. It was the RSM's voice. He cleared his throat.

You are being sentenced tomorrow Monroe. You say anything of this and I will fucking make what little time you have left even more miserable. He cleared his throat again. Said, I will. Mark my words.

David was lying on his side. He had been put in the shade of the wall and was shivering from the shock and the water. The sun-warm woollen blanket across his shoulders held great comfort. His body shuddered and he held his hands out into the sunlight. He nodded and made a noise of acceptance.

The RSM looked down at him. Touched his leg with the pace stick. You hear me?

David nodded again and said nothing. He watched the sun on his black hands. He began to move his fingers, turned them towards each other. The fingers and thumbs just, gently, touched. A tingling sensation made them jerk. That was enough for now. The sun, and that he could feel his fingers touching each other.

He whispered yes Trevor.

The RSM blinked and bit his lip, shook his head and looked up and over his shoulder. Made that noise in his throat again. Looked back at David and said, I lost my temper Monroe it was the shit you talked I...you shouldn't have said that stuff. The fucking English look down their noses at us enough now. We have to be better than them.

David was nodding, whispered, don't worry it is all right Trevor. It is.

The RSM stopped. He turned to the sergeant. Get a medic to look at his hands and feet and feed him some soup. He needs to be ready for sentencing tomorrow.

The RSM cleared his throat for the last time, put the pace stick under his arm and marched away from the prison courtyard.

It is my sad duty to tell you Sergeant David John Monroe that the court martial convened here finds you guilty of desertion, aiding an enemy officer to escape and theft. It is the ruling of the court martial that you have become a traitor to your King, your country and the Empire and therefore that you be taken from this place of trial and be executed by firing squad. The sentence is to be carried out immediately. May God have mercy on your soul.

All three officers stood up to attention. Each wore a black armband. The New Zealand major and Australian captain did not look at him. They looked straight ahead, their faces set. The Guards lieutenant smiled at him and moved his head down and looked at him beneath his brows. An ancient gesture of superiority.

David nodded. He looked down. Began to tremble. He brought his hands around and formed them into a bowl. The thumbs touched. The British smile seemed so cruel that all his earlier stoicism evaporated. Suddenly he understood that he was going to be shot to death. Whispered, Mahmoud? O God. Dry retched then.

Escorts, the RSM said with a firm but low voice. Hold him. The RSM stood to attention and saluted.

The inside of the cell was dark. David could see nothing. He was staring straight ahead into the darkness as if waiting for something to be revealed to him. He sat on the bed in the cell and knew when he heard the marching steps that it was the time. The approaching cadence of hobnails on the stones had a clashing sound that could only mean the time had come.

He whispered, Mahmoud. Thought, help me. Help me to die well. I am so terribly frightened. It is not supposed to be like this.

The voice of Mahmoud was saying to him *courage and dignity are manifest in an individual but are of the cosmos in origin. Once we understand that we may simply surrender everything of who we thought we were and just ask.*

Light appeared under the cell door. The sound of keys. The cell door opened and the RSM and the escort sergeants stepped in. The two escort sergeants were carrying Coleman lamps. They held them up at shoulder height.

You, the RSM said. Stand up Monroe.

David stood. The pale yellow lights of the Coleman lamps swayed and met and threw shadows around the walls.

The Australians won't do it the RSM said. That Guards lieutenant almost had a bloody seizure.

David said nothing. He offered his hands to the RSM.

The Aussie boys told them to go fuck themselves they will not shoot one of their own. That's what they called you. One of them threatened to give the Guards lieutenant a hiding. Spank his arse he said. Called the lieutenant a *fucking-cunt*. David heard one of the escorts stifle a laugh.

There are no other troops available. They have all been shipped off to France. There is only the Australian Light Horse left awaiting deployment to Palestine. They refuse to carry out executions. Especially of Australians or New Zealanders it seems. They know about your service at the Cove. They know what you did. Most of them just said turn it up mate where's the right of it? Y'know in that bloody Aussie accent they have?

The RSM cleared his throat. He started to speak again and a high-pitched snort came from his nose. He shook his head and laughed. Bloody Aussies. Aren't they bloody wonderful?

Then after a moment he regained control and said, sit down Monroe.

David sat down. He held his hands in front of himself, again like a bowl, thumbs just touching. His whole body continued to shake.

Yet again the RSM cleared his throat.

What the major is officially saying is that he is appealing to HQ in Cairo for a review, given your service. But it is to save face. To avoid a possible embarrassment. Even whiffs of mutiny he said.

There will be clemency shown I feel, is what the major said. And that I could convey that to the prisoner. Demoted to private of course. A prison term. Probably in France with field punishments. There is some talk of penal units or battalions like the French have. Clearing mines and carrying supplies. There we are.

One of the sergeants holding the lamp sneezed.

David looked at the RSM. Whispered thank you Trevor. You are a good man.

The RSM was staring at David. I still think you are what you are Monroe. A bloody idiot.

I know Trevor. I know you think that.

As acting RSM my rank should be Warrant Officer First Class. Bob Brierly was, as you probably know, killed on the Daisy Patch. I am awaiting promotion to the appropriate rank for RSM but for now my rank is Warrant Officer Second Class. You Monroe will address me as such. Not Trevor. Is that clear?

Yes Sar'major.

The old man stood outside the Ruatane police station. Closed his eyes and breathed in the late-afternoon air. A wet, cold smell with somewhere the tang of woodsmoke through it.

Opened his eyes and looked at the small town. The main street was wide and there were no trees in the street and the buildings were all built since 1914.

A bushfire had destroyed the town and thousands of acres of felled bush in the late summer of 1912. A great roaring destructive thing it was. He remembered how the land seemed to moan and shift and then wail as the fire came over it. The day become night.

It's bloody biblical all right, Bluey Finer the head shearer in his gang had said.

He looked across the street at the Ruatane Hotel. It was single storey and made of Huntly brick, pale and dappled black. Two mud-splattered and dented Land Rovers were parked diagonally in front of the hotel. Dogs were chained alongside them.

Directly across from that was a Caltex service station. Reynolds Motors painted in large black letters. Repairs and Petrol. Refreshments. Rust stains had bled from where the sign was fixed to the wall.

To his left was the general store.

A blackboard with *Rua Spuds* written in yellow chalk. *10 shilling a sugarbag.*

It was a three-mile walk back to the Papango Valley and Papanui Station. The government men had offered him the use of a telephone but he declined.

The old man hadn't moved at first when the inspector said there were no more questions. After a few moments, Inspector Ogden had looked at his watch and said you can go now Mr Monroe, thank you. Repeated to himself, bit of a bloody wild goose chase. Forty bloody years ago. Who next?

Sergeant McMillan had said all right old timer?

Yes, the old man said as he stood up, I'm all right.

He crossed the wide street and entered the general store. As usual the owner Chung Moon stood behind the glass-topped counter. A full white apron. Suit and tie.

Ah, he said, Mr Monroe, long time. His accent reversed the 'r's and 'l's. Long time became rong time. No see. Bull sale last time. Yes.

Afternoon Mr Moon.

Chung Moon chuckled. This old man mad Dave, shell-shocked Monroe, was one of the few who still accorded him the respect of a title. Not Chung or the more insulting Mooney. Never mocked his accent. Carazy man. They all too should be carazy like him.

What you want? Chung Moon said still smiling.

The old man pointed towards a line of glass confectionery jars.

Which one?

Those peppermints.

You always get these ones. Ten shilling. Chung Moon laughed again. Everything was 'ten shilling', followed by an inviting chuckle.

I have no money on me Mr Moon. I'll pay you the next time.

OK OK, Chung Moon smiled and shook his head. Passed the old man a white paper bag of peppermints. Tuppence only. Next time. Bull sale. No idea. Mr Moon laughed then, a little shrilly and shook his head once again. You, he said. You funny bugger you. I don't know.

Thank you Mr Moon.

He left the store and stood under the veranda for a moment. Took a peppermint and put the bag in the pocket of his coat. Then he moved to his right and sat on a bench seat. Behind the seat was a red and black advertising board for Coca-Cola. The painting of a smiling child holding a green glass bottle.

The old man leaned back and crossed his feet at the ankles. The hobnails clicked. There was still mud on his boots and the insides of his calves. A smear of blood from the dead sheep he had skinned earlier in the day. His hands rested on his lap, palms up, fingers very still.

Some time passed like this. He nodded and thought about what the men from the government had asked him. Once he groaned and said no no. Ah well then.

He looked up as he heard a car horn beep twice. A large American car came into view. He turned, saw that it was Mrs Catherine McKenzie, the owner of Papanui Station. And then as he stood and looked again, absurdly, within a moment of his second seeing, his own mother's open mouth. Heard her laughter. The wavering sound of her last words, you make me remember when I see you and am unsure what it is I remember. Small waves.

Shook his head. Whispered no you don't.

The woman Catherine McKenzie almost-smiled and rolled down the window. Leaned her head out of the car. Her left hand on the top of the steering wheel, her wedding ring removed from the third finger. A pale circle of skin. A headscarf pulled up and tied under her chin. Dark glasses with white rims.

Are you all right Mr Monroe?

The old man had stood up from his seat and removed his hat. He was staring at her quite intently.

He walked towards the Chevrolet and said Mrs McKenzie how do you do? Mud splashes above the wheels.

She grimaced at the formality of the greeting, said good thank you, and then, do you need a ride back? The men from the government called this morning and asked if they could speak to you. They said they wanted to bring you into Ruatane. I came in to see if you needed a ride? A ride back to the station.

No thank you Mrs McKenzie, the old man said and stepped away from the car. That's very kind of you but I'm fine. Just fine thank you.

The afternoon wind blew and pushed his beard away to his right. He nodded and sniffed. Said, yep. Good.

He watched her close her eyes and then open them and look away for a moment, gathering her thoughts.

She is of her mother he thought.

Felt his heart beating in his throat. Sarah, the way she would place her fingers on the artery pulsing there. Ask him what it was saying.

And he had replied that it was probably unable to be spoken.

Sarah and her face behind a window in the rain.

He almost cried out. Instead looked down. Wanted to say, you Catherine, you too make me remember.

How Sarah had raised her hand and the smell of freshly baked bread on a wet Saturday morning. How he had walked backwards as he left through the mud of Mimi Creek. Wanting only to keep seeing her for as long as he could. Falling over a stump and her mouth open then in laughter and he knew she was also weeping behind the wet pane. How he had come to her not an hour earlier and the crash of a wire stand as he brushed past it. How, she asked, and then his name. David. How did you know to come to me? Two loaves of bread on the floor. Her saying oh the bread and him whispering *shhhh*. His fingers large and clean and work-rough alongside her face as he kissed her. The tiny cleft in her chin in the crook between thumb and index finger. The tip of his ring finger beneath her ear. Her mouth tasting of tea and milk. The smell of yeast and white flour. The arching of her spine.

Nobody saw me.

Somebody saw you, she replied. The how-did-you-know in her throat a pleading as if he was something other than what he was. The ninety-first psalm? Repeating the words you know again and then again. Asking him don't you? Yes he said. Yes I know.

Your hair, he said.

Catherine smiled and touched her hair beneath the headscarf. What? As if something was wrong.

He was staring. I. No, it is like your mother's. The colour is the same.

Catherine looked at the old man Monroe standing there in his old-fashioned clothes. Cropped white hair and wide beard. Woollen trousers, bowyangs and leather boots with hobnails and tricunes. Blood and mud on the inside of his legs. Braces and collarless shirt. A black woollen vest and jacket. A pocket watch and chain. Broad leather belt with a knife pouch behind his left hip. Old felt hat in his big hands curling and uncurling the brim.

Everybody knew he was crazy. Her Auntie Mem said he was the *koro porangi* the crazy old man. Keep away from him.

Old Dave who left gifts at their door on her birthdays when she was a child. A small black and tan bitch pup she called Missy that drowned in the river; once chocolate; a pineapple; a rag doll with red spots on its cheeks she named Cat and kept for years; a book of poems by Lewis Carroll and five pounds.

Auntie Mem had shrugged and said if it rains at night you get the eels in the morning. It's him up there on the high ridges...*Koro*. And pointed a finger to her ear and made circling gestures.

She thought he got the gifts from Chung Moon's store. They stopped when she went away to the coast to train as a nurse.

The best lamber in the top country. She remembered seeing him spinning around and around with his arms held out all alone on the Abernethy Flat. Falling and crying out to the sky. She

45

remembered waiting for something to change but all it did was rain on him.

Only shearers wore bowyangs now. Nobody had pocket watches.

My mother's? she said.

Yes. The same colour.

Catherine studied the old man in front of her for a long time. You knew my mother?

Yes he said then, yes. Sorry.

She waited and then said Mr Monroe. It's all right.

After some time he said I am so very sorry for your recent loss.

She stared at him and at the white-bearded face. The scars coming up from his chest, across his neck and disappearing into the white hair. The ragged edge of an ear. His eyes held a hazel tenderness that she only recognised in her eyes as something lost. Something no longer there.

Oh she said. Thank you.

Ken Scott the station manager had mentioned that he had come to Saint Mary's, the church in Ruatane. He told her that the old man had ridden into Ruatane to Drew's service. Sat at the back of the church by himself holding his hat in his hands. Almost six months now since the plane crash.

Tied the horse to the cemetery railings, let the stirrups irons up and eased the girth strap, looked a little out of place.

The only bloody horse. It was his best, a chestnut he called Majnun. He had blackened and polished the saddle. Cleaned the bridle linkage, bobbed Majnun's tail. Embarrassing really. Lines of cars were parked diagonally all along the street as far as she could see. She didn't remember seeing the horse. At least he left the flipping dogs at the station, Ken said.

She had said of course he would Mr Scott. Of course. Flipping dogs have no place at a funeral.

~

Papanui, 1946

David was skinning a dead lamb the morning he first heard the Tiger Moth fly low over the Papanui lambing flats.

He finished the last cut and dragged the pelt off the small red body and stood watching. The skin of the lamb held, dripping in his left hand, the knife in his right.

The yellow Tiger Moth banked high above him, fell away to its left, yawed and straightened to fly straight down the valley. The wings waggled left and then right.

It came lower and lower, following the river and the lambing flats, just above tree height and directly at him. A cloud of white dust came out of its undercarriage and the plane climbed steeply and the sound of its engine came over them like a wave. Superphosphate and boron rained down. The man crouched away from it. He heard his horse snort and turn away. He immediately regretted not tying Majnun to the fence.

Majnun, he called, but the horse had begun to run. Tail high in alarm and white eyed, he ran away from the thing come out of the sky, roaring now above them. Majnun knew some ancient terror and flattened in a desperate gallop to outrun this death as the plane swept over them.

47

Majnun, he called again. But Majnun was beyond hearing, he was running as he had never run before as fast as he could towards the sheltering trees and high ground.

Then as Majnun reached the shelter of the kanuka and was running alongside the treeline, David saw his head snap forward and his front legs cut away from under him. He watched as the horse fell, somersaulting forward. He saw him pitch onto his nose, his back legs kicking out as he flipped. His tail pointing ludicrously, for one moment, in the direction of the departing plane. And then he was gone from sight.

David was half running half walking towards him. His hip ached and his legs didn't work quite as well as they used to. He remembered how he had let the reins trail as he had dismounted and gone to the dead lamb. He always did this, Majnun had learned his manners. There were no planes in the sky. How could he teach him that? It was probably those reins, hanging in a loop, that had taken the legs out from Majnun.

Walking now, breathing hard. His hands on his hips as he walked, chest up and out as he puffed. He saw in his mind the small buckle where the reins joined and thought if only I had undone that. He had dropped the lamb skin but still held the small Green River skinning knife in his right hand. Dreading what he might have to do with it.

It took him ten minutes to get to where he had seen the horse tumble out of sight. The ground was gouged and the grass flattened but Majnun wasn't there.

David stood for a moment and then squatted to touch the torn earth. He noticed his thermos flask and a flattened metal cup off to the left. He stood and looked up into the trees. He studied the ground again and saw where Majnun had righted himself and gone into the sheltering bush.

Waited and listened. A silence settled over him and there was only his breathing and the beating of his heart.

Who the Majnun? he said, who the boy now? Whistled as he would a dog. He had left his dogs back at his hut this morning. But he whistled to them as if to reassure Majnun. It was a soft come-here whistle. And then he began to speak the nonsense he always spoke when handling his horses. Majnun Majnun the fine boy now where are you hiding? Would you ever come to me. I know the bloody thing frightened you but have you ever played the piano when you fell in love with a Chinese river and... mad boy of one thought, how would Mahmoud know I was to become such a tormented fool along the enchanted way?

Majnun whinnied softly from the trees.

Come on now, the man said in a low voice.

Majnun stepped out from between a fern tree and the low branch of a kanuka. The saddle had slipped down beneath his belly. The reins were behind his front feet and he was bleeding from one nostril. There was mud on his neck and caked into the bridle. A gash from a branch on his chest.

Who the boy? David whispered and slipped the knife back in its pouch.

He stepped up to Majnun and waited for the horse to nose him. Then he quietly reached up and ran his hand down his neck, circling his hand on the tight muscle.

And all the time he was hushing the horse. Soothing him. Majnun was trembling but settled and stood still as the man began to examine him.

He held Majnun's head and looked at his nose. Rubbed the blood out of his nostril with his thumb and palmed off the mud. Lifted his head and looked into his mouth. Examined the colour of the blood on his hand. Nodded.

Then holding the reins he ran his right hand down across Majnun's shoulders and front legs. Pushing his thumb and forefinger into his legs to detect any soreness. Majnun shifted away from his hands. David nodded and said good good the boy. He touched the edges of the gash on Majnun's chest. Ah now you are as sound as a bell my darling. Sound as a bell.

Then he thought, that bloody aeroplane. Young Drew McKenzie all himself new home from the war mad spiralling through the air like a tormented angel. Drunk no doubt.

Well if you are sure Mr Monroe? Catherine said.

The old man was still looking at her.

What?

About the ride home?

The old man nodded. Oh yes Mrs McKenzie. I will be fine. Thank you. No.

Are you sure? I drove in. Just in case. It is quite a walk and I…

Thank you, the old man said again. No.

Catherine frowned and wound up the window. Raised a hand then leaned over the seat as she backed out.

He stood there with his hat in hands and watched as she stopped the car, put it into first gear, turned to him, seemed to force a smile. Looked ahead and drove away.

He had raised the hand which held the hat.

He waited for some time before stepping back to the bench and sitting down. Leaned forward and opened his mouth, whispered Sarah she is just fine. Just fine.

Moved the peppermint around his mouth, touched his tongue onto the stub of his front tooth. Thought Trevor whenever the stub pained him. Always reluctant to have Crawford, the Ruatane dentist, remove it. Stood up. And held his hands on his hips as he arched his back.

A green 1955 Ford pickup truck drove past with its lights on. A hand-painted picture of a horse head on the driver's door. Winthrop Stud painted under that. A black and white dog stood on the tray. Nose lifted into the wind.

The old man stepped out and looked up at the darkening sky. Wind flattened his beard. Across the street the light that shone on the Ruatane Hotel sign came on. He could hear laughter from the public bar.

Catherine could not look back but she knew old man Monroe was there.

Standing with his hat in hand under Chung Moon's veranda. His white beard. And short cropped white hair. Those two lines that ran down from his eyes. The scars. The ear. He knew my mother she thought. And probably my father too.

It began to rain.

She turned her head and looked up at the sky and saw the

cloud coming down off the high country. The air was cooling and the rain was bringing the cold mist.

She turned on the windscreen wipers and eased her foot off the accelerator. The road fell away and twisted as she drove down into the Papango Valley. A heavy shower of rain came across the road and across the car.

Rain was falling when he crossed the first of the two bridges on the road back to Papanui Station. It was dark and he could see no more than a few feet in front of himself. The rain came from the west and was strong enough so that the old man had to lean his head forward to keep it out of his eyes.

A Holden utility passed him and stopped. He could hear the motor idling and the sound of the wipers on the windscreen. Red brake lights sparkling in the wet. Rain drummed on the roof.

Is that you old Dave? The shape of a man, silhouetted against the light of the interior, leaning out of the opened door and looking back at him.

Yes it is, the old man said holding his hand up to shield his face from the rain. Who's that?

Charlie. Charlie Baird. You better get in boy.

Charlie Baird was young enough to be his grandson. He called everybody boy.

Thanks Charlie. The old man closed the door and sniffed. The inside of the vehicle smelled of tobacco and dogs, burnt oil and dry hay. Charlie looked at him.

Bit damp?

Yep. Bit damp all right.

Walk from town?

I have. The old man watched the windscreen wipers. Blinked and sniffed. Wiped his beard. Charlie glanced at him then he too looked at the wipers.

Take you to Papanui if you want.

It's out of your way Charlie. Your turnoff on the River Road will be fine.

It's no bother boy, Charlie said. No one home. Lorraine left and took the kids. Went to her mother's down on the coast.

Sorry to hear that.

It's all right. Have to be born to this country I suppose.

As they drove through the wet night, Charlie hummed a tune of the sea being too wide to swim over and he being seldom sober. Not having wings to fly. He attempted to roll a cigarette with one hand while he drove.

Here you want me to do that? the old man asked.

Charlie handed him the unmade cigarette. Thanks. Bottle of beer under the seat if you...?

No thank you. Here. He handed the finished cigarette back to Charlie.

They followed the twisting and dipping road until they reached the flats of Papango Valley. Drove along the straight, passed the old Lawrence General Store, unlit and boarded up. The headlights swept over the building. A passionfruit vine had claimed half the roof. Paint peeling; blocked and rusted through gutters. A lone, dirt-covered Pegasus petrol bowser.

Papango Valley General Store on a sign hanging near the

entrance. Faded and dirt smeared. Cold Storage and Fresh Provisions. The old man wondered if the little bell that used to tinkle when you opened the door was still there.

Charlie looked over at him. The old Lawrence place he said.

The old man nodded.

Good milker that Mrs Lawrence. Raised in the Valley. One of the original families. Smiths I think. Outmilk most men by hand they said. Her boys went to Queensland. Roy became a tennis coach I heard and dunno what the other one did. Peter I think it was.

The old man cleared his throat. Dunno.

They drove through the night, quiet then except for the sound of the engine, the tyres on the wet road gravel. Stones rattling under the utility. The rain.

I don't blame her, Charlie said after some time.

The old man looked at him. Mrs Lawrence?

Lorraine.

The old man looked back to his front. No.

Lonely, Charlie said.

The old man nodded.

After a while Charlie said you been alone all your life boy?

Yes.

All right?

Has its moments.

The rain continued to fall and the wipers flicked back and forth. One of the rubbers had frayed slightly and a thin curve of the windscreen remained unclear, covered with moisture. A metal claw was beginning to scratch at the glass.

The headlights swept around a bend and along a wire and post fenceline, shone briefly on a padlocked gate.

The old Mitchell farm Charlie said, and looked over to his right where there was an overgrown driveway that ended in a flat paddock. House burned down years ago.

Charlie slowed the utility and turned in his seat, looked towards the paddock.

An orchard of plum and apple and pear trees remained. They could just make out the darkened shadows of the trees black against the black sky.

They were flowering this morning Charlie said. The damsons always flower around lambing time. That old orchard runs right back to the Mimi Creek. We used to say it was haunted when we were kids. He gave a short laugh. Old lady Mitchell the mad witch. Hiding in the trees.

The old man said nothing.

Saw Catherine Mitchell in town earlier. Y'know Cat?

No.

No, well she is a McKenzie now. Charlie laughed. Your boss. Owns the station since Drew was killed.

The old man nodded.

Married fifteen years or so, I still think of her as Catherine Mitchell. From school I suppose. He was a bit older.

Charlie waited and glanced across. You could of got a ride with her boy. Didn't you see the car?

No.

No?

They were quiet again for some time.

The old man was holding his hands in a bowl shape. The

55

ends of his fingers interlocked and thumbs barely touching. He looked down at them.

Charlie held the steering wheel in both hands, the unlit cigarette in his fingers. He spoke while staring straight ahead, you know they found Catherine in a basket on the front step of Mem and Rangi's place? Two weeks old.

The old man cleared his throat.

Old witch Mitchell, she'd disappeared. Catherine's mother. Into thin air.

Sarah.

Charlie shot a look at him. You knew her?

He shook his head. Knew of them he said softly. The Mitchells. Sarah and Gerald.

Charlie looked back to the road. They found him in the orchard, he said. *Jesus* bloody *christ* sad all right. Never found her. What did you say her name was?

Sarah.

Sarah, Charlie said. Sarah Mitchell the witch.

There was a fire, the old man whispered. Nothing anyone could do.

He was hanging from a plum tree, Charlie said, probably one of those damsons. Des, my oldest brother Des told us there was a blood-stained axe in a stump. But then he would make those *whoo-ooo* noises y'know? Frighten the shit out of us.

Then there was only the sound of the motor as Charlie shifted gears. They drove down into a sharp descent and bend in the road.

The old man was staring at the windscreen. Wiped his beard.

After a time Charlie spoke again into the dark. Made good

bread that Mem. She said the secret was potato water.

The old man nodded and looked out the side window at nothing.

Charlie glanced over at him.

Still as talkative as ever boy? Never shut up do you? He gave a short laugh. Blinked and hummed.

I wish I was…

Only for nights in Ballygrant.

Picked up a box of matches from the dashboard, shook it. Took a match from the box with the heels of both hands still on the steering wheel. Struck it and cupped his hands around the box and the flaring match-head. Bent forward with the cigarette in his mouth. The light of the burning match surrounded his head, bright inside the car.

Charlie inhaled smoke and breathed it out, coughed. She'll come back he said. Holding his breath. Hates me smoking around the kids, Lorraine. She'll soon get sick of her mother.

After a while he wound down the window and threw the barely smoked cigarette out into the wet night.

They turned off at the side road marked Papanui Station Wharekaka House.

Listened to the hollow sound of the vehicle on the supports as they crossed the Papanui Bridge. Stopped at the road gate to the woolshed and the old man's hut.

The old man got out and opened the gate, waited until Charlie drove through. He closed the gate and got back in the utility. Shut the door and nodded to Charlie. Righto.

Got the early ewes along the flats I see. Lambing.

They looked to where the headlights laid a white path across the wet paddocks. Three Border Leicester ewes stood watching them. Their sides bulging. Eyes glowing yellow-green in the glare of the headlights. Walked away from the approach of the utility. The grass shone wet in the light.

They're lambing now, the old man said. I didn't go round them this afternoon. In town.

Too late now boy, first thing in the morning.

First thing.

Rain's eased, Charlie said and drove up to the small musterer's hut where he knew old Dave lived. Stopped the vehicle.

There you are. The motor still running.

Thanks. The old man got out and leaned his head into the cab. See you Charlie. The old man nodded in appreciation. Charlie not asking him why he was walking back from Ruatane in the rain. Knew Charlie was the sort of man who would never ask such a thing.

Charlie nodded in return. Good-oh boy.

The old man stood on the small veranda and watched the tail lights. He raised his hand. Listened as the utility crossed the bridge and turned onto the bitumen road. Heard the growling sound of the motor climbing away as Charlie accelerated.

The wet nose of the dog Floss touched his hand. The rattle of her chain.

Floss the girl he said and bent down. She had been chained up next to her kennel on the porch. Patted her and held her ear for a moment.

Good, he whispered and opened the door to his small hut. He knew it would a long time before he could sleep.

Étaples Military Prison France 1916

He could hear the strange boy whispering in the dark of the cell.

Why are you here?

Sssh.

Why are you here?

It doesn't matter. You must be quiet. If they hear you.

I am here because I loved my father.

Sssh.

I can feel small animals and birds in my blood. In the veins of my arms. When they cry and sing I feel it. I cannot bear the death of anything. I know I shouldn't be so but I cannot help it. My mother said I have an appreciation. My father said I am a catastrophe. I joined the army to make him proud of me but I cannot.

David put his fingers against the cold wet wall of the cell. Be quiet will you? Don't say such things.

The boy was weeping in the dark. Did you know he said that when man wants to become God, he sins. He transgresses the natural order of things. Makes death, thinks he makes life. Becomes so proud he thinks he is God.

There was a loud metallic rattling. A nightstick dragged along bars. Silence, one of the military police guards called. No talking.

The boy whimpered.

What did Mahmoud mean then, David thought, when he called me God? David lay in the stone silence. He said it was about trembling awe not pride. Humility.

Somebody began to sing Abide With Me and he heard the

running feet of the guards. The cell door being opened and then the crying out and shouts. Silence means fucking silence ye conshie bastids. The thuds of the batons. Traitorous god-bothering bastids ye.

He could hear the strange boy weeping softly until he slept.

It was always dark when the morning bells began to ring.

They were getting out of their beds.

My name is Daedalus Giacomo Cranley, the boy said above the ringing bells. I promise I can teach you how to fly. That is why I have this name. What is your name brother?

He was speaking as if he had become another person from the terrified voice in the night. Defiant, brave and smiling. Something of who he was resolved to be who he is become.

Hush, David hissed. Are you mad? They will hear.

You have to fall into love. Watch me.

The prison lights came on. Harsh, almost blue electric lights.

They were standing by the prison beds. David looked at the young man who had been speaking to him. He could not pull his eyes away. O God I know you are at work in this one.

The cell doors were being opened. A military policeman stalked along the landing bawling orders. Out you weak bastards. Shit buckets in your left hands, face left and stand still. Stand still.

Daedalus smiled and said in a very loud voice: some say I resemble Teresa of Avila. Seven houses to my angelic soul. It is not my name I just made it up. I am Daedalus not Icarus. A maker of things.

Then he ran through the cell door and dived over the railing, his hands held to his sides.

The military policemen were gathered around the broken, sprawled body.

A fucking dead loss no danger. A harsh English accent, Midlands. Laughter.

Deed-a-what-ulus Gee something. What sort of shite name is that? Dead fucking loss is what he is all right.

The single blue eye of the military policeman turned and fixed on him and David thought Nelson, Lord Nelson and did not really know why.

You. The pace stick pointed at him. Did ye see what happened?

He dived Staff, David said and stared at the wall in front of him. Over the railing.

Did he say anything to ye, ye weak dog ye?

No Staff, nothing.

⌐

There was autumn rain over Flers-Courcelette the morning David was taken from the barbed-wire enclosure of the newly formed Punishment Battalion and subjected to Number One Field Punishment.

The corporal who escorted him was Canadian. He was humming a tune that sounded vaguely like a hymn and peeling a pear with a knife as he walked.

David obeyed his directions, gestures with the knife and his eyes and chin, as they followed a sunken road. Turned to his left when told to turn left, stepped up an embankment and then emerged onto the open fields. The ground was heavy underfoot and the sound of their feet in the wet mud was loud.

David could smell the cooking from the kitchens. In the distance the landscape rose towards a smoke-shrouded seam he knew was the front line. There were tall denuded trees sticking up like shattered imitations of themselves. Bits of what they had been hung off them. He could see the haze that was the barbed-wire forest in front of the German positions.

There was no sound of gunfire or artillery. A shout in the distance. A dog's bark and a rippling of laughter. Coughing.

Ici, the Canadian said. Stop. Here it is, turn around.

The tripod was between the reserve trenches and the latrines. It had been made from three willow poles about six inches in diameter and twelve feet high. The ends of the poles had been driven a foot into the ground and the tops were secured with rope. The front of the tripod was leaning forward, just out of the perpendicular. The rearward legs had smaller brace poles tied at intervals. Approximately ankle, knee, waist and shoulder height.

The Canadian cut a piece off the pear and carried it up to his mouth on the knife blade. He spoke to David before putting the pear slice in his mouth.

Put the back of your heels against the poles, legs apart. Up and your arms there. *Ah oui.* Stand still. *Bon.* Now, look at me Private. *Regardez-moi.*

He ate the last piece of pear. Made a noise of appreciation and threw the core to his right. Wiped the blade on his trousers.

David looked at him. The Canadian's face was lean and he had a heavy growth of facial hair. He had shaved not long ago but the growth was again clearly visible. A man with a navy blue face, David thought. There was a cast in one eye so that when he spoke to David only the right eye focused. The other looked above David's head. Two deep lines ran down his face on either side of his large nose. His mouth was red.

He sucked air into his mouth to taste the pear again. I am a trapper, he said. Where I come from, *les bois du Lac à l'Eau Claire*, the lakes and the woods, no? His English bore a strong French accent, so that trapper became trappeur. Suffering means nothing to me. Do you understand?

David nodded.

Eh bien. So if you make my life, my duty, difficult in any way, I will make you suffer more that you are to already. Do you understand New Zealander?

I understand. David looked towards the German lines. Smoke was rising from their fires.

Bon. Up on your toes. The Canadian tied David's elbows to the poles, then his hands and knees and then his ankles.

He was kneeling on the ground in front of David finishing the knots, when there was a loud whiplash crack above them. He dipped his head.

A rifle, David said. One of ours.

Somebody doesn't like you back there.

They don't like any of us.

Là, fini. I will warn you that I have tied you so that you will not lose circulation unless you struggle. Then the knots will tighten and the blood supply will be cut off.

David looked at him. Nodded. The Canadian crouched.

If there is a barrage I might not be able to come for you until it is over. Last week an English boy had his hands amputated because of gangrene. From struggling against the ropes during an artillery barrage. We didn't get him until the next morning. The Canadian shrugged. It is up to you.

David nodded. Thank you Mr Canada.

The Canadian frowned. One eye stared at David, the other seemed to follow the passing clouds. Did you say thank you Mr Canada?

Thank you, yes. This is not your fault.

Hooh, don't thank me for tying you out here. You might be shot or blown to pieces.

As God wills, David said. But I think you have a kind nature. You are, I believe, a good man.

The Canadian knelt and held his face and rubbed it. David could hear the rasping sound of his whiskers against his palm. David waited and watched the French Canadian as he seemed to think. Watched as he took a pipe out of his pocket and filled the bowl with tobacco. The Canadian spoke as he tamped at the pipe bowl with his thumb.

It is God this and God that with you fools. The English boy whose hands we cut off seemed to be in love with God. He said something about Galatians, the chapter I forget, verse something or other. Cursed is everyone that hangeth on a tree. I remember that. Today thou shalt be with me in Paradise. He said that too.

David felt the backs of his legs beginning to cramp. His legs were wide apart and his elbows were tied almost into his body. He was, in effect, tied on an A-frame and therefore into an A shape. The ropes at his elbows were digging in.

The Canadian cupped both his hands around his pipe as he lit it. Puffed. Smoke surrounded his head.

And now, he said, with the pipe stem gripped in his teeth, this Englishman he cannot even wipe his own arse.

He stood up and laughed. Looked at David. I am not a good man, he whispered, I am a *cunt*, shrugged and began to trot back towards the sunken road. And, he said as he turned, I am not a Canadian. *Je suis français. Comprenez-vous?*

David watched him go and tried to ease the pain he felt in his legs. The ground slipped away from beneath his toes. He was standing on his tiptoes and as he slipped forward, the ropes around his ankles and knees and hands constricted.

His legs were agony. He could no longer feel his forearms. His head hung down on his chest and then every now and again he would look up. The rain had swept across the landscape and there was a break in the clouds. Sun broke through and he heard the song of a skylark spiral high into the sky. There had been no more rifle fire after that single shot from the lines behind them. He was beginning to pant. The image of his mother's face came to him. He had run from her and was hiding in tall grass as she cried out where are you?

A long time seemed to pass.

I am not God he gasped Mahmoud that was nonsense. Why did you tell me such things? What was I thinking? Everything you said was shit. Just shit. If it wasn't I would be somewhere else.

He thought he heard Mahmoud say *if you are not of God then, David, who are you?*

Fuck off you, David yelled out at the space in front of himself. I am nothing. Go away Mahmoud, look at me. I am such a fool. Loving you did this.

Did you think that to say I believe was enough?

No, I...

That you would not be tested?

This is too much.

Too much?

Yes too much. If we are...are divine we...

David.

Yes.

David where is your pain?

My pain is everything that I am. It is everywhere.

Look at me. Do you think God has betrayed you?

Yes. David cried out, fucking God has betrayed me. Has betrayed us all. Look around you.

This is absolute? Unchanging?

David's mouth is wide open in a soundless scream. White flecks of spittle on his lips. He is shaking his head.

Trench mortars begin exploding away to his right, the crackle of far-off rifle fire. The rhythmic pattern of machine-gun fire being laid down across enfiladed lines.

Occasional shots come near him, throwing up dirt. An artillery shell detonates about a quarter of a mile in front of him. He sees a tulip of earth thrown up before the sound breaks over him.

A hundred yards west, another explosion. Much closer this time; the sight and the sound of it are immediate.

David looks up towards where the skylark was. He is swallowing convulsively. Veins standing out on his neck. He is thirsty. Christ, so thirsty.

Willing the shells even closer. Let this all end, let it be finished.

Take me, he yells. Then he leans against the ropes and cries out louder, take me.

Now the fall of artillery shot begins to advance towards him.

The voice of Mahmoud.

Who do you think you are? You are no better than the next killer of men, why should you be different? Are you finally becoming the mad man? If everything is lost then this is truly a time to rejoice my friend. A time of forgiveness.

David growling, noises of disgust. Shaking his head.

The creeping explosions rip great smoking gouts from the earth. Cloudbursts of mud and tree branches raining. Screaming metal tears through the disbelieving air.

The sound concusses: like placing a metal cooking pot on your head and hitting it with a wooden bat. There is nothing else but this. The deafness, almost a relief.

Nitrogen vapour drifts, white and soundless from the shell holes. He opens his mouth, a false yawn so as to hear again. The sounds come back to him in staccato. Heartbeats of noise.

He leans his head back as far as he can, mouth yawning again to hear. Wonders at forgiveness. Then he bows his head onto his chest. Yea, he weeps. The psalm we all know. Yea though I walk through the valley of the shadow of death, I will fear no evil…amid the rocks and the white desert of loss, Mahmoud you intrude. That is the desert of unbelief. Of dry-mouthed obedience. The twenty-third psalm returns me. Suffer us to endure. Kiss me in death.

Let my cry come into thee.

Je suis fou, j'suis complètement fou. David heard the words and then the sensation of release. *Et toi là?*

He looked around. The Canadian corporal had crawled out and had cut the ropes around his ankles. He then reached up and cut the ropes around his elbows and hands. David was still tied at the knees.

Fool, the Canadian said. Here. He passed the knife up to David who had turned and twisted to look down at him.

You cut them.

David took the knife and leaned down. The knife was razor sharp and the ropes came away immediately. He fell down next to the Canadian. He began to laugh and cry. Thank you thank you Mr Canada. I knew you were a good man.

No, the Canadian shouted, you are an idiot. Not me. I am a survivor. Don't call me Mr Canada. It is a foolish thing to say. *Tu me dégôutes.*

David shook his head. He was lying in the mud next to the corporal.

I thought you said you would not come back for me.

Hah. The Canadian was beginning to crawl back towards the safety of the sunken road. *Tais-toi, parle pas.* Don't talk. Crawl. *Allons-y.*

The fall of machine-gun shot across them.

David saw the man swell as if someone had suddenly pumped air into him and then collapse like a punctured balloon. His hand reached out and grasped the earth. He rolled over and twisted. A wheel of blood fanned out.

David stood up and ran to him, bent over.

The Canadian lay face up. *Eh toi là*, he whispered. Why did you have to say I was a good man? He turned his head. I am a

68

trapper from *les bois du Lac à l'Eau Claire*. I feel nothing for the suffering of others. Do you understand New Zealander? Nothing. The beaver and the fox they mean more to me than you. You are a fool. *Je te déteste*.

David smoothed the hair back from his forehead. They were lying side by side. The rain was falling on them. The Canadian looked at him with one eye. He put his palm over the other look-away eye. My knife is sharp no?

Another line of machine-gun bullets fell near them. Earth splattered. A high round ricocheted from something metal and whined away.

Oh yes, David whispered. It is very sharp.

My mother would kiss it you know.

What? Your knife?

No you *cunt*. My eye. The one that looks to other things. My father thought it was the work of the Devil. He taught me to sharpen a knife. The Canadian coughed and the blood came up and out of his mouth and over his navy blue chin.

Ah non he said and put his hand onto his mouth and chin and throat, wiped at the blood. Looked at his hand. *Ah non*.

Did you love your father?

Oui, j'aimais mon père. Yes, I loved my father. He was shaking his head. *Tu sais*?

Me too.

David held his hand as he died.

The old man woke with the sound of rain blowing hard against the iron roof and thought immediately of the new lambs.

How many born this night? He spoke the words: how many. Imagined the newborn as he had seen them every spring for most of his life. Still yellow and blood-streaked from their mother, rising on shaky wet legs, splayed out in the mud. Frantic ewes turning this way and that in the dark. Threads of clotted blood and afterbirth swinging from the vulva.

The wind like…The thin sound of the lambs calling. He cleared his throat in the dark and spoke, crossing over from what he spoke in his mind to what he spoke aloud. The wind is like it is.

He listened, heard the steady ticking of the clock beside his bed and then the rain and the wind. Felt the thrashing movement of the trees on the river side of his small musterer's hut. Held his breath. The vision of the trees coming to him through the earth.

It was coming from the south east. There would be ice in it from the mountain, killing the newborn. Killing the mothers.

He breathed out and in, held his breath and then sat up in the narrow bed. Found the box of matches next to the candle stub and lit one.

The match flared and then settled on the wick. He sat there and studied the colours of the flame. And then thought of the government men, the inspector and the sergeant. Wondered if they knew what they had touched. Of course they couldn't know. They were just doing their job. Everybody is just doing their jobs. When they came for him they said, we called the owner. Mrs McKenzie your boss. She said it was all right.

Catherine in the dark red Chevrolet. The blue *papa* mud splashes above the wheels. Her hair, the colour of her hair and her incomprehension.

He thought of the forgiving smile of his friend. He lay back down in his bed. Pulled the blankets back over his shoulder and remembered Mahmoud with a paintbrush in his hand. Smiling up at him. How those few months on Lemnos changed everything. Nothing would be the same. Blinked as he stared at the candle.

Mahmoud was asking have you ever been in love David? Truly in love so that the mountains become rivers? Rivers mountains? Woodgrain water, fire becoming water falling up and every individual thing become as one thing?

No.

When, like me, you take off all your clothes and put them back on again. But this time they are inside out and back to front and then you run out into the streets waving your arms up and down convinced, absolutely convinced you can fly, ascend into the sky like a pelican?

No David said. Of course not. That is nonsense Mahmoud.

Yes David, it is isn't it?

It is madness.

Yes. That too.

Sarah Mitchell placed two pots of jam and one jar of pickled onions on his table and began to speak.

We have finished milking the cows for the morning David, she said.

He nodded.

Gerald said he would sweep and bucket the shed and told me to come back to the house. And to bring these to you. I had asked if I could. After the dance the other night. You left without taking anything.

Thank you. David was standing at the door.

He barely speaks to me now, she said. He has never been one for that but he used to sing well on Sunday at church. A tenor. It is the Welsh I suppose. But he doesn't sing now either.

David said nothing. He closed the door of his hut and walked over to the table and picked up one of the jars.

Thank you Mrs Mitchell.

Sarah walked over to the window and looked out. Next to her was the prayer rug Mahmoud had sent to him. It was red and black and orange. Pearl spirals representing plants. Blue flowers and birds. Geometric shapes. Persian script.

She put four fingers on it and pressed, moved them down a few inches, feeling the wool.

This is very beautiful. I have not seen the shades of these colours before.

Yes it is beautiful.

Do you know what the writing means?

David nodded. Yes Mrs Mitchell I do. It says, You are the cure hidden in the pain.

She turned her head and shoulders and looked at him. Sunlight coming in from the window lit her. Her mouth open in surprise at the words.

David continued to speak while looking at the rug.

Concealed in anger and betrayal is your compassion and loyalty. You are not only in Heaven. I see your footprints every-where on earth.

She looked at him for a long time. Then she said oh David. Waited for another moment.

Shook her head. You know I used to look for Jamie's footprints in the mornings sometimes when I was going to the cowshed.

David nodded.

One morning after the telegram came I got lost. She smiled to herself. Well. I shouldn't have of course. I had been walking the same path to the cowshed for five years. Twice a day. Then suddenly I didn't know where I was.

When Gerald found me I do remember I was sitting on a matai stump and unpicking a little woollen jacket I had knitted. Winding the wool around my hand. I recall what he said. Come on now love. Come back to the house.

David said nothing. He kept looking at her.

Sarah had turned back to the window. She was staring out at the long flat paddock which ran down to the river. The sweeping

S shape of dark trees following the river. Up to the dark green hills and beyond there to where the mountains would be. Her arms were folded. Her back to him. He could see the colour of her hair in the sunlight.

The wool, she said, it was blue and white. A little sailor's jacket. Come on now love he said. Up you get. That's what he said. Up you get. He never calls me Sarah. Mostly it's love. Or sweetheart. And dear.

He made me a cup of tea. And then I went to bed. He asked if I was all right. My feet were so cold.

I heard the floorboards creaking as he walked in the night.

She turned and looked at David. He could not see her face. The sun had shadowed her.

I was all right in the morning. We milked. Gerald said I didn't have to if I wasn't up to it. He could manage.

But I wanted to milk. That small jersey cow with the black ear and white star between her eyes, Sally. She was like an old friend. A warm cow on a cold morning is a good thing. She just stood still for me and I leaned my head into her and cried.

And then when she was empty she just walked off. Stepped high over the bucket and walked away. I thought then it will be all right because I was holding the bucket so she wouldn't kick it over.

Gerald was sweeping the yard with a stable broom and looking at me.

He just kept looking at me as he swept.

She stepped away from the light and looked again at the rug.

Where did you get this?

A friend sent it to me.

She waited.

Did you know our Jamie, David?

David picked up the jams and pickled onions and was placing them on a shelf. He had his back to her.

You see, she said, Peter Whiting's mother told us that he wrote and said that you were with him and that you were a blessed saint and not to take any notice of what anyone might say about you. They lost him on the same day as we did our Jamie. They were in the same unit, they are buried together at the Euston Road Cemetery at Colincamps in the Somme Valley.

David stared at her. He opened his mouth but couldn't speak. He was shaking his head.

She turned back to the window. I wanted to know how he died. If it was peaceful. If he suffered at all. I just wanted to know.

She looked over her shoulder at David who had not moved.

That is why I so wanted to see the clairvoyant, Madame Kerensky at the Winter Show. She turned once again to the window. It doesn't matter I suppose. She had a cold. Let's hope it's not the flu.

No. David was looking at the table. His fingers pressing down on the wood. He touched the grain. Thought, this is the shape of water. Ran a fingernail across it.

Sarah continued to speak. I saw little Annie Smith down in the river paddock yesterday. She was walking along and whipping thistles with a stick. I called out to her but she didn't hear me.

She stopped speaking then. Her hands holding her arms.

They were both silent for a while.

Then she said, he had a stutter. Peter did.

Yes David said. He did.

Peter Whiting who they all called Fish dry retched and then farted, loose and wet in his pants because he knew. He had done this before. He was smoking and looking at the fingers which held the cigarette, watching the blue smoke curl and the pale mud ingrained in the whorls of his fingertips.

There was a red raised flea bite at the wrist. He bent his head forward, bit and sucked and then put the cigarette in his mouth, drew on it and inhaled the smoke into his lungs with an in-hissing noise. Held the butt in front of his face for a moment and then, opening his fingers, let it fall into the mud at his feet.

He looked down at the cigarette and stepped on it. Kept looking at his boot.

Then he sniffed and shook his head. Looked up, turned and winked at David who was sitting on an ammunition box at the back of the trench with a Red Cross armband and holding a folded stretcher. He nodded back at Fish. Whispered, Fish.

All along the trench there was movement and low, rumbling talking, some laughter. David heard *Hail Mary Mother of God*. And then there were some French boys, a flame-thrower section, some of them were also in prayer, *Sainte Marie Mère de Dieu prie pour nous pauvres pêcheurs maintenant et à l'heure de notre morte* and the Australians and New Zealanders *fuck this for a game of soldiers, jesus. Holy Mary mother of God pray for us sinners now and at the hour of our death. Amen. The stupid bastards*. The sacred and the profane. Like the beautiful song and the rotten breath from the same mouth. *Oh God*. The sound of metal on metal rattling back and forth.

David watched Fish pick up his rifle, balance the body of it in his left hand, palm back the bolt. Check with his thumb the magazine lip and breech. Touch the firing pin with his index finger, circle the breech block face and inspect the end of his finger. Rub off the brass-coloured metal dust with his thumb. Look at his thumb and finger.

He stopped and glanced at David. Winked. Asked, yes? Yes you tr tr traitorous bastard? Laughed. Deserter boy? You still here then? Haven't run off? Tell me Davie.

He looked at David and blinked. Nodded in question.

Yes, David replied. You have not been deserted by God. I promise.

Fish laughed again, nodded and went back to his preparations. He reached into a webbing pouch and extracted a clip of ammunition. Blew on it. Turned the clip in his fingers and rubbed some dirt on the back of the clip off onto his thigh. Then he moved his left hand back to hold the bottom of the magazine, letting the Lee Enfield rifle swing slightly forward with its own weight. He placed the clip of .303 ammunition into the top of the open breech and with a push of his thumb he loaded the brass rounds into the magazine. The empty clip bouncing off the body of the rifle made a pinging noise and fell into the mud next to his boot. He used his thumb again, to depress the uppermost round in the magazine, sliding the bolt forward onto an empty chamber. Eased the firing mechanism by closing the bolt with the trigger depressed.

Fish grunted as he lowered the butt of the rifle onto his left boot and with his right hand reached around and found the handle of the bayonet just behind his right hip. He pushed the handle of the bayonet downward and extracted the whole of the blade in one movement. Brought it around and looked at the spring housing, blew on that also and then positioned the bayonet at the muzzle of the rifle. He held the sight with his left hand. Clicked the bayonet into place with his right and ran a finger along the back of the blade. Held it between thumb and index finger, moved it back and forwards to check it was secure.

A heavy shower of rain came over them. David looked at Fish in the rain. He saw the rainwater beading on the steel of the bayonet and running down the blood groove. All along the trench as far as he could see, curving lines of bayonets in the rain.

Have I? The boy on the right of Fish had turned and was looking at David.

What son?

Been deserted by God. Have we all? The boy had muddy fingermarks on his cheek. The beginning of facial hair on each side of his chin. His upper lip. One eye was red and the lid was swollen. A sty. David thought his mother would rub her golden wedding ring on it to make it go away. He saw the image of a mother holding the forehead of this boy and rubbing the edge of her wedding ring against the swollen red infection in her son's eyelid. Stay still son. His mother would do this thing for him. Her thumb pulling the skin on the side of his head tight.

What's your name?

Jamie, he said. I know you David you worked on a farm near ours.

Where are you from Jamie?

The Papango Valley. I am one of the Mitchells.

Fish laughed. I know your dad, Jamie.

Do you really Fish?

78

A g g good bloke. Gerald.

God has not deserted any of us, David said. Look to your gear Jamie.

Do…d don't listen to him Jamie, Fish said frowning. He is a conchie traitorous bastard. And he thinks he is g go god. Then he laughed at the look on Jamie's face. No mate, Dave here is the one that will keep you alive. He w wi will be right there behind us. Pretty good for a fucking deserter and a piss poor half-back. He he he will pro protect…ah fuck it.

Jamie smiled. His lip trembled.

Fish put a hand on his shoulder. Yep Jamie I I knew your dad. Mum too. Good coo cook your mum. Shore some two-tooth wethers on your place…she made scones for morning smoko. Home ma ma made plum jam if I remem mem… Fish stopped talking, shaking his head.

Jamie laughed, coming to Fish's rescue, speaking quickly. Mum's jam, yes, I loved it.

A hand-held bell sounded. A schoolmaster's bell to summon the children to class. And then the voice-chatter approach of a message passed from mouth to mouth along the line. Full magazine, bayonets fixed, nothing up the spout. Good luck boys.

David watched Fish as he closed his eyes and bent his head forward, leant his forehead against a sandbag. The brim of his helmet bumped. He looked back at David and said I was shook on Annie Smith you know Davie I can tell you now. Can't I? She was your girl for a b b bit. I'm sorry.

You can tell me Peter. She is a terrific girl. Small one who works like a man. Bit of a temper, sits a horse well though. Heart of Archer. David smiled.

The bell sounded again and then a voice called out. Up we go lads onto the firestep. Wait for the whistle. That's when we go over the bags. Steady now.

David watched as they stepped up. Wet bayonets along the sky.

The boy on the right of Fish, it was Jamie, said Fish.

Fish turned to him.

I think I have pissed in my pants. He was looking down at his groin. Look at me, he said. Jamie looked as if he was about to cry. His eyes dark with fear and then horror at his own body's betrayal.

It looks like the ma map map of Africa son, Fish laughed. It's all all all right. I think I shh shit my my myself before. Farted and followed through. Don't worry young Jamie. That will be the la la last of our fuckin' worries…

German machine-gun fire began exploding along the lip of the trench and moving along to their left. Another machine gun came back crossing over. Some of the rounds striking the back of the trench.

Fish turned back to David talking. David couldn't hear what he was saying because of the machine guns. Something about I always was fond of her I think but a rugby team or being enfiladed and the Ranfurly Shield has been won by Taranaki for the last few and do you she is she is don't you think David. Little Annie Smith like a hedgehog in her shyness.

David was shaking his head.

There was a lull in the firing, Fish turned and knelt down in front of David. He spoke clearly, one hand up as if to shield his words from others' hearing. Down in the river paddock on the lambing flats, between the thistles we walked and I first kissed her on the mouth. I told her my left foot said, I love, and my right, you. But I never to her. It was just in my head. But the way she smiled it was like she knew what I was saying. Y'know Davie?

I know Fish.

Then Fish squatted down and put two fingers down his throat. The morning coffee and rum came up in a wet surge.

The young man with the sty watched with his mouth open. Said, Fish.

Fish was standing and shaking his head. Spat out drooling saliva, smiled. Better, he said, if you are gut-shot. To be empty. Ask g god there. Winked at David.

Explosions began coming down the trench line from their right. David saw Fish's eyes wide. Great roaring explosions. David could hear nothing but the roaring. Then the sky became filled with earth. The earth opened under them and became the sky.

The young man called Jamie Mitchell with the sty in his eye was somersaulting above them. A gust of hot wind and a shower of blood rained over him.

The high ringing deafness went on for a long time. He could not get his balance. Kept falling over.

Sarah turned away from the window as she heard the footsteps of David on the floorboards coming towards her.

He was speaking. The words were just coming out of him.

I am sorry. He said. I am sorry I could not keep him alive. Your son Jamie, he had a sty in his eye and I saw you rubbing your wedding ring on his sty and saying shush be still. There were wet bayonets all along the sky at Mont Saint Quentin. He was above me before we lost him Mrs Mitchell. I couldn't keep him with me. I am so sorry. Fish was speaking to him of you just before and he smiled when he said your name…Mum. He said Mum's jam.

⁓

The candle stub in the tin gave off a circle of light at Mahmoud's knee. He smiled as he slowly drew the brush along the curving line which was the beginning of God is merciful.

Have you been to London? David asked.

The centre of your Empire? Mahmoud asked and looked up from the calligraphy.

Yes. David stared at what Mahmoud was doing.

Yes I have. Mahmoud replied and waited a few moments thinking. I remember I arrived with a pocketful of currants and dried apricots. My grandfather insisted I take them. He smiled.

I have never. My mother…

A great river fog covered the city and the air was brown. When I ate the apricots I ate the sunshine of home. That is what my grandfather told me would happen anyway.

You studied there?

Yes Mahmoud said. The British surgeons were unsmiling gods. And the crowds of London immense. Everyone seemed to walk in straight lines. A friend of mine who studied in Berlin and London said only the Germans walk in straighter lines than the English.

My mother wanted to go to London David said.

To the famous hyacinth gardens?

What?

The gardens?

I don't know David said. I remember her saying she wanted to go to the heart. Where it all began.

Mahmoud looked at him. Rising wind moved his beard. The candle guttered.

The colour of the dawn on Lemnos was the colour of ripe apricots. They had been unable to sleep.

The sun rose and the light came over them, bronzing their faces.

On our small farm in Anatolia we grew apricots Mahmoud said. When I was a small child I remember asking my grandfather why the fruit has such a colour.

As he spoke Mahmoud's undamaged fingers touched the shrapnel scars along the inside of his right leg. The torn tissue was raised and purple.

Some of the wounds were still stitched. A few open, red and weeping. He drew invisible lines between the scars and wounds.

The Southern Cross here, he said. And here, I discovered Scorpio. You call this one Canis Minor I think. The little dog. He traced the shape of the constellation on his calf, knee and thigh. Your British Navy gave me such lessons in Astronomy.

David was watching him.

Well I have Orion's belt across my arse, he said. Compliments of the same instructor. Remember?

They both laughed. They could hear the far-off sound of early morning naval gunfire coming on the wind. The morning sea wind still smelled of the cleanliness of itself. The fighting was far enough away. But they could hear the fire and steel of the guns. The deep crumping sound.

Remembering what it did.

So what did he tell you?

Mahmoud had been looking to the east, down towards the sea. The day was clearing, brightening in the sun. The dawn was no longer the colour of apricots.

He turned to David, said David? as a question. His eyes were heavy from the morphine.

Your grandfather. Did he have an answer for you?

Yes.

And?

David I will not be able to whirl anymore. My foot is gone.

David shook his head, that is not an answer.

Later, passing Mahmoud a bowl of stew and rice. Mahmoud nodded in thanks. David, imagine if we have forgotten why we are here?

What do you mean?

If you lived your whole life certain of everything. Like an animal.

David knelt next to the cot bed where Mahmoud was propped up on pillows. He leaned onto his elbow.

How is your foot? David asked.

Missing. My foot is missing David.

David opened his mouth.

Mahmoud continued, that is what I am saying. I was certain

my whole life of my foot and then…

I mean, David said, what is left. He looked at Mahmoud. How is your leg?

Mahmoud shifted his weight on the cot. It is all right, he said. It aches. It itches. The morphine helps. Then he looked at the bowl David had passed him. Is that meat?

Yes, David said. Mutton ragout the cook said. Whatever that means. No pork. And there is a potato. Under the rice.

Potato? Well, get the chair David please, Mahmoud said. Eat with me.

David laughed and opened up a small canvas folding chair. Sat and put his bowl of rice next to Mahmoud's. I have also, David said and waited for dramatic effect. Curry powder.

Mahmoud looked at him.

I got it from a Sikh gunner. He lost an eye poor feller.

David carefully unfolded a piece of newspaper. Smell, he said and held the curry towards Mahmoud.

I know what curry powder smells like. What did it cost?

Well, David said, it cost three of those cigarettes you don't smoke.

Hah. The Sikh drives a hard bargain. Perhaps the loss of an eye…Mahmoud didn't finish the sentence.

Eat while it's warm. David said.

Do you think the Sikh has almonds?

David ate. Made a noise of not knowing.

Mint? Parsley?

David swallowed. I'll ask, he said. The next time I see him. Do you have any more of those Turkish cigarettes? They seem to like them.

Mahmoud nodded at David. We'll see.

They were silent for a while as they ate.

There are three hundred angels with us, Mahmoud said, when we eat. They accompany our meal. Be aware of every bite. They watch and smile.

David looked up at Mahmoud, a spoonful of rice suspended. Really? he said. Three hundred.

Yes Mahmoud said. Really.

David nodded and said three hundred again.

Mahmoud sat up and held his hands in front, palms facing upwards. He recited a prayer of gratitude, smiled and began to eat with a spoon.

So the question is how do we remember?

Remember what?

Why we are here. Do you want me to teach you?

What?

Why we are here. David are you listening to me?

I have never thought about it, David said. He paused with his finger and thumb holding a pinch of curry powder above the rice. Do we have to have a why?

Mahmoud swallowed and made a sound of appreciation. Only animals don't ask, David my brother. Everything humans do is asking that very question. That is what is behind everything. Have you heard of Darwin?

No. David said and started to rub his thumb and index finger together again, spreading the curry powder over his meal.

Mr Freud?

No.

No? One said what, the other asked why.

No.

Who have you heard of David Monroe?

David took a spoonful of rice and ate. King George the Fifth.

Mahmoud stared at him, laughed and continued to eat but was laughing at the same time. Grains of rice fell out of his mouth. You have heard of King George the Fifth?

I have heard of King George the Fifth.

He is a memorable king?

Yes, David said, King George the Fifth. Our king. He is important.

The old man smiled as he watched the candle, whispered King George the Fifth. Married Queen Mary.

Looked at the clock. Not quite four-thirty. At least two hours before the dawn. He sat up in the bed. Drew a blanket over his shoulders and sat for a long time. His hands pulled the blanket around himself. He lifted his chin to allow his beard to come outside the blanket.

The small spearhead of light around the candle spread dim sepia colour out into the space of the room. The smell of the candle wick caught at him and he cleared his throat, paused and then cleared it again.

He sat watching the flame and then he made a noise, said his thanks to God and stood. He walked through the light. The shadow swayed and then righted. The walls and ceiling of the hut were lined with newsprint as wallpaper and insulation. He read the walls as he walked through the light.

Winston Churchill – Our great wartime leader dies aged 90 – Nations mourn.

Morinsville Bull Sale.

The old man stopped and pressed a finger on the black typeset of Winston Churchill. There was a photograph of him with his famous V for Victory gesture. A cigar jutting out and his bowler hat. Mouth and jaw set in that absolute obstinacy that he had.

He touched the face of Winston Churchill with two fingers. Smiled and said my. Turned and walked towards the window. He didn't read any more of the pages he had stuck to the wall, he was surrounded by them, it was just wallpaper.

Hallenstein's sale of men's and women's autumn clothing.

3,500 US Marines arrive in South Vietnam.

For sale: Fenceposts, number 8 wire and 350 battens. Offers.

Palm Sunday Tornado 1965 outbreak across Midwestern US States. Estimated 51 tornadoes killing between 256 and 270 people.

He didn't know where these places were. Perhaps they are places of pilgrims and saints, dogs and lion skins on which to fly to Paradise, the old man smiled.

⌒

They were standing on the beach. The sky a vast, still, blue-grey dome.

David stood slightly above and behind Mahmoud who had gone down to the water's edge. The sea was moving gently; as if sleeping. Swelling up and back. Moving as a sleeping man's chest moves.

Mahmoud was pointing towards the south east horizon. He held his bandaged leg up, behind himself, bent at the knee.

I come from there, he said. A place called Hajibektash. Beyond Iconium or Konya.

How is that? David asked. He was looking to where Mahmoud was pointing. Hajibektash?

89

Yes Hajibektash, Mahmoud said and lowered his hand. He regathered the crutches into his armpits. The missing fingers had healed enough for him to use the heel of his left hand to hold the crutch. His hand and forearm were still bandaged.

David was looking to where Mahmoud had indicated. He suddenly remembered his mother. Her arm held out, pointing. The sea wind in her hair. The sound of her sniffing and apologetic laugh.

Mahmoud had turned away and begun to move off. He began to propel himself along the beach with a series of jerking motions. The wooden ends of the crutches sank into the wet sand and pebbles. He used his remaining foot to lever and push off, and by swinging the weight of his body, he was able to move at a fast walk.

Starting and stopping were the most difficult. He fell often. David had to stretch out to keep up with him.

Mahmoud turned his head slightly as he vaulted along, and spoke to David.

It was named after the saint Haji Bektash Veli. Hence Hajibektash. Haji. It means pilgrim who has been to Mecca. The Haj. My grandfather named me.

A saint? David said, slightly breathless. Can you stop Mahmoud? You are going too fast.

Mahmoud stopped, swayed awkwardly and then fell over.

He sprawled out, the crutches making an L shape. His face in the sand.

David said shit and stepped forward to help him. He sat Mahmoud up. Knelt beside him. Are you all right?

Mahmoud smiled and then laughed. Jalal al-Din Muhammad Din ar-Rumi would be so very proud of me. I am what you infidels call a whirling dervish of the Mevlevi order. First rate. Now I am falling on my face. He kept laughing as David got him upright. Thus it all passes away.

There was sand on his beard and forehead.

There was no strength in the damaged left hand, blood had stained the bandage. David steadied him and looked at his hand. Said yes? Wiped some sand off his cheek. Yes?

Mahmoud shook his head and regained his balance and turned back to David. He propped his crutches. One slightly behind and to the left, the other ahead and to the right. He lowered his bandaged leg, until where the foot used to be rested gently on the sand. A club of white bandages. His hip cocked.

Perhaps we shouldn't have come so far.

The sea had begun to waken. Small urgent waves washed up the beach. They both stared at the sea and the movement and sound of the water, the sun spangling through it like musical notes. Further out the colour changed to a cobalt blue. The white caps of small waves as far as they could see.

A light wind blew across them. It smelled of the sea and far away the coal smoke of battleships.

They were breathing hard. Weeks of convalescence.

He walked on the sea David, Mahmoud said.

David frowned. Who did? Jesus?

Mahmoud smiled. No David, Haji Bektash Veli did. He also flew to Paradise on a lion skin.

David was staring at him. A lion skin?

Yes. And he gave sight to the blind.

Your saint?

My saint. Veli. It means saint.

David nodded. He took the rifle off his shoulder and placed it between his feet. Held it by the front sight and let the flat of the bayonet rest on his stomach.

I was twenty-three last week, he said. Tuesday. It was my birthday.

Mahmoud was smiling at him. Happy birthday my friend.

Thank you.

Mahmoud moved forward and kissed him on first the left cheek and then the right and then on the mouth.

Happy birthday.

David had never been kissed by a man. He looked at the sea. Mahmoud was watching him. They were silent for some time before Mahmoud spoke.

He called Christians *Quizilbash*.

Quizilbash? David said almost laughing in relief at the passing of the moment.

It means redheads. It came from the disgrace you call the Crusades.

David stared at Mahmoud and then shook his head. Said no mate, the crusaders were heroes. Brave men.

Mahmoud was laughing at him. They were disgraceful murderers. Infidels. When you betray a sacred oath it is called infidelity. No?

David turned away from him. You haven't read the books I did.

No, Mahmoud said. I have not.

They looked up as they heard the approach of a group of prisoners.

There were about ten Turkish prisoners escorted by three soldiers wearing the tartan kilt and bonnets of a Highland regiment.

The prisoners wore untidy turbans on their heads; these were just wide strips of cloth loosely wound around their heads. The headdress of peasants or slaves. They all carried shovels.

The Scottish soldiers each carried a rifle with a fixed bayonet, slung at the shoulder. One was at the head of the group and to the left, the other two were at the rear of the party and about five paces behind.

One of the prisoners recognised Mahmoud and called a greeting. *Assalamu alaiküm.*

Cut the fuckin' gash Abdul. The Scottish soldier at the rear left of the group yelled. He winked at David. Morning Sergeant.

David said Corporal.

The work party moved down the beach. David watched them. One of the prisoners turned and smiled back at them, raised a hand called out *giaour* and shrugged at the escorts. Winked at Mahmoud.

Eyes to the front you horrible wee man.

Mahmoud was leaning on his crutches. He raised a hand at the prisoner who had turned back into the group.

Wa alaiküm assalaam, he said softly. Peace be with you also my brave friend.

They watched the work party until it turned off the beach to the right to follow the road that led back to the hospital.

How is your hand?

Mahmoud looked at the bloodstained bandages. Inspected them with the fingers of his other hand. It hurts.

We had better get back.

Yes. Mahmoud paused.

David looked at him and then to where he was looking. So that's where you come from?

Yes.

How do you say it? Hapbentash?

Hajibektash.

Is it far?

Several days.

How far on a lion skin?

Mahmoud looked at him and laughed. That my friend is immediate. You are becoming a Sufi. Never mind. Let's go.

Mahmoud pivoted to push off but his bandaged hand slipped off the crutch handle and he twisted, paused for a moment and fell forward onto his face.

Oh no David said, *jesus* not again.

Mahmoud rolled over and groaned. He said something unintelligible. Then, sorry David.

It's all right mate. David put the rifle down and bent over to help him up.

He got his shoulder under Mahmoud's arm and began to lift him. Said up we go Mahmoud. Up son.

Mahmoud cried out as he put weight on his foot. David, he said, I think I have twisted my ankle.

You what?

He said something again that David did not understand.

What?

Suddenly Mahmoud was yelling at him. His mouth was open, close to David's face. His teeth. David could feel the spit landing on his cheek. His ear hurt.

Did that English bomb blow your brains away too? How I have to repeat everything to you? Or do all New Zealanders have brains of fuck donkey? Isn't it my ankle twisted now. I even can't...

It was so unexpected, so unlike this man Mahmoud that David

had come to know that he was for a moment deeply shocked. He thought it was as if someone had dropped a bottle of precious spirit and the contents flooded everywhere. He was stepping among broken glass.

And then Mahmoud began to yell at the sky. Waved his remaining good hand. As if imploring sense to be made of what was happening.

David shrugged Mahmoud off his shoulder, pushed him away and stepped back. Watched as he toppled over.

Mahmoud fell into an awkward heap on the beach. His bandaged leg waved in the air. Tried to sit up. Yelled out again as his ankle got caught in one of the crutches.

David stood watching him. He put a finger up to his lips, smiled and made a long *sssssshhhh* noise. Crossed his arms.

Mahmoud eventually sat up, glaring at him.

David returned the stare.

They both blinked.

The waves continued to wash in. The wet rattling sound of pebbles. They came in and out.

It is probably just me, David eventually said.

What just you? Just you what? Mahmoud's English syntax became jumbled when he was angry, but David had only just learned this.

That has the brains of…what did you say…a *fuck donkey*?

Mahmoud looked down. Shook his head. Kept making small shaking gestures with his head.

Most New Zealanders I know are quite bright really. Much brighter than the Australians. *They* don't think so of course, at all. Because they imagine themselves better at cricket. But if

95

anything I would say the Australians have *fuck donkey* brains. David laughed.

Mahmoud was trying to arrange his crutches. He said nothing.

You probably don't understand the joke Mahmoud. It's a thing between the New Zealanders and Australians. It's funny, like cousins teasing each other.

Cousins?

Never mind. David sighed.

I am too—I...I lose my temper. It hurts. I am sorry David. I became like a child. Mahmoud was looking at him.

David smiled. I am going to resist the temptation to say what. You won't take the morphine anymore. And you are in pain. It is no wonder.

Mahmoud looked at him. He had tears in his eyes. I am a *Djiin*, a demon from the mountains of Kaf, of the desert. And it is your birthday. The morphine frightens me, I like it too much. It takes me, I don't take it. I am sorry David, my brother. Mahmoud had struggled up to stand. He was leaning heavily on the crutches.

David stood still and looked out to sea for a long time.

Don't give it a thought mate. Looks like I'll have to carry you again though. At least this time you won't get your blood on my flash uniform. Eh? Better leave the crutches here. I'll come back for them.

David knelt in front of Mahmoud and held his left hand up. The right still held the rifle. Just lean your weight over me mate, he said.

Mahmoud leaned forward across David's back. Let them go, David said. Mahmoud dropped the crutches in the sand.

David took Mahmoud's hand and then his weight and stood up. He spoke as he moved Mahmoud into a more comfortable position across his shoulders.

Tell me about your mother Mahmoud. I had a lovely mother. And I miss her. She died when I was sixteen. Her name was Mary O'Connell and I don't think she ever really grew up.

Your mother? Mahmoud asked. His voiced was strained from the pain.

Yes David said. I loved her very much. She was only thirty when she drowned.

⌇

Mary Monroe née O'Connell was lost in a green sea off a black sand beach known as Pungarehu. On the beach there were great piles of tangled driftwood driven high up on the upper tide mark. The air hazy white with fine salt spray.

She had loved the shapes the storm-driven and sea-smooth wood had been sculpted into. She would collect the wood and gather shells and stones and make them into what she called My Arrangements.

Had placed them around the house and garden of the small cottage they owned next to the Gill family at the southern end of the Papango Valley.

As a boy David would often come upon these small shrines to place. The sea and wind.

We live on an island, his mother said, at the bottom of the world. The Arrangements tell us where we are. Look how beautiful and strange the wood is. The sea did this.

David's father was good with a horse everyone said, as if that was enough to be said of a man. He was most often away on the large coastal sheep station known as Te Taurangi breaking in the young horses. There had been a demand for them for the war in South Africa. He called them remounts.

His mother apologised to David often for his father not being there. It is what we have to do until we can buy a proper place of our own. David had looked at her and almost said there is no need to say sorry. It is better without him.

David remembered whenever his father came home. The heavy sounds of walking in the house. Jingling. And the smell of horses and dogs and mutton fat. Stockholm Tar and fresh meat. He always brought freshly killed meat. Usually wrapped in cloth and draped over the front of his saddle. Sometimes he would come walking out of the big hills with the carcass of a wild pig on his shoulders.

David's mother knew how to smoke and salt the meat, hang it in the chimney so the cottage smelled like wild bacon for weeks.

Sometimes she named the Arrangements. One was called simply How Great Thou Art after the hymn and another The Soul's Star. Her favourite was The Flight across the sky of God who we can see as a Meteor.

There was an unspoken agreement never to tell his father who, they both knew, would have dismissed such things with silence and turning away. A raised hand as if to strike out, a gesture almost to his own long-dead father. An imitation.

She told David that the arrangement she called The Flight across the sky of God was named after the old chief Te

98

Whiti-o-Rongomai. That when she was a girl of ten, her father had introduced her to him. She remembered him looking into her eyes, his hand on her cheek, holding her face. His laughter making everything possible. And the gentle rumble of his voice. *Kia ora hine.* Hello girl. He gave her a white feather she told David and said *taku awe kotuku,* this is my feather of the white heron. Here take it. His fingers big and so very soft as they touched hers. Hold it up into the sea wind. Listen to it.

Later she would hold the feather up and face it into the wind. Feel the feather come alive between her thumb and forefinger. The edges curling, eager to be off, longing to be away from the earth to soar high above the ground. To glide effortlessly, the power of a thousand sea-borne winds contained in the delicate perfection of each feather hair, the whispering of far-off places, of magical forests and unknown lakes.

This is what she told David. A thousand sea-borne winds. He loved her stories.

Whenever she spoke of Te Whiti her eyes would fill with tears and she would look away. To the south usually and sniff and say, he lived there. Pointing. In a *Pah*, a large village named Parihaka. There were so many unjust things. She often could not finish speaking, her throat closing with noises of grief. As if what she would feel was best borne in silence. Left half said or not said, gestured at. The power of utterance holding qualities of destruction and betrayal. The thing and the thing done remaining true. Thus a flower placed on a table bespoke love more eloquently than any words.

David could not always see the connections between the names and the Arrangements. The placing of shells, stones and wood. His mother had laughed and said it doesn't matter. You can see whatever you want. It is like finding animals in the clouds. Some find lions and some lambs. Dragons or horses. This is the wondrous part my darling, all that to a world of possibility.

Mr Gill's nose David said and pointed at a bulbous-shaped cloud. They both laughed at this.

Mahmoud's weight was distributed over David's shoulders in the fireman's carry as they made their way along the beach. David held Mahmoud's wrist and ankle with one hand and carried his rifle in the other.

My mother would point out to sea, David said. Just like you did today. Well not exactly but it reminded me. And gather things from the beach. Stones and wood. Shells too, all kinds. She felt sorry for the ugly shells.

Mahmoud groaned and said we have a saying, a *hadith*, David. We say Paradise lies between the feet of mothers. Remember I told you of this? he whispered, then made another small groan.

David was silent.

You're a bit heavier than a lamb Mahmoud.

What about a donkey?

Don't make me laugh mate.

They moved down the beach, David concentrating on the weight, on keeping his back straight. On his feet sinking into the sand and stones. Mahmoud trying not to think of the pain. Silently praising Allah. Praising Allah for the pain.

There is a brotherhood in the Caucasus that uses physical pain, Mahmoud said. His voice becoming hoarse.

David said nothing.

Physical pain to shock the seeker into a state of being beside themselves. To experience being as non-being.

David shook his head. I don't understand. Shush now.

It is not unknown in the Christian world.

I don't know about these things. Please stop talking.

In some of your monastic traditions I think. To become closer to God.

David felt his feet sinking further into the soft sand. It was becoming more and more difficult to keep walking.

If we can separate ourselves from what many of us believe is the false reality of this world.

David stopped. I doubt that mate.

You are very ignorant Mahmoud said. But it is not your fault.

I think we have to rest for a moment David whispered. He was almost panting. His shirt wet, starting to spot with blood from his wounds.

Yes. All right.

David slowly squatted and lowered Mahmoud onto the beach. He rolled onto his back and made a groaning noise. Mahmoud too was lying on his back looking up at the sky. It was enormous, blue.

And it had been there, it seemed, forever. He was holding up his leg with the amputated foot.

They were both quiet for a while.

Have you heard of *jihad* David?

No.

It is a holy war.

Right.

But the Faithful of my order believe it is a war against unbelief.

David made a grunting noise. He was sweating heavily. Still lying on his back, his hands on his chest. He could feel that his wounds had opened and were bleeding freely. Blood was warmer than sweat. Like oil.

David began to breathe as if going to sleep. To relax.

He called himself a dog, Mahmoud said.

Who?

Hajibektash Veli. For humility.

The lion-skin man? Who walked on the sea?

Yes.

A dog?

A dog.

Jesus Mahmoud you are heavy. Why would he do that? Call himself a dog?

Humility and fidelity. Mmm. I think we will have to get going David, my hand is bleeding. Leg too, quite badly I'm afraid. Please do not blaspheme the prophet Jesus Isa peace be upon Him.

David rolled onto his side and then slowly got to his feet. Sand and pebbles sticking to his back. Moved over to where Mahmoud was.

All right mate. Sorry about that. I forgot you are a little sensitive about Jesus. Hold on. He knelt in front of Mahmoud. Just get your arm across my shoulder.

David your back is covered in blood. It is quite bad enough. I should look.

Mahmoud, he said, just brush the stuff off and get on would you?

Mahmoud paused. David, he said. I should look.

David made a noise of impatience. Do I have to swear at you? Call you animal names?

Oh David, Mahmoud said. He leaned forward and rested his damaged hand on David's shoulder. Gently brushed the clinging sand and stones from David's shirt with his other hand. Then he leaned across David's upper back and whispered brother.

Up, David said and stood. Blew air out through his nose like a fighter. Steadied himself. Took a firmer grip of Mahmoud's wrist and ankle. Stood up. They swayed as David got his footing on the beach.

Your rifle. Mahmoud said.

The rifle was still lying flat on the beach.

David groaned no. Stood for a moment, shook himself like a horse would and then, keeping his back straight, lowered them both down. Still looking up, felt for the rifle.

To your right a little Mahmoud said. A little more. There it is.

David felt for the rifle, found it and stood up again.

You would think I would weigh a little less with one foot and a few fingers missing, Mahmoud whispered.

Don't make me laugh Mahmoud.

Dogs also eat shit by the way David.

David began to walk, shrugged Mahmoud a little higher onto his shoulders. Mahmoud gasped.

Sorry.

No don't worry.

Dogs what?

Eat shit.

David began to laugh, coughed. I told you not to make me laugh.

Sorry. Mahmoud was smiling. But they do. Happy birthday my friend.

They do. They certainly do. Thank you.

David could feel the blood running down the backs of his legs.

Thank you Mahmoud, he said. No more walks for you for a while. *Jesus christ.*

David do not blaspheme.

Sorry.

David you are bleeding. I can see the blood on the stones behind us.

You are bleeding too Mahmoud.

There is a lot of blood.

Don't look at it mate. Close your eyes.

꩜

The old man dressed slowly and stepped to the window. Pulled back the curtain. There was no light from outside, the morning was still dark. Rain beaded the window. He noticed his half-reflection slide across the glass, turned and rubbed his hand across his face. Stood for a moment with his fingers in his white beard, a prophet figure. Smiled to himself.

Looked up as he heard the thunder.

The eye dog Floss whined and then there was another solid rolling sound of thunder coming down the valley from the eastern high country. He looked to the door where Floss was waiting and whistled to comfort her.

The rain came again across his hut, harder this time with a lashing squall. The candle light moved away from the direction of where the weather was coming from, the shadows towards it.

His left hip ached and he moved his leg from side to side. Rubbed his hip where it hurt most.

Yet another breaking-open sound of thunder came over them and Floss made a small bark this time. He spoke out, said that'll do Floss girl. Then the rain came down as if in answer to the splitting of the thunder.

In the half-brown darkness he reached to the table where the

Coleman lamp was, lifted the glass off the lamp body and lit the wick. A helix of smoke funnelled out. He turned the small brass finial until the flame was steady, replaced the glass. Replaced the lamp in the centre of the table.

Soft lamplight spread down and across the inside of the two-roomed hut.

He returned to his bedside and blew out the candle.

Crossed the floor into the kitchen area, lifted the stove lid. He leaned forward over the stove and blew onto the embers, a small cloud of ash rising up around his face. Nodded as he saw some were still red. Newspaper, kindling. Opened a ventilation lever. Waited until the flames took and replaced the lid. Put a kettle on the stove top.

It was three days before they left the tented lines again and late morning when they came across the funeral.

There were twelve graves. They had been dug in a straight line. The pale, rocky soil had been piled up along one side to form a long shallow trench. Around the edges of the graves the ground was cleared and spaded flat. At one end of the trench there stood a chaplain and a padre. On the left hand side of the trench a firing party, and opposite them a group of nurses in long khaki dresses, scarlet shawls and wide hats. They had been joined by some other wounded soldiers and medical staff. Major Aberhard was there and two of the other surgeons. Three Sikhs stood alongside the nurses. One of them held the reins of a white horse. Another had a bandage over one eye. A photographer had set up his camera nearby, his head under the cloth folds of a darkening hood. A flash-rod held up in one hand.

The chaplain was reading from a bible he held in his hands. The wind was lifting and ruffling the purple ecclesiastical stole around his shoulders. Dust blew up from the newly dug earth. The padre, standing beside him, smoothed down the front of his surplice and began to intone a blessing. He raised his hand to make the sign of the cross as he spoke.

The wind took the words, it seemed to hold them suspended and carry snatches of them to David and Mahmoud who stood and watched the funeral from a small ridge above the plain.

They heard the chaplain speaking in English, followed by the padre who recited the blessings in Latin. In the name of the Father *In Nomine Patris*. And Son *et Filii*. And Holy Ghost *Et Spiritus Sanctus*.

And then they spoke together, through Christ our Lord. The wind keened. They could not hear any more of what was being said.

We too have our schisms, Mahmoud whispered. The Sunnis and Shiites just like you Christians. Catholics and Protestors.

Protestants, David whispered out of the corner of his mouth. Then there was a silence as a small whirling dust-devil carried itself across the flat ground to their left. A stack of wooden crosses fell over.

The funeral party watched this phenomenon unfolding. The nurses put their hands on their heads to hold down their hats. Some of the soldiers made the sign of the cross.

There, Mahmoud said very softly, the word of God. No?

I doubt it David said.

Genesis 1...In the beginning God.

Mahmoud was leaning on his crutches. David stood next to him. They both held broad-brimmed Australian hats in their hands. David was wearing a short-sleeved white shirt with no collar and a sweat cloth tied around his throat to stop the chafing of his healing wounds. He had wide khaki braces that held up baggy khaki trousers. Puttees wound around his lower legs above leather hobnailed boots. Mahmoud was wearing blue and white striped pyjamas and an Australian khaki jacket. He had a single hospital shoe on his foot and his other leg was held up behind. The bottom of the pyjama leg pinned up to cover the bandage. One hand was still heavily bandaged. He whispered Allah from time to time as he watched the funeral unfolding below them.

Revelation 20...And I saw the dead, small and great, stand before God.

David nudged Mahmoud. Do you want some honey? He held out a glass jar with a screw top. A small spoon under his finger on top of the jar.

Mahmoud frowned at him. Looked down at David's hand. A piece of the waxy honeycomb was on top, oozing golden liquid.

David, he said and gestured with his bearded chin towards the funeral.

No? David said. The bees feed on rosemary I was told. It is very good.

Mahmoud ignored him and turned back to the funeral. Shook his head.

Psalm 23…Surely goodness and mercy shall follow me all the days of my life: and I will dwell in the house of the Lord for ever.

Blessed are the peacemakers: for they shall be called the children of God.

Amos said, Prepare to meet thy God.

Ashes to ashes dust to…

Then they were singing a hymn. How Great Thou Art.

David heard the refrain my Saviour come to me and remembered his mother's funeral. I hear the rolling thunder…

They had no hymn books and only a few of them knew the words. There were gaps and silences.

The broken, open-air singing ended and there was the sound of coughing.

The Last Post was playing and David heard the command called out: Firing party.

Shoulder arms. Ready. The rattle of rifle bolts.

Fire.

The flat smack of sound. He saw two of the nurses had their hands to their mouths. The officers were saluting.

Ready. Again the rifle bolts. Fire.

And then it was over with the last volley. Ready.

Fire.

Shoulder arms. Order arms.

The officers began to file past the graves. Each of them dropped a handful of soil in each grave. The wind whipped the hat from the head of one of the officers and sent it spinning away.

The nurses began to file alongside the graves. Hands to their heads as they bent, seeming almost to curtsey as they dropped their handful of soil. Next the wounded and accompanying medics.

One of the locals who had been recruited to dig graves was running after the officer's hat wheeling on its brim down the slope towards Mudros harbour.

Mahmoud was watching the gravedigger. He said something.

Do you think he will get it? David said.

I hope not.

David nodded to himself. I am sorry I offered you honey before Mahmoud. I hope I didn't offend.

Mahmoud turned to him. No, he said. No of course not. Why?

I thought the...never mind.

Mahmoud stared at him.

My foot that is not there aches, he said. My fingers that are not there ache. But you David. You are as clumsy sometimes as a child and yet also a dangerous man. You make me laugh. King George the Fifth.

Look, David said.

The gravedigger was running back towards the British officer holding the man's hat in his hand. The officer took his hat and patted him on the shoulder. The gravedigger was smiling and began to bow. The British officer stopped him. He patted him again and reached into his pocket.

David heard Mahmoud make a noise in his throat.

The officer handed something to the gravedigger. The gravedigger smiled and bent his head, to kiss the officer's hand, then as the officer snatched it away, he took two steps back, moving his hand and head in gestures of gratitude and humility. The officer waved his dismissal and turned away.

You English have an expression, Mahmoud said. A vulgar expression. I am not sure I should say this at the moment. Funerals are a sacred time.

They must have been officers, David said, separate graves. And the bugle.

Four more gravediggers had appeared, and began to shovel earth into the holes. The wind caught the dirt and dust flew away towards the sea. Another of the gravediggers was carrying the stack of wooden crosses under his arm. He began to lay them down at the head of each grave.

Major Aberhard, the Australian doctor from Melbourne, had allowed David to accompany Mahmoud during their joint convalescence. Called it escort duty. Most irregular. Mahmoud said probably only an Australian would allow such bending of regulations. And after all it was his nickname: Major 'Ave-a-heart.

But Mahmoud's qualification was from the Royal College of Surgeons of London where the major too had trained. And Mahmoud had been most persuasive. As indeed had the young New Zealand sergeant David Monroe who, it was reported, had carried the Turkish doctor down to the beach in spite of his own wounds. Impressive, the bond that seemed to have grown up between these two.

That they were both clearly a bit doolally was unsurprising after having been being blown up by a 15-inch naval shell. Apparently the Turk had been rendering first aid to an Australian boy and was most distressed over his death.

It is the eighteenth of October Sergeant Monroe, Major Aberhard said. Your new battalion commander Colonel Fulham has cabled us and asked when you will be returning to unit. Short of experienced men it seems. He speaks highly of you. Exceptional, he says. This is bloody rare for you New Zealanders. Bloody stoical lot. Adequate bespeaks high praise. Major Aberhard smiled and winked.

How are your face and shoulder David? he said. The shrapnel across your lower back and buttocks also wasn't it? A beard one day perhaps? Cover most of the scarring.

Yes sir. Fine sir. Thank you.

Major Aberhard looked at him, raised his eyebrows. Good.

David cleared his throat, waited.

The major was reading from a sheet of paper. You have been mentioned in dispatches. And there is a pending promotion to acting platoon commander for your actions on Chunuk Bair in August.

The major took off his glasses and put them down on the desk. Smiled.

Yes sir David said. His voice was quiet. Thank you.

How is your...friend, Sergeant?

David stared at the large man behind the desk. The surgeon, Major Aberhard. He was balding and had a large protruding forehead. There were lines around his eyes and he looked very tired. He had grown a moustache. The hair seemed to stick straight out like a blonde toothbrush. David knew that the major was both highly capable and compassionate.

In pain sir. Still.

Major Aberhard was squeezing the bridge of his nose. Yes. He cleared his throat. I expect he is David. I expect so. However. He stopped and cleared his throat again. Tapped the desk with the pencil he held in his fingers.

He will be shipped to a prisoner of war camp in Palestine next week and you will be RTU also next week. Orders from on high I'm afraid.

The major held up his hand, paused and then lifted it as if thinking of something else, almost spoke and then suddenly sneezed.

David was looking at the canvas wall of the tent behind the major. A small lizard moved across the canvas in a short rush and then froze. The major sneezed again.

Quite, he said and took a handkerchief out of his pocket. Blew his nose. Turned the handkerchief over and looked at what was there. Winter coming.

The old man took the lamp and stepped outside onto the small veranda of the hut. The wind moved the lamp to one side and blew against him, flattening his trousers and pushing his beard across his face. He used one hand to smooth his hair away from his eyes. He found Floss and let her off her chain one-handed. Then, holding the lamp at shoulder height, peered out at the morning. He could see nothing beyond the weak light cast by the lamp. Floss ran out onto the wet grass, squatted to urinate and ran back to him.

The sky was black and the wind-borne rain continued to come in squalls. Water ran in a line from a blocked gutter. He could smell the wetness of the grass and trees and the slightly metallic tang of lightning in the air. Then the old man sneezed. Cleared his throat and took a handkerchief out of his pocket and blew his nose.

He knew that dawn would come soon enough and there was no use riding out in the dark, you could see nothing riding in the dark but he would get everything prepared that he could. The old man nodded to himself and rubbed his eyes. He would have to wait until first light.

He put the lamp onto a piece of wire bent into an S shape and hung from one of the timber supports. The light swung back and forth in the wind. He took a hat and an oilskin coat off another hook and stepped onto the wet path that led to the nearby horse paddock.

The grey gelding he had named John was waiting at the gate, his backside turned into the wind.

The old man retrieved a rope lead looped over the fence and snapped the catch onto the halter ring under the gelding's chin. Whispered who the good boy John who the boy? Bad morning mate. Walk back now. Made a kissing sound with his mouth. Opened the gate and pushed against the wet front of the horse to let him open the gate and walk through.

He brought the gelding through the gate and then turned him to close it. The horse's hooves made wet sucking sounds in the mud and the chain was cold and wet in his hands. Floss stood off to one side, a shadow in the dim light cast by the swaying lamp on the veranda. Her head turned to one side against the weather.

There was a tearing crack of thunder and John went up in the air and pulled away from the old man, snorting in fear, straining away from the rope.

He held onto the rope with both hands and dug his heels into the mud.

Whoa now whoa the boy whoeey now, he called to the gelding. Don't be silly.

John stopped pulling back, stood and listened to the soothing of the old man's voice. Stood still in the rain. His nostrils distended as he smelled the metallic air. His eyes rolled, seeking out the source of the terrifying noise.

Who the good boy? the old man said. Stepped forward and

patted his neck. Rubbed a wet hand across his nose. Come on now you give us both a fright here this morning old mate.

He waited. Felt John's long neck muscle relaxing under his hand. He chuckled. Good boy.

The old man led the horse to an open-sided machinery shed that had been built onto the back of the woolshed. He turned on the light. Electricity had been connected to the woolshed for the shearing. A single cobweb-shrouded light bulb glowed orange in the rafters. He stared up at it and sniffed. Made a humming noise, whistled to Floss.

Inside the shed it was still and dry and it smelled of hay and creosote and oil. There were two horse stalls and a benched area where equipment and various pieces of machinery were repaired. In one of the stalls a red and grey Massey Ferguson tractor was parked. A bale of hay was on the carry tray, an old coat across the engine cowling. Some loose and knotted baling twine across that. A six-inch spanner. A Lister shearing handpiece. Wide metal combs and cutters strung on a loop of wire.

He led John into the other stall, turned him in a tight circle and faced him out. Bent over to secure the two holding chains onto the halter. Looped the rope lead over the edge of the horse stall and began to remove the wet cover.

When he had finished taking off the cover, he found a towel and rubbed the neck and ears of the horse. Dried off the tail and mane; all the while talking softly to him.

The John he called him. He had been named after a lot of horses that had come before him. It was thus more than a name or an individual; it was an affirmation of memory, a respect of that which had been. For as long as he could, he had always kept three horses and he had named them The John, The Layla and

The Majnun. He had refused to answer anyone who asked where such names came from. Looking at them as if they should know better than to ask a man his ways or his whys.

Mahmoud had said that if you want to find what you are looking for, you have to follow your footsteps to where you have come from. Thus everything is. Be quiet man. Just be and stop trying to know. Everything will reveal itself as it should in due course and if not who cares? It is as it should be.

The government men walking here into me and my world then, he thought, and now. Asking such questions. The memories have no sequence to them. No path or footsteps to follow. They are like the moving picture shows but somehow played backwards and out of order. Am I the only one to make sense of it? Of course Mahmoud would say, you are. Who else?

But God? Allah?

And that is, after all as it should be. The nature of a horse is that of a horse. Who are you or I to sit in judgment of others? To say that they be more or less worthy than us of this life? This is not why we are here. Wake up now.

He had said, sell certainty buy bewilderment. You are a fool. You will have nothing. Don't even try.

Another time he said, do not expect to eat dates from a willow tree.

And it would not matter in the least. None of it. It will be as it should because if it was supposed to be anything else, it would be. You cannot make Paradise from this, Mahmoud held up a handful of earth. From this you make pots and bricks. Not Paradise.

Catherine Sarah's daughter was another matter entirely. The old man shook his head and scratched at his damaged ear as if he had heard something he didn't want to.

The John, he said to the horse and left his fingers in the stiff hair of John's mane. Threw the towel over his shoulder and stood still.

Who the boy?

He squeezed the bridge of his nose between his thumb and index finger. Then pressed his thumb and middle finger into his eyes, gently palpated, easing the pliant globes beneath the lids.

Whispered again, who the boy John? The good boy now.

David rose quietly and walked out of the tent. He squatted in the cool early morning air and looked to where he knew the sun would rise. He heard the coughing from the different lines within the surrounding camps. And in the very far distance the occasional deep booming of artillery fire.

The first touch of dawn began to grey the land and he could make out the shape of the beach and the boat harbour. He studied the jetty and the headland area. There were no sentries. The sea was flat, glittering in the moonlight and barely moving in the still air.

He thought of the dream he had been having, as real as the scene he was watching now. Even blind men dream, Mahmoud had assured him. Men blind from birth, they dream in colours and shapes. They see that which they have never seen.

The movement of Mahmoud. He was getting out of his hospital cot and urinating into the chamber pot. David heard his wooden crutch fall against the cot.

He came out of the tent and breathed in the morning air.

David he said quietly, where are you?

I am here David said, knowing that he could sense him being there but not see where he was. I was dreaming of my mother and I am wondering what will happen.

They sat in the darkness and listened. They could hear each other breathing and then the wind coming over the sea and the sea beginning to move with the pull of the earth. The moon waned. The tide was coming in. Waves washing in, clearly heard, washing out.

Hear the waves? Mahmoud eventually said.

Yes.

How many waves we hear is a question that should not be asked.

I was just wondering what will happen, David said.

I know, Mahmoud whispered. Excuse me David, I must pray.

David watched the night shapes of the coast and listened to the wind bringing the sea to him. He heard the ponderous movement of Mahmoud return to the tent and clumsily wash his hands and face and foot before prayer.

Then he heard the recitations begin as Mahmoud kneeled and bent forward.

David only recognised some of the words, but their cadence and rhythm stilled him. He found himself raising his hands to his face and then lowering them as he had seen Mahmoud do. It seemed like the most natural thing to be doing. He felt the

peace come over him. He sat still and thought of the countless thousands of men and women and children who would be
moving with these words. How their bodies would bend and
poise and sway and rise up, again and again. How they would
move back and forward and back and forward always with the
recitations and affirmations. How they would all, countless
thousands of the humble faithful, rise to sway forward in adora-
tion and submission and would then rise again and ease back and
be still. And then David repeated what Mahmoud was saying:
la ilaha illa Allah. He knew what it meant. There is no god but
God. And he too felt the peace be almost physically upon him.
The next line he thought was, and Mohammed was his Prophet.
But he wasn't sure.

After a while Mahmoud returned to where David was sitting. He
said, this future, as he sat.

What?

Some believe it is predetermined my friend.

David looked at him. What, Mahmoud?

Mm, yes, while others believe we can create our own future.
Our own fate.

What do you believe? David said.

Mahmoud did not reply, he seemed to be thinking. David did
not ask again.

They sat in silence and watched the light change over the land.
From deep violet to grey and blue to the blood orange, apricot and
yellow. And then the clarity of the morning light. Smoke from the
early-morning cooking fires began to rise and drift over the island.
They heard the coughing of hundreds of men as they woke.

That evening David returned to visit Mahmoud.

Assalamu alaiküm, he said.

Mahmoud had looked up from the book he was reading when David entered the tent. *Wa alaiküm assalaam* David.

David approached and Mahmoud indicated for him to sit on the cot next to him. Mahmoud moved over.

David shook his head and instead half-squatted half-knelt next to Mahmoud. We can go tonight, he whispered.

Mahmoud said nothing. Looked down and nodded.

I have a boat and a fisherman to take us.

This is dangerous David. What do you have in mind brother?

He will take us to the mainland and then I will help you return to your village and your wife Aisha, your daughters.

And then?

And then, God willing, David whispered. *Insha'Allah.*

Insha'Allah, Mahmoud repeated.

I can return, once you are safely home. Or…

You can stay with us Mahmoud said.

David nodded.

Mahmoud smiled and then stopped smiling. This fisherman?

Yes?

Does he have the face of a spider?

David looked at Mahmoud. What do you mean?

Is he to be trusted?

I am giving him my rifle and ten English pounds.

A fortune.

Yes.

What will he do for this fortune?

David looked over his shoulder. The lines of tents were quiet. Mahmoud was the only Turkish officer on Lemnos with serious wounds. David had been assigned to him as both aide and guard. As a result Mahmoud had enjoyed a rare privacy and respect.

I cannot sail a boat. I wouldn't know my arse from my elbow in a boat.

Your arse from your sorry I don't understand? Mahmoud said.

Doesn't matter. He will take us to the mainland. It is only fifty kilometres. He will say nothing. From there we can find our way. I have saved some supplies and still have money. There is morphine if you need it.

Mahmoud lifted his head. Blinked and touched his bottom lip with his tongue. Bit his bottom lip. Inclined his head to one side and smiled.

If you need it, David repeated.

Mahmoud nodded. Sometimes it sings to me in my dreams.

David made a noise of impatience.

The song is like…

Ssssh Mahmoud, you know you…We can buy a donkey for you.

Mahmoud was staring out to sea. Then he turned as if hearing what David was saying. Did you say a donkey? Mahmoud said. David are you making fun of me?

David laughed. No no. Of course not.

Well then David. If you are serious.

Yes?

I have to ask you again and for the last time. And I should know better than to ask. Allah is wise.

What?

Why? Why are you risking everything for me?

David looked into Mahmoud's eyes. Do you remember when

we first came here? And they had taken off what was left of your foot and hand? I was bashed up too and had lost some of my hearing. But not like you.

Some.

I came to visit you often and then was assigned to guard you. I asked Major Aberhard if I could because of what had happened and when he spoke to you it was...

Yes.

You asked me once to look into your eyes. That is one of the reasons. The other is your blasphemies. David laughed.

There was a lot of morphine, Mahmoud said smiling. Turned his head to one side as a form of smiling explanation.

Remember, you said: Look at me.

Yes.

They were both silent trying to remember.

Mahmoud said something in a language David couldn't understand and then in English, I cannot explain it. If I turned, whirling to the music that is so beautiful that it keeps me here on this earth instead of ascending to Paradise then, perhaps.

David studied the man sitting next to him, smiled and shook his head. Said, you...Waited and then spoke again. We were both still recovering from the wounds. Mine weren't as bad as yours. It was the second visit I think. It doesn't matter but I think it was the first or second time.

And...David stopped speaking.

You brought me a can of sardines?

Yes and you asked how my wounds were and I began...The tears.

Yes, Mahmoud whispered now. It was quite beautiful. I could taste the salt of your tears. I beheld Majnun. The truth of you.

And, David said very softly, you said I was God. That we all are and that it is a death sentence.

I asked you to look into my eyes, Mahmoud said. Yes I remember now.

David was frowning.

David, Mahmoud said. It is *wa Mohammed rasul Allah*.

What?

And Mohammed was His Prophet.

How did you know?

You were speaking to yourself David, Mahmoud laughed. As I prayed this morning Mahmoud snorted slightly as he laughed. If you could see your face now.

David smiled and then laughed also. There is something, he said. There really is.

Shall I tell you what Shi–ites say in *Shahada*? The affirmation of faith.

No David said. Please. I am confused enough.

Do you remember?

Yes David said.

How are your eyes?

They are fine you barbarian. Be ready Mahmoud I will come for you tonight and we will go.

Yes David.

David stood. He placed his hand on Mahmoud's shoulder. Mahmoud reached up and put his hand on David's. He was still looking down.

Soon, David said, you will be with Aisha and your children.

The tears were running down his face. Thank you David. I am afraid.

David said nothing. He squeezed Mahmoud's shoulder.

I know he said. And took his hand away.

Mahmoud didn't want to say that he wasn't afraid for himself.

David turned and walked out of the tent.

Mahmoud noticed he was unarmed. Perhaps he had already sold his rifle.

His name was Alexis and he waited for these two strange men who seemed to love each other, sitting in the prow of his small fishing boat, with his shoulders below the gunwales and his head just visible. He was smoking a perfumed Turkish cheroot. Alexis thought about these two unlikely fools. One of them had lost a part of his leg. He wore the uniform of the hated Ottoman. The hat of the Australians. The other an Englishman. He too had been wounded from the war on the Gellepoli coast. And was probably mad.

Alexis thought about the coast line along the Dardanelles. The Thracian Sea. As far even as the Sea of Marmara. He had fished those waters with his father. What had the English been thinking? To land there was madness. He shook his head and whispered madness again and then who am I? Shrugged. Threw the cheroot over the side and scratched under his jaw. His beard itched and he wondered if they would come. The boat rocked in the darkness from side to side. Unfamiliar currents from the ballast waves of foreign warships came into the harbour. Everything was changing. He touched the wood of the English Lee Enfield rifle the soldier had paid him with. Put his fingers to his nose and smelled linseed oil. Why would he not accept? He was a boatman and he was paid. He did not ask questions. Did the ferryman ask his passengers why they wanted to cross? Even Charon required only a coin under the tongue and no explanation.

He heard his name, a whisper.

Alexis. Alexis.

He saw them coming slowly down the jetty. One of them was on crutches. That would be the Ottoman. The Englishman was carrying a pack on his back and two sacks in his hands. My Lady, he whispered these nights are getting colder. Then he hissed, mister. Mister here. Here.

The freezing October night and ice-clear star-filled black had given way to a hot mid-morning sun. The fishing boat moved silently through the water. The two heavily mascaraed eyes painted on the prow staring, almost in surprise. The bow barely raised a wave as the boat passed across the headland and entered the sheltered waters of the bay. The sun ran alongside the boat and caught in the sea, reflecting itself in crazed hexagonal shapes, forming and reforming in constantly changing variations of light in the clear water.

David could hear the water running under the boat like liquid at the back of his throat. Vibrato with an indrawn breath. His hand trailed in the cold salty sea, it seemed as blue and pure as the cloudless sky.

The cross mast swung slightly and the main mast creaked. They had passed yet another headland and the winds changed. The triangular sail collapsed and then turned and pulled itself open as the fisherman stood and pushed the boom to one side. He sat down, sniffed and held the tiller. The canvas of the sail creaked as it opened. It smelled of fish and wax; tallow and hot pine gum.

They were tilting and moving into the small bay now. The fisherman had followed the headland around into the lee of the bay. He lifted his head and put his tongue between his teeth as he swung the tiller sharply against the prevailing current.

They yawed. The bow of the fishing boat swung around to starboard and pointed directly at the beach.

Mahmoud was sitting in the bow, facing aft. A blanket around his shoulders. He had his eyes closed but David noticed that his lips moved from time to time. Alexis spoke to him, saying something in Greek which he didn't understand and pointing with his left, free hand and his facial expression towards the beach.

David was kneeling holding the blue painted side of the boat. He nodded in reply to Alexis and crawled forward and touched Mahmoud on the shoulder. The boat lifted, caught on the soft swell of the incoming tide, and began to gather speed. Small waves carried them forward.

Mahmoud opened his eyes as the bottom of the boat scraped onto the sand and pebbles of the beach. They were stopping. David overbalanced and tipped forward, almost sprawling over Mahmoud's body. He put his hand up and grabbed the wooden prow.

David looked behind him to see Alexis leaping over the side. He held the bow, paused and then with the next incoming swell pulled the boat as far up the beach as he could. He looked at David and motioned with a leaning of his head for David to join him. He said, mister.

David jumped over the side and held the bow on the other side. They waited and then with the next lift of the incoming wave, Alexis said something in Greek and David said now, and they both pulled the small fishing boat as far forward onto the beach as they could. The tide coming in overtook the boat almost as soon as they had pulled it up. Alexis shrugged and made a digging motion with his hands. David nodded, unsure what he meant, but held onto the prow while Alexis returned to the stern and collected the anchor and ropes. He ran this forward onto the beach and dug the metal fluke into the sand just beyond the high water mark.

The small waves began to turn the fishing boat sideways.

Alexis returned to where David had got back into the boat and was helping Mahmoud to stand. Alexis held up his hands to help. David nodded to him and passed him the sacks. He took them and, holding them at shoulder height, well above the water, walked them up the beach and put them on the sand.

David was back in the water alongside the boat, now holding up his hands and speaking to Mahmoud.

It was nonsense: do you know, my friend, the difference between a pint of milk and a river?

No, Mahmoud said gently and smiled.

Lean forward Mahmoud, take my hand.

The boat juddered sideways as the keel resisted the beach in the tide. Mahmoud took his hand. He placed the forearm of his injured hand on David's shoulder, shaking as he was caught between the movement of the boat and his friend's outstretched hands. The remembered trauma of his wounds had made his body afraid, David knew. Knew too how he detested this cowardice.

Mahmoud made a noise of insecurity and then another noise as if to resist his fear.

Go on David said, Mahmoud trust me now. Just let go and lean forward. Trust me mate. Let go.

Mahmoud trembled and said what? What's the bloody difference David?

They both can't ride a bicycle.

David walked back two steps into the surf as Mahmoud collapsed forward and let all his weight fall onto David. He was laughing.

David said *jesus*, laughed also and swayed in the surf as Mahmoud slid down his front. He held him and said Mahmoud my friend. It is all right. It is. It is.

David held onto his undamaged arm. Mahmoud held his bandaged leg and hand up and looked at the sky. Thanked Allah. David moved his hip next to Mahmoud's hip and put an arm under his.

Come on mate, he said.

They began to wade, hop and half stumble onto the beach. Both trying to synchronise their limbs in the moving sea and at the same time support each other. They formed a strange three-legged shambling creature joined at the hip and shoulder. Stumbled and fell in a confused tangle as they reached the shore. Alexis watched them and said *cunt of a goat*. Turned away touching the top of his head.

The beach sand was a dirty pumice stone white, grey pebbles and white shells. Wild olive trees grew down to the high water mark. There was an ancient limestone wall and a ruin behind that, further up on the flat ground just above the beach. A flat series of plinths of what had been a walkway with the plain scroll lines of a series of small Ionian pillars, the fluting chipped as if it had been shot away. Behind the flat ground, great rocky cliffs rose up, sheer until there was nothing but the cliffs and then the sky above them. David looked to the left and right. There were headlands on both sides of the bay that also rose up in stark relief against the sky.

They were in a small half-moon bay about half a mile across.

You can…Alexis said. He pointed to a wall.

Alexis approached Mahmoud carrying the crutches. He leaned them against the wall, ignoring Mahmoud's outstretched hand, then turned and walked back towards the beach. He spat and said, Ottoman. The crutches were just out of Mahmoud's reach. Mahmoud stood and hopped, holding the wall with one hand until he reached the crutches. He positioned them in his armpits and swung himself back towards the beach, following Alexis.

Eh. He called to Alexis.

Alexis stopped, he didn't turn for a moment. His shoulders seemed to lift.

Mahmoud saw David look up from what he was doing.

Eh Mr Lemnos man, Mahmoud called again.

Alexis turned slowly. He said nothing, raised his chin as if to demand what.

Thank you for your insults. Mahmoud said. If you would listen I would tell you a story. I doubt you would sit to hear but may Allah bless you for delivering us safely here. The blessings of Allah and Mohammed His beloved Prophet be upon you.

Alexis looked puzzled, paused and then shrugged with his hands up as if he had not understood.

David glanced at Mahmoud, smiling and holding onto the wall.

Alexis approached David and held out his hand, palm up. Rubbed his thumb, forefinger and middle finger together. Money, he said. I go now, you pay me.

David reached into his pocket and took out a leather purse. He extracted several coins from the purse. Counted them into the man's palm

There. Thank you. You have my rifle. I gave that to you as a down-payment.

Alexis lifted the weight of the English coins in his hand, smiled at the sound and made no other acknowledgment, walked back to the fishing boat. He held the side and leapt in.

David was walking up the beach, carrying the pack on his back and the two sacks in his hands to where Mahmoud still leaned on the crutches. He heard the oiled metallic sound of a rifle bolt being opened and slid forward. Alexis' voice saying, *English.*

Mahmoud whispered Allah.

David turned and said Oh no. Don't.

Alexis was walking up the beach towards them pointing the rifle at them from his hip.

Give it, he said.

David knelt quickly and shrugged off his pack. Opened the straps and took out a Webley service revolver. He pointed it at Alexis.

Alexis was pulling at the trigger. The rifle would not fire. David stood up and walked towards him, holding the pistol out. The fisherman was slightly crouched over, he opened the bolt again and slid it back; a brass-coated live round flicked out. He reloaded, closed the bolt and lifted the muzzle of the rifle up and pulled at the trigger again. Again it did not fire. He hissed at the rifle. Cursed it. Crouched over and lifted it up to within a few inches of his face. Shook it.

You do that one more time and I will shoot you, David said.

Alexis straightened and looked at David. He dropped the rifle and took off his sheepskin hat. Dropped to his knees. Holding the hat to his chest as if praying, please, he said. Please mister.

David was standing above him. The muzzle of the pistol at the left side of his temple.

Please mister.

David touched the wet hair of Alexis' temple with the front sight of the revolver.

Alexis cried, I have two daughter. Only five, eight year old. David did not know what he was saying, all he could hear was his own breath.

He was breathing in through his nose and out through his nose. His eyes saw everything very clearly. His breath calmed him. He felt the growling coming up from beneath his testicles, twisting around his spine in a thrilling clasp and release. He opened his mouth and sighed. Something coming up making him want to laugh and feel the explosion of the pistol in his hand and the shattering of this betrayer's skull, his body driven over. The diseased unworthy blood spraying out. The fisherman's legs flexing out and fitting as David would step over him and shoot him again. He was the death of Alexis the disloyal Limnion. This unfaithful fisherman who should have listened more closely. He started to smile, lips moving over his teeth. He started to kill the fisherman with the smallest movement of his finger and the hammer of the pistol arched.

David.

Mahmoud's voice.

David. Stop. Remember the Australian. Remember who you have become. Spare this idiot. Look at him. I ask for your mercy.

The moment held. Mahmoud lifted one hand, the damaged one, and then as if trying to break into David's thoughts, he said, the noise. We don't want any attention. Someone might hear.

David's arm sagged. He stared at Mahmoud, hesitated. Then he turned back to the kneeling fisherman and he saw himself cutting this Limnion's throat as he would a sheep. Pushing the knife into his neck between the windpipe and spine and cutting out, through both the carotid artery and the jugular vein in a singular motion. The gush of blood soaking his knife-hand and feet. The blood in the trachea smothering all noise. A redemptive thing of flood. The crack of the spine across his knee. He pushed the revolver into his waistband and quickly took out a clasp knife from his pocket. Opened it and automatically tested the blade with his thumb.

Please stop. Please David.

David was holding the hair of the fisherman who had closed his eyes and was making whimpering noises.

Drop the knife David my brother.

David turned and the hand that held the knife drooped. It was so heavy it sought the earth.

Mahmoud?

No please. Spare him. Mahmoud said and raised a crutch almost in benediction. Do not kill this fool. He is not worthy. He was still extending his bandaged hand. Both of Mahmoud's arms were out, wide apart. A supplicant. A supplicant on one leg,

David thought. Smiled in a dazed fashion.

David looked into the face of Alexis. He had closed his eyes. His contorted face. Mouth open and moaning no. His rotten teeth. The tears running into his black beard.

See the light that is shining upon your arm. Mahmoud held both hands out towards him now. See it David my brother.

David looked down to his right at the hand that held the knife. The sun was reflecting from the blade up onto his arm. He looked back to Mahmoud. His eyes asking questions.

Most of what the old man whispered and cooed to John was nonsense. His voice gentle, encouraging. His father's way with a horse. His father's voice with a horse.

And how the John isn't it, was your night now in the wet were you frightened all over your self by the thunder but not you even though we took your balls because you couldn't bear the sight of us alive we cut you proud the John John and look what we have in you now my boy a fine and strong brave horse who will carry me now and not be too grumpy. Ah there you are now. Did you know why there is no difference between a pint of milk and old Floss there? Well they both can't ride a bicycle. Or for that matter a bull through China backwards. The old man chuckled. Who the John? Look out there at the sky it's raining on us.

John's ears moved back and forth as the old man spoke and worked. He moved his feet and once bent his head forward to scratch an itch on his eye with his knee.

When he had finished rubbing John down, the old man laid a dry towel across his back and on top of that, a full wool sheepskin, then he laid the saddle across that. He put on a crupper and a breastplate but left the girth strap undone for the moment. He hung the bridle on a nail next to John and looped the reins back up onto the nail. He took the *pikau* which had been hanging over the side of the stall and put that across the front of the saddle. The *pikau* was an old chaff sack that had been sewed shut and then split halfway through the middle of the sack to form a makeshift saddlebag across the neck of the horse. The old man used the *pikau* to collect wool plucked from dead sheep and to carry orphaned lambs.

Once the *pikau* was secured with a length of baling twine to the saddle rings he placed a strip of oilcloth cut from a worn-out coat across the withers to waterproof the *pikau* as best he could. Threw a light canvas cover sheet across John's backside. He bent over again and, in turn, lifted each of the gelding's feet and using a small metal pick, cleaned out the hooves. Pressed with his thumb at the sole around the frog to check for soreness. Nodded, stood and patted the horse's neck. He collected a white plastic bucket and filled it with chopped lucerne chaff. Returned to the stall where he placed it in a wire ring for John to feed. John put his head into the bucket and nosed at the chaff. Blew out through his nose and began to eat.

Good, the old man said and put both his hands into the small of his own back and arched. Then, holding on to one side of the stall, he cupped one hand under his knee and lifted his left leg as high as he could into his chest. Put it down, turned and rubbed his aching hip. Stood and listened to the sound of John eating.

Whispered again in his father's voice, good boy long day ahead son. That's the boy now.

Waited for a while. Looked at the open side of the machinery shed. To the lifting morning of navy blue light and the glow of a waning moon behind mottled rain clouds.

The canvas sheet moved in the night wind and David stood and checked the ropes. Mahmoud studied him. He was sitting next to the small fire between two columns in a corner of the ancient white-stone ruin. The shadows and light of the fire played against the stones.

David had made the fire from old rosemary twigs and dead pine branches, the smell of the burning resins mingled with the smell of the tea they were drinking.

David looked at Mahmoud. Do you think it is true?

What David?

What the fisherman said.

That we are still on Lemnos?

Yes.

Perhaps. I would not know where we are.

This was a bad idea, David said. I am sorry.

Mahmoud made a face. You are probably right, it was a bad idea.

David sipped his tea.

But not as bad as the idea of the English to attack the heights of Gallipoli no? Mahmoud smiled.

David was watching the light of the fire playing shadows against the ancient stone. He could feel Mahmoud's eyes on him.

What? He turned and looked at Mahmoud.

Mahmoud shook his head, nothing. It doesn't matter.

They were silent for a while. It was getting colder. David stood up and gathered some more branches.

They watched the sparks race into the black sky as he threw

them on the flames.

David, Mahmoud said, why didn't the rifle fire?

David gave a laugh. I took the firing pin out. When you asked me if he had the face of a spider I thought I should be careful.

Mahmoud chuckled. Then he waited for a moment and said, you would have killed him wouldn't you?

David was looking into the fire. His eyes glassy.

You wanted to tell him a story, he said.

I did. I did want to tell him a story. Is that better than shooting him in the head? Or cutting his throat?

What was the story?

Mahmoud smiled. It is a good story. It is a story about a man who wanted to be admitted to a particular city. He went to an honoured teacher and asked how he could enter this Forbidden City. The teacher told his student to pay money to anyone who insulted him for the next two years. The student carried out these instructions and for the next two years faithfully paid whatever money he had on him to anyone who insulted him. After the time had elapsed he returned to the honoured teacher and asked if he could now enter the city of his desires. The teacher asked him if had done as he was instructed for the past two years. The student assured him he had carried out the instructions of the teacher. Well then, the teacher said, perhaps you are ready. We shall see. The teacher told the student to travel to the city of his desires. The student did so, and found a gatekeeper barring the entrance. The student asked if he could pass whereupon the gatekeeper started to abuse him. The student began to laugh. The gatekeeper, incensed, abused him even more, at which the student laughed even harder. Finally the gatekeeper stopped and asked, why do you laugh when I insult you so? The student replied, for the past two years I have been paying anyone who insulted me all the money I had in my pockets and look now I am getting it all for free!

The gatekeeper bowed and opened the gate. Welcome to the city he said.

Mahmoud was chuckling.

You would have told him this story? David said and shook his head.

I would have. But he didn't have the ears to hear it.

I wanted to shoot him, David said. He reached out to put a long, thin stick into the fire, held it up and watched the flame. I really wanted to kill him like nothing else I have ever wanted. I have never felt that way before…It was like being…It wasn't like the fighting at the Cove. Or on Chunuk Bair. It was different. I wanted to kill him like I would desire a woman.

I thought so. It is as it should be.

David turned his head sharply. How can you say that?

I must tell you about the Conference of the Birds. Not now, soon. Now we must sleep but just remember my friend that when the sun is brightest the shadow is the darkest. And you are still only in the second valley with your head on fire. The valley of love. There are seven valleys.

I don't understand you Mahmoud. I don't know what the hell you are talking about most of the time. But I also have never felt.

David stopped. He tried again to say what he felt. With me being…Us. I am not saying this as I should, but I think.

Sleep David. The night is cold. Mahmoud said, rolled over and faced the stone wall, his back to the fire. Then as an afterthought said, it is not hell I am talking about David.

David pulled a face at Mahmoud's back. Poked out his tongue.

You are being a child now.

What do you know Mahmoud? What do you know about anything?

I know that a few hours ago you were a killer of other men and now you are a child.

It was still dark when David rose up and walked out to where the beach was and sat with an olive tree at his back. He had a blanket around his shoulders and the wide-brimmed slouch hat with both sides pulled down. A woollen scarf around his ears. It was colder as the dawn came.

The sun was rising beyond the sheer rock walls behind him. The light fell on the waves several hundred yards out from where he was sitting. It formed a moving line between the two horns that marked the edges of the crescent shape of the bay. He studied the movement of the sun on the sea as the sun rose further in the sky.

After a while he stood up and walked back to where they had made their camp among the ruins. Mahmoud was lying on his side and blowing on the embers of the fire. He had laid some pine needles and small twigs on the embers and when he blew the white ash flew off and the coals glowed red. He closed his eyes against the ash.

A flame appeared and caught onto the pine needles. Mahmoud clumsily righted himself and coned larger sticks onto the flames.

He smiled at David. Good morning. Some of the ash had settled on his beard.

We are on the west side of somewhere, that's for certain David said. Good morning.

Mahmoud nodded and placed a blackened billycan next to the flames. He held up the army-issue canteen. We will need water.

David nodded. There is another canteen and a water bag. The goatskin.

Yes, Mahmoud said, but we will need water soon. It is best to find it now while we still have some, is it not?

I heard naval gunfire. David said. It was coming from the east. From beyond those cliffs.

Here.

David looked at him and stared, he didn't seem to see what he was looking at. I think, he said, we are still on Lemnos. On the west coast. The fisherman surely betrayed us.

Mahmoud nodded. We are in trouble, I believe. They will hate you David, even more than me. You will be condemned as an infidel by your own people.

Never mind, David said. Then, it's not infidel Mahmoud. We call it something else.

He remembered the face of the fisherman. His parting words as he sailed out of the bay, he called out in Greek that they didn't understand but knew to be insults. And then his accented English. You are still on my island. I have left you on Limnos.

And how he had lifted his mouth to the sky and laughed in the open-mouthed mocking way that such men had.

Here is some bread and sausage. It is not the last of the bread. Mahmoud held a small tin plate towards David. We have enough for three more meals. The bread.

Thank you. David took it and they ate in silence.

When David had finished he stood. Well I had better go and have a look around. See what I can see. He bent and picked up both canteens and his pack. You keep the goatskin.

Mahmoud nodded.

I will be back before dark.

Be careful my friend.

David followed a stone-paved path that appeared to lead from behind the ruin directly towards the cliff face. It was framed by two low walls and heavily overgrown with weeds and yellow flowering broom. The stones were well placed and well worn.

After about two hundred yards, the path opened out onto long, flat ground that had perhaps once been an orchard and garden. He examined the black curling bark of a long-unpruned almond tree; the leaves were turning a dark autumn yellow. Along one side of the flat ground there were five apricot trees, their leaves a lighter yellow, fruit hanging thick and deep-dappled orange from the branches. Two fig trees between what looked like old vegetable or herb beds, purple fruit drooping.

There was fallen fruit at the base of the trees. A tangled mass of grapevines, their support structures long rotted. The stone posts that supported the wooden trellis still standing among the tangle of untended vines. Stone benches around a semi-circular space, which looked like a small amphitheatre.

David knelt and studied the area. His eyes moved back and forth, looking through the trees and bushes and not at them. Through a screen of Italian cypress he saw a small aqueduct coming from somewhere near the base of the cliffs and dropping down in a series of yard-wide channels to a long central rectangular-shaped pool. No water flowed from the mouth of the channel.

David waited and listened for a long time. There was silence except for the high call of an occasional sea bird and, as always, the deep crumping sound of gunfire in the distance. The autumn day warmed as he knelt there. He smelt the air and the sea wind that came over him. Wished suddenly he had a dog with him. Cicadas came awake in the sun.

He stood and walked quickly through the orchard area to the pool. It was about ten yards long and two yards wide, dry and filled with weeds. A small fig tree had begun to grow there. The stone channel at the far end that had once fed the pool was similarly full of sand and wild grass. On each side of the pool there was a wide walking space and then beyond that a line of stone figures, defaced and smashed into scarred and wounded shadows of what they had been.

Again he knelt and waited. Listened and raised his nose for the smell of tobacco smoke. The smell of burning tobacco carried a long way.

He waited and watched.

A long time passed until he stood and followed the stone channels to the base of the cliffs. There he discovered a natural spring now reed-choked and silted into a thick, still pond. It curved away to his right, following the base of the cliffs. The ground was spongy underfoot. He began to clear away the reeds and dug the silt out in thick handfuls. An ancient terracotta field tile emerged filled with silt and the roots of reeds. He cleaned it out and positioned it into the mouth of the spring where grooves had been cut into the rock to accommodate it.

The water welled up from the rock, clear and cold; it seemed irrepressible. David took a palmful and drank. The first water he had drunk for over a year that had not been distilled or chemically purified.

Holding his hand to his mouth, he watched as the water from the spring ran and fell into the first of the stone channels, soaking quickly into the sand and weeds, building up to form a tiny pool and then run away on top of the sand and to feel its way down the channels.

He stood and walked with the leading edge of the water. Following it with his eyes as it ran, snaking and seeming to gather speed until eventually a muddy, finger-thick stream began to flow into the main pool area.

He returned to the source. Used his hands to scrape away the wet sludge that had accumulated in the channels and found they were lined with smooth crushed-marble cement. The white surface sparkled in the sun. The water built up behind his diggings and flooded forward as he removed each handful. He found himself smiling and humming. He had no idea of the time passing.

Mahmoud breathed in and held his breath. He waited and then breathed out through his eyes and saw the carved broken symbol of the Byzantine cross before him.

He was sitting still with his damaged right leg crossed before himself and his other leg up so that his knee was in line with his chest. His left hand with the missing fingers rested on that knee, while his good right hand lay palm-up on his upper leg, just below his groin.

He was sitting so that his body was in the sun and his head was slightly shaded. His eyes were open but hooded as he studied the shape on the ground before him. His *Pir* had led him to the technique of seeing with his whole being. It began with breathing with your eyes. Seeing with your breath.

This thing before him was a spiral shape. The points of departure and points of return indistinguishable. It was the galaxy from where we came and would return. The navigational tool of angels.

Mahmoud breathed again the shape with his eyes. And then slowly let the air escape from his lungs.

The symbol before him began to be seen.

Mahmoud too had no concept of time passing.

The sun had moved across the sky sufficiently for his body to be in the shade when David returned.

Mahmoud?

Mahmoud blinked and smiled at the sound of David's voice. Ah David, he said and turned from his meditation.

David was holding the front of his shirt up in one hand and a canteen in the other.

What have you got? Mahmoud indicated David's bulging shirt.

Look, David said. Knelt and carefully lowered the makeshift carry-all. Apricots. The fruit rolled out onto the ground in front of Mahmoud. And I found a freshwater spring. Taste this water it is beautiful. And figs.

Mahmoud picked one up and lifted it to his nose. Smelled. Said, figs.

The water is fresh, David said. I have not tasted sweeter water. He held the canteen out to Mahmoud, who took it, smiled and tilted it towards David in a salute, and drank. He closed his eyes and opened them again, smiled. This is good water. Where?

There, David said and looked behind him towards the cliff face. There is a spring, an orchard, old gardens, a watercourse.

Paradise?

Paradise.

Mahmoud laughed. Are there any virgins? I want at least forty. He laughed. Forget I said that.

David smiled. What is that thing you are touching with your foot?

I found it in the corner. Over there, Mahmoud indicated behind himself. It is a common symbol in the old Byzantine ruins. They have it in Buddhism too. It is good fortune. The future.

David was looking at the symbol. It was carved from stone.

A wheel? he said.

Or spiral Mahmoud said. It can represent eternity, the four winds, the sun.

Ah.

They are very common in these old ruins. It reminds me of the spiral where the point of departure and return are the same.

That sounds terrifying.

Mahmoud bit into a fig. Why?

I don't know, David said and picked up an apricot. Perhaps I am afraid of returning to where it all began.

They were silent for a long time.

Do you think the light shining in your heartbeat began in semen?

Semen? David shook his head. I don't know what...

No of course not, Mahmoud said, and who you are did not originate from a groin.

No.

And that is why, to me, returning to our point of departure is not a terrifying thing. Perhaps this is why I...

You. David said and shook his head. I have no idea what you are saying but you really believe that it is good there? At the heart?

I do.

What if it isn't good there? At the, what do you call it? Point of departure? The point of return. What if it is not good there? That we are all like me when I had the pistol at the fisherman's head and I wanted, so badly, to feel his blood hot on my arms. What if we are like that there? The beast in me. All of us full of horror.

Mahmoud stared at him. Have you ever been in love? Madly, madly in love?

No. Well. David looked at Mahmoud. I don't know what it means really.

Well this perhaps will mean very little to you but to answer your doubting I will try to explain.

How?

Take off your boots, Mahmoud said.

David looked at him.

Go on.

David shrugged and sat. Leaned forward and removed his boots and socks.

Jalal al-Din said that all loves are a bridge to Divine love. The love of God, Allah. I am going to give you a taste of what it is to know this. What we call *dhikr*—the remembrance of God. We have always known God you see; we just have to remember.

David stood, barefoot with his hands on his hips.

But first Mahmoud said, you also have to take off your head and put on a pumpkin.

David looked at him and laughed.

Mahmoud smiled, when my Brotherhood gather we call it *kharabat* the temple of ruin. Look David we are in a perfect place for *sama*—a journey—this journey back to ourselves.

David stared at Mahmoud seated on the block of white stone. The skewed arch behind him, in the bright sun, covered with a grapevine. The leaves turning orange and red in the autumn. To his left and behind him there was another colonnade, the fluting of the limestone pillars also all shot away; a walkway with pieces of orange terracotta roof tiles broken across the ground, standing alone supporting nothing.

Weeds in the jagged gaps. A dandelion head. Above them blue sky.

He turned his head and looked at the wide steps and low wall that ran to the beach, wild thyme and yellow broom almost obscuring it. A fallen column, the stone rounds broken apart like an articulated spine. White blocks lay scattered. Angular plinths levered out of place and the remains of great vases broken into pieces.

The gouged remains of a sparkling mosaic figure set into a once-interior wall. Black scorch marks from an ancient thieves' fire.

I am no-thing, Mahmoud said softly. There is no hope. That is for children. I am no-thing. I expect no-thing and *insha'Allah* there will be all things.

David watched this man before him smiling and holding a hand up towards him.

Mahmoud reached into his small bag and extracted a long pointed peg with a metal ring on one end.

This, he said, is a camel ring. Here. He threw the peg to David.

David caught the ring.

Take it over there and push it into the earth Mahmoud said, pointing to a piece of open ground. Clear away those small bushes.

David followed Mahmoud's instructions. Pushed the camel ring into the earth. When it stuck he stood on it until it was all the way in. Looked at Mahmoud.

Now, Mahmoud said, good. Loosen your clothes so you are comfortable and you can move. Good. Step into the camel ring and hold it between the big toe and second toe of your left foot.

David did so.

Place your hands on each of your opposite shoulders.

Again David did as he was told.

Close your eyes. This symbolises your oneness with God. Be silent for a moment.

They were quiet.

Some time passed. Sea birds called and they could hear the waves washing up against the beach as the tide began to turn. The sun was hot and cicadas were singing in the orchard grass. An onshore breeze came through the white ruin. They could smell the sea, the saltwater and rich wet-fish smell. Hot sand and olive-wood.

Mahmoud recited something.

Then he said, we of our Brotherhood wear a camel-hair hat when we gather in *sama*. It is the tombstone of what is known as *nafs*. What westerners call ego. Our made-up notion of who we think we are. The construction before the ruin. You have only an Australian soldier's hat. No matter.

David opened his eyes and put his arms down to his sides.

Hold your arms out, turn your left hand to the earth and right hand heavenwards. Towards Paradise. Now you will begin to turn, off your right foot, moving clockwise and all the time watching your left hand. Hear the words in your mind—I am no-thing as you turn. I am not...*who who who*. Watch, watch your left hand David. I love you.

David is turning. The world around him is whirling as he stares at his left hand pointing down to the earth. His toes, awkward, hold the camel-ring peg.

Mahmoud calls to him, feel the dance, focus on your earth-hand, turn brother, whirl. This is our *sama* this is our journey. Our journey of remembrance. Back to ourselves. There is no god but God. *Ashadu Alla Illa Allah wa Ashadu Alla Illa Allah wa.*

David sees the colours the shapes of where he was. Transforming into bands and then surrounding circles of light and dark and the faces of prophets coming out of the darkness. Desert birds and red winds. Sun-spots reeling before him in horizontal lines. A green field and black trees. The ruins transformed into a thin white line encircling him.

Mahmoud's voice reaches out, in our *kharabat* there is beautiful music. It is only the beauty of our music which keeps you here David. I cannot say but *Ashadu Alla Illa Allah wa*...

David is whirling faster and faster.

A huge sun begins rising from an unknown desert. Grasslands, mountains and moons appearing through mist. Lakes reflecting the sky. They become a hundred suns and a hundred colours of suns whirling in crazed bands of light around him. The moving sea and his mother's hair blowing out like tree branches in the wind. He can see the stars beginning to race over him in the shape of men's faces; the life season of a plant in the space of ten breaths.

Then suddenly vomit rose in his throat. He began to retch as he spun. He had veered away from the peg.

Breathe brother, Mahmoud said, and love. You have come too far. Then he began to chant *who who who who. Ashadu Alla Illa Allah wa Ashadu Alla Illa Allah wa. Ashadu Alla Illa Allah wa Ashadu Alla Illa Allah wa.*

David began to slow and then he staggered. He ran off to one side and held both hands up as he collided with an olive tree. Held onto the tree and then sat down. Got onto his hands and knees and retched again. He made a groaning noise and spat out the saliva. His eyes filled with tears as he looked at Mahmoud.

Mahmoud smiled at him. David, you went a little far. But there it is the beginning of the revelation. Fool.

David retched again and through his tear-filled eyes he saw Mahmoud struggling to stand.

And so, Mahmoud said as he rose, this is our point of return and our point of departure. Drunkard.

David sat back and wiped his hand across his mouth. He began again to hear the sea washing on the beach. Felt the breeze on his face. The cicadas singing in the ancient orchard.

What, he said after some time passed, has this to do with being in love?

Mahmoud was leaning on his crutches studying David. I am going to pray, he said. I will speak more to you later.

⁓

He had sat for a long time looking at the sea. He knew Mahmoud had finished praying some time ago and had used some of the spring water to wash before prayer. It is called *wudhu* David. It is a purification. Sea water is fine, even sand when there is no water.

The sun was beginning to disappear into the sea when he stood and returned to the camp they had made in the ruins.

David stared at the man sitting now before him in the fading light. His bearded face was open, his glasses in his hand. His undamaged foot on the Byzantine symbol that he had said was a sign of good fortune. A small fire was burning. David felt the smoke blow over him.

I think there is a path up the cliff.

Mahmoud frowned. What?

I found goat droppings, David said, and no goats.

Mahmoud sighed. Reason is a God-given thing David.

I will look for the goat track tomorrow.

That is good. Mahmoud said. Very wise.

We will have to get more food than this. David indicated with an open hand the apricots and figs.

Mahmoud nodded. Perhaps we can fish?

I have no hooks.

No.

But we have been lucky. The fisherman could have taken us anywhere.

He could, Mahmoud said and then looked up. There are date palms here also. He pointed.

David turned and saw the two date palms. He had walked under them oblivious this morning on the way to discover the spring.

Those yellow bunches?

Yes, they are dates.

—

It was mid-morning the following day when David found the small goat track at the base of the cliff. The spoor of goats and a small human footprint in the earth near where he had cleaned out the spring.

He knelt under an olive tree and studied the area. His eyes moved through the trees and bushes. He looked to where he would walk, where animals would move. Saw how they would have come down and spread, walking out among the trees and old gardens.

But the signs of animal presence were few. As if they had strayed here and been hurried away by the owner of the footprint. He rubbed some of the droppings between his fingers and noticed their dryness. At least a week old.

He stood. Began to make his way along the base of the cliffs until he came to a large boulder which leaned forward, saw the marks of sliding in the stones and gravel. Up behind the boulder he found a set of chiselled stone steps, the beginning of a track about three feet wide which led up the side of the cliff following a natural fault in the stone wall.

He retreated to the shade of the trees and again, knelt and studied the area. Looked up to where the track would go, traversing the cliff face on an angle it was almost impossible to detect if the onlooker didn't know it was there. He waited and listened. Smelled the air, alert as always for the trace of tobacco smoke that would tell of the presence of other men.

He could smell only the sea, the brine and washed-clean limestone smell. The air coming across the water. A faint prickle of woodsmoke. A sea bird calling. Gulls above.

And then he thought he heard the far-off sound of bleating.

He swung the army 08 pack down from his back, took out the revolver and looked at it resting in his hands. It was heavy and oiled. He cocked it, pulling back the hammer with his thumb. The double click of the cocking mechanism seemed to enter into his bone. He felt it travel up his arm. He paused then and turned the pistol from side to side, studying the lines. His thumb rubbed the wooden grip, the forefinger of his left hand touched the front sight. He held it in both hands and tested its weight. Waited for another moment and then nodded, eased the hammer of the revolver back and opened the cylinder. He removed the bullets and held them in his palm, as last night he had held salt in his palm when they ate.

He took the clasp-knife from his pocket and cut out a piece of oilcloth. Wrapped the bullets in the oilcloth. Folded the bundle over and placed it in the bottom of the pack. Pushed the pack under a rosemary bush, a stone next to the bush to mark the hiding place.

David stood up and walked to the goat track that led up the side of the cliff.

He was high above the sea when the track turned and widened onto what he first thought of as an ending point. There was a small shrine to his right and to his left the opening of a cave. The track disappeared around a protruding rock cornice.

David stopped, he found himself on a flat area about three yards wide that seemed to jut out over the cliff face. The alcove that was the shrine at the edge contained a crucifix with the body of Christ in white wood and next to that a statuette of a woman with a veil over her lowered head. Her hands in an attitude of prayer.

The wax of hundreds of candles melted into pools and beaded runs at the base of the figures; flowers and a small cloth doll also lay there. The ground was neatly swept and two terracotta pots had been placed near the entrance to the cave.

Below him he could see the bay and the ruins. The beach a perfect half circle. The date palms and old gardens. The watercourse, and now the sun flash of the reflecting pond.

Gulls floated on air currents across the glittering blue of the sea below him. The wind was stronger and cleaner where he stood. He could feel the wind in his mouth when he opened it to breathe from the exertion of climbing.

A voice from the cave. Who are you?

An English voice. It held the curvature of sound that he associated with the large property owners, the wealthy and privileged. The *who* arched and accused.

David crouched and peered into the entrance of the cave, high on a cliff on a Greek island above a Greek sea.

He could see nothing but the shadows of the cave. After a while he said, my name is David Monroe. I come from New Zealand.

There was a long silence. Nothing came from the darkness.

Then David said, who are you?

I am you.

What? David said. Where are we?

The voice emerged from the cave. Are you a wayfarer?

I was a shepherd. David said. I have been a soldier most recently.

Ah. Pilgrim. The voice had softened. I fear you may be lost.

~

David said all right Mahmoud. I know. Tell me.

Then there is the lunatic Al Hallaj, Mahmoud said.

Al Hallaj. David attempted the name.

His words, his name, his death sentence, *una-al-Haq*.

What does that mean?

He said I am the Truth. The Creating Truth. And they cut his dancing legs off for this on the scaffold.

Wait, you say they cut his legs off for saying I am the Truth?

Yes. Men of my faith are very serious about these things.

David was staring at Mahmoud.

The greatest of stories about this mad fool Al Hallaj is one by Jalal al-Din.

David nodded.

It is of a man who was seeking to be one with God. We call it *ahadiyyah*.

He knocked on his friend's door. His friend asked: who is there? The seeker answered, I. It is I.

Be gone from here, his friend said. It is too soon to be at my table. There is no place for the raw. And how else can the raw be cooked but by the fire of absence?

You, David said, once again you are talking about love.

Yes of course David. That is the great gift. The transport. But *sssh* let me finish.

Sorry mate, David said.

So the seeker turned sadly away and for a whole year the flames of separation consumed him. Then he returned and he paced up and down outside his friend's house. Eventually he knocked on the door, terrified that a disrespectful word might escape his lips. Just as we do when we love another.

I wouldn't know, David said. Go on.

Who is there? Cried the voice of the friend behind the door.

And the seeker answered, It is you, oh charmer of all hearts.

Now at last the friend said to the seeker, since thou art I, enter. There is no room for two I's in this house. *Sulh-i-kul*. Love and peace with all.

There had been no sound coming out of the cave for some time.

What are you doing in there? David spoke in the direction the voice had come from.

Waiting.

Waiting for what?

For you to go away.

Do you know where I can buy a donkey?

There was silence from the cave.

A donkey? David repeated, you know, *hee haw*.

I know what a donkey is and I am aware of the sound it makes.

Well do you know where I can buy one?

What do you think this is, a bloody stockyard?

David straightened. No. He turned away from the cave and looked out to sea. In the far distance he could see the shape of hills following the horizon until they disappeared into a shining white haze. He thought it was the mainland of Greece. The only sounds were the wind and cries of sea birds.

Eventually the English voice came out of the cave. Keep following the path. There is a girl who brings me food. She may have a *hee haw*.

Thank you. David waved at the cave's entrance.

Goodbye wayfarer. God willing you will find your way.

David said nothing but raised a hand and turned away from the cave. He followed the track as it curved around to his left and up towards the top of the cliffs.

When he got there the track flattened just below the summit and followed the cliff face for about two hundred yards. It ended with a flight of steps that took him up onto the flats.

He was standing on a plain which stretched away for as far as he could see and ended with the sharply rising mountains. The land was covered with outcroppings of rock and small, wind-bent trees and bushes.

He turned quickly as he heard a small cry on an indrawn breath.

A girl was standing there. There were goats behind her. They were standing off and looking in his direction. The kids continued to move about.

Hello, David said.

The girl stared at him. Shook her head. Looked behind herself.

She was about thirteen or fourteen. No shoes, bare feet with wide toes and scratched knees. A gash on her shin.

She was wearing a rough woollen dress tied at the waist and a sheepskin cloak across her shoulders. Unkempt black hair blowing in the wind. She pushed it away from her face. She was holding a wooden walking stick.

Donkey, he said and pointed his fingers on each side of his head to imitate the shape of ears.

She looked behind herself again and then back at him. She was frightened and bit her bottom lip, a pink tongue. Looked away towards the sea. She was becoming a woman. David could see the shape of her small breasts under the dress.

Hee haw, he said and stepped forward, he put his hand in his pocket and took out a leather purse. *Hee haw*.

159

She stepped back. Her eyes became large and she raised the stick. The small herd of goats that seemed to be attached to her also started in fright and scattered.

David was standing there with the purse in his hand, holding it out towards her. She had thrust the walking stick before her as protection. They stared at each other. Her eyes narrowed and watched him. She looked him up and down and then after a few more moments she said *hee haw*? as a question.

David nodded, yes, he said. Donkey *hee haw*.

She smiled and then giggled. Lowered the stick and put her hand to her mouth. Laughed. *Hee haw.*

Half an hour later the girl returned leading a white donkey. She said Aristotle as he paid her. He thought she said thank you.

The face of the donkey drooped, there were dark smudges beneath its eyes that looked like tear tracks. It had baskets strapped across its back. Terracotta pots in the baskets. A loaf of bread. Its tail hung down and small midges floated around its ears.

＝

We shall call him Israfel, Mahmoud said and looked at the mournful face of the donkey. Has he sung to you?

What?

Has the donkey made a noise David?

Not a peep.

Mahmoud began to laugh. So the name is perfect.

What is so funny?

Oh David, Mahmoud said. Israfel is the angel of music. He possesses the most melodious voice of all Allah's creatures. And you told me that you asked for a...? Mahmoud waited, one hand suspended.

Hee haw. What else was I going to say? I can't speak Greek.

Mahmoud howled with laughter. None sing so wildly well as the angel Israfel.

David was holding the left ear of the donkey. He was smiling but his lips felt crinkly.

Mahmoud was bent over. He wiped his eyes with his bandaged hand. The girl?

She thought it was funny too. I think he is a bargain. Good ears. They both stand up nice and straight when you talk to him. Bit mournful looking about the eyes but donkeys are prone to that. David smiled at Mahmoud.

Mahmoud was looking out towards the ocean. He sniffed. David.

David was speaking. You can ride Israfel and we can.

David.

What?

There is a boat coming.

They looked out to the entrance to the bay.

It was a naval lighter and it was motoring towards the beach. In the bow was the Limnion fisherman Alexis and he was pointing. Next to him was a sailor with a rifle. They saw the recoil jerk the sailor back before they heard the shot and then the high-pitched fizzing crack of a bullet passing over them.

There were other uniformed men gathering towards the bow. Soldiers, and at least one had the cap of an officer. More aiming of rifles. More shots. They heard a smack and the donkey barked.

They turned. A round had hit the white donkey in the chest. It had gone down on its knees.

David and Mahmoud were lying in the sand next to the donkey. It had its mouth open and coughed, snorted, blood poured out. It was trying to breathe but the blood made a gurgling noise. It lifted its head and then spasmed, its legs straightening and then relaxing. Coughed again and became still. Eyes open, framed with long lashes above the black stains that looked like tears.

Israfel, Mahmoud whispered. He looked at David. He reached out a hand. You must run David.

David reached out his hand towards Mahmoud. No mate.

You must, they will hate you more than me. The betrayal will be greater do you see?

It's too late anyway.

I love you my friend.

Yes.

Well what have we got here? a voice said.

They lay in the sand stretching their hands out towards each other. The ends of their index fingers almost touching. They stared into each other's eyes. Look into my eyes Mahmoud whispered, and smiled.

A right pair of bicycle riders.

And a dead donkey.

I give up. What next? They look like they given each other a walk under the trees.

162

And a helping hand. One of the sailors laughed and stood on Mahmoud's damaged hand.

Alexis stood above David and said *English*. Looked at Mahmoud who had opened his mouth in wordless agony. Turned his head and spat. Ottoman dog.

David got to his feet, pushed the fisherman back and swung a clenched fist at the sailor who had stood on Mahmoud's hand. Yelled out as his fist connected with the sailor's jaw, don't you touch him. Leave him.

The sailor staggered back, raising a hand to the side of his face.

Mahmoud had cried out and rolled away from the sailor. He sat up cradling his bandaged hand. He looked at Alexis.

Why?

A sailor had David in a headlock, pulling him down. The one he had struck was kicking out at his backside. Then cursing and using the butt of his rifle on his lower back.

The last time he saw Mahmoud the sailors were dragging him towards the sea. He turned his face back towards David and smiled. Mouthed something, nodded and David saw again the overwhelming tenderness. The look he had first seen in this man's face the second time: when he brought him sardines.

He thought perhaps Mahmoud had been trying to say I am become Haji Bektash the dog. But he would never know.

David would piss blood for three days.

It was just daylight when he called to Floss the eye dog come on the girl.

As he walked back towards the machinery shed, he looked up to the sky and land around him. High cloud had massed and was tumbling over on itself as if seeking the earth. What wet light there was came filtered through grey and bone-coloured air. Tendrils of mist clung to the high country and fingers of cloud covered the gullies and folds in the hills. Everything was dripping wet. He felt as if he was breathing the cold edges of his world.

He heard his walking boots in the mud. The splashing through the puddles. A flurry of wind sent a shower of rain across him. He noticed how the rain falling into a flat puddle to his left made such perfect rings. How the rings spread and touched each other, merging, overlapping. Perfectly round. Who would know to make the shape of raindrops falling into water so round? What hand in this?

He stopped walking.

Floss stopped too. She looked at him. Then towards the machinery shed, then back to him.

The old man was looking at his hands. He turned them over. Continued to look at his hands. Then he looked at the sky, shook his head and said to Floss hold on girl. Hold on a minute.

The saddlebag slipped off his shoulder onto his forearm. Water ran in a line off his hat.

He felt the rough wool rub of old wounds across his shoulder and flank. We are pattern makers, Mahmoud's voice as his fingers touched the scar tissue. But there is no sense in these David.

No David said, none.

Perhaps the night sky.

It was quiet except for the rain and a gusty wind coming from the mountains.

The old man knelt on the wet ground.

Papango Valley 1922

In the small upland valley, the rain became distinct above the cleared land. The scarred and returned man, David Monroe, stopped work. Put the axe down, leaning it against the upright spade, and looked at the falling rain.

Looked at his hands. Turned them over, looked at the shape of them. Then he stared at the raindrops in the puddles around him. Thought of their perfection of shape as they fell and opened to touch and lap and merge, and fell again and again to open to touch and lap. Who would make them so? The noise of the rain almost like a woman hushing comfort to a child. Such circular circles. And what a silly thing to think.

He turned and looked to the east. Where the sun rose.

His feet stuck in the mud as he turned. They made wet sucking noises, his movement slightly clumsy, jerking as his feet came free of the clinging mud. Water ran off his hat in a silver line.

He saw the hills and ridges rising up from the valley floor and then beyond that into the dark green of the high inland forests. Beyond there now the unseen mountains. The rain merging with the trees and the sky, becoming a moving white mist.

As he watched, the mist began moving towards him. Strong weather coming from the interior. A prelude of cold white air rolled down on him, surrounding him. It smelled of wet wood and rotting leaves and yeast and of lightning strikes on mountains.

Wet bayonets in the rain. 1918.

The linseed oil of the wooden handle. Number three Enfield oil. Perfumed with cardamom. And his friend Peter Whiting in the rain at Mont Saint Quentin. He closed his eyes and remembered.

He was still for a long time. Waiting for it to go away.

It was spring two years ago when he had returned to the Papango Valley. His post-war service ended in Berlin late in 1919 when a drunken officer with one ear signed the papers of pardon and recommendation shortly before falling unconscious. His forehead banged on the desk in front of him.

David waited, then took off the officer's hat and turned his head to one side. The burnt nub that had once been an ear facing up.

A grateful government had allocated the land at the southern end of the valley for returned soldier settlements for which David was ineligible. When he went to ask for work on Balmoral

Station the Australian owner Eoin McKenzie was still wearing his captain's uniform. His right sleeve pinned up.

He asked David if he had been over there.

Yessir.

At the Cove?

Yessir.

In Belgium and France?

Yes sir I was.

Why didn't you take a settlement block Mr Monroe?

David told him.

He listened and then said you can start today. There is a musterer's hut you can sleep in by the woolshed. Do you know it Mr Monroe? There are some old Rimu trees around it.

I know it, David said. Thank you sir.

David bent down and picked up the leather suitcase at his feet. He put his hat back on. Turned to go.

Captain McKenzie reached into his pocket and said Mr Monroe I have something for you.

David turned back. McKenzie was holding a five pound note folded between his index and middle fingers and a red paper flower.

David took the flower. Said, it is a red poppy.

Yes, it's a new thing, Captain McKenzie said, for remembrance. Some of the returned men are forming associations. To help.

A lot of people would not allow me this.

They would not have been there.

Thank you sir for your...I will earn the money. He put the paper flower in his pocket.

I believe you have earned it Mr Monroe. McKenzie reached

forward and pushed the folded note into David's top pocket. It's an advance on your first wage. Get something to eat man. And you may call me by my name Mr Monroe, not my rank. If you wish.

Thank you Mr McKenzie. He paused, touched his shirt pocket. I will.

Captain Eoin McKenzie showed Helen, his wife, David's service record, obtained from Defence HQ in Wellington. He had expectations that it might be a moment of epiphany for her. A revelation. They read it together in the library of the homestead. She let her hand fall from the paper and walked out.

It was later that day she spat in David's face when he came to the homestead Wharekaka to collect his wages.

He knocked on the side door and stood on the veranda. He had taken off his hat and was holding it in his hand as a mark of respect.

She called him a damned traitor. Her father had been killed at Gallipoli with the 10th Light Horse. Her brother still mad and hospitalised in Greylands, a Perth asylum, after Fromelles. Holding hands with the Irishman O'Meara who had crawled out sixteen times at Moocow Farm to bring the boys back. Most had died after only the once. I will never let his hand go cobber. Never. They gave him the VC but he sought only morning porridge and the hand of his friend, her brother. I would rather only the top milk, father gets the cream. And a little brown sugar. Like I once had in the mother mornings, he called them. By the stove and lapping cats.

How dare you, she said to David. And, how dare you to her husband.

Eoin used his handkerchief to wipe her spit off David's scarred face. Wept as he stepped back and saluted with his left hand.

David grew a beard and did not return to the homestead. Eoin McKenzie always addressed him as Mr Monroe. He arranged for his wages to be paid into the branch of the Bank of New South Wales in Ruatane.

The cold mountain air was rolling down across David and he opened his eyes and was back in the valley. Three years, he thought.

The rows of felled trees. Late last summer he had burned the trees. Terrible, blackened winnows. A pile of fence posts stacked. Two rolls of barbed wire he had for the top two strands of the valley fence. A pile of surveyor pegs to mark the boundary lines between Papanui Station and Wit Abernethy's place.

He made his way to the tree line and squatted against the trunk of a white pine. His back against the rough bark. Pulled his legs up and felt his back rasp against the bark of the tree. Thought about his friend Fish, Peter Whiting.

Never saw him again and I promised him, yes. I did, he said aloud, I am so sorry Fish I did. I promised. I would be right behind you like a halfback behind you the best last man down I ever saw and had the...You. You bugger you. I can see you laughing at me for being a sook now. Sulking like a jersey cow cow gone down in the bail. You have to say cow twice you see because...ah now Peter Whiting. Because you stuttered so...

David looked at the boundary fence again. Wit was supposed

to help with the fence but it didn't look like he was doing anything with his farm.

Wit Abernethy had a soldier settler's block next to Papanui Station. Land that the owners had given to the government for the returned men. Not men like David.

Wit was Fish Whiting's cousin. Another Gallipoli man; a Mounted. David had seen Wit talking to himself as he walked up the Ferntree Ridge. Hatless and waving one hand about as he moved between the trees.

Mrs Lawrence, the owner of the Papango Valley General Store, said her boys heard him talking to an invisible horse, apologising over and over again. Called the horse Gone on Down Wounded or Lightly the John Lightly they said. Something like that.

He himself, Mr Abernethy, the boys said had told them that was the name of the horse. Except he had no horse, not any longer. He was alone in that hut on his 125-acre allocation. Some government men tried to call the farms selections. Like the men had a choice. There was a dog though. Black and white, they thought its name was Tom.

Mrs Lawrence had asked David if he would call in on Wit seeing as he was a returned man also and had been in the medicals wasn't it? Red Cross? She didn't know what had happened.

She had known Wit's mother. They had a farm just under Mount Messenger coming down from the North Country. They had gone to dances together as girls.

He said he would.

They threw the donkeys overboard at the Dardanelles you know, she said. Wit told them. They had to swim ashore. Yes he said, he knew. A line of ears all pointed forward swimming towards the gunfire. A swimming donkey is a funny sight. He didn't tell Mrs Lawrence that. Chins up and such gentle little faces, so sad looking at the best of times.

I never had a donkey Mrs Lawrence he said. I became a stretcher bearer after I was wounded. In France. That was the English boy Jack Simpson, he was with the Australians. And some of the other boys used donkeys. Henderson of the Auckland Mounted. He was killed too.

I did not, he said, use a donkey in France. They only understood Hindustani.

Wit's mother was a Smith before she married big Tom Abernethy. A cousin of mine actually. There was a brother Samuel too. Lovely boy with curly hair and a sweet smile if I recall the one. Lost him at Gallipoli. Both the boys with the Wellington Mounted Rifles. Wit rode to Damascus. Saw Bethlehem. I was at Mary's and Tom's wedding. Do look in on him won't you David. He seems so troubled. And he has done no work at all to speak of on the place. None at all. It's going back.

It takes time he said and repeated that he would call in on Wit.

Joseph used a donkey for his wife, she said.

Sorry?

For Mary, David. You know the Mother of Jesus.

Ah David said. Yes. Yes Mrs Lawrence. Bless them.

Bless them indeed David Monroe. She eyed him. Yes, your mother's name was Mary wasn't it David?

He bent to pack his supplies into his pack.

Good with an axe.

Pardon me, he said.

Never saw a better man with an axe. Big Tom Abernethy.

Oh yes. The Spanish flu wasn't it?

A crying shame. Well, him and hundreds of thousands of others. Oh before I forget David I have another letter for you. I think it's for you. Someone playing a joke; Mohammed ibn Monroe? Foreign by the look of it. Funny handwriting.

She held out the letter to him and said Turkish?

He took it from her. Said thank you Mrs Lawrence.

Anyway David Monroe it's good to have you home son. A nickname is it? Mohammed.

⟶

David's knees were becoming cramped and sore. He stood up and walked back into the clearing. Looked around.

The jagged ends of the scarfed tree stumps could be fingers in this fog. He looked at his feet. Mud-covered boots. The perfect circles made by the raindrops in the foot-hollows he had left in the shining blue clay.

The clay was blue at Fromelles and Pozières. Sometimes it was white. Along the Somme plain. Imagine white clay. From all the chalk. A darker blue than this though. Passchendaele was not white clay. Passchendaele was Passchendaele.

The mist was rolling through. He opened his mouth again, closed his eyes. Tasted the iron mountain, the iron in our blood. Thought of gas. Shook his head, said I am here Mahmoud I am here. He thought he heard a whistle.

The words of the crazed and wounded priest of Polygon Wood came to him: I once went to the ocean seeking redemption and found only fish.

No, he died up by the Windmill Farm. In the fifth attack along with the youngster Jamie Mitchell from the valley. August 1918.

Here there is rain. And wet clay and dead trees and the only clarity is of remembrance. He stamped his foot in the mud. As if to focus.

The mad priest who had been taken from the line suffering from shock. The final act had been when he crawled up behind a concealed sniper, grabbed him by the balls and asked him, yelling it out, if he had anything to confess.

Laughed suddenly at the memory. Felt the laughter pull at him, like a thread, tugging at him, pulling him back to here and now. The cold mist on his teeth and in his mouth.

Saw himself. The laughing man in the valley.

Saw himself as if he was looking down on himself. Learning again how to know. Thank you Mahmoud. Memory was making sense of this, making him laugh.

Remembered the laughter going through the battalion lines as the story was recounted of Father Hickey.

David had helped tie the weeping priest to the stretcher.

Regimental Sergeant Major Noel McCormick, unsure what he would do next, said tie him down and get him back to brigade. If you gave this bloke a cricket bat he'd probably try to fuck it.

Gag him if you want. God knows what he'll say.

Probably, someone piped up.

Oh no David said, no need to gag him. No no. And looked at the other stretcher bearers who all shook their heads, looked at their boots and made noises of negation. They were not going to miss a moment of this. The sergeant major frowned, said belt him if you have to. Then waved a hand and made a noise of disgust. You conchie bastards wouldn't hurt a flea.

It was well known that the sergeant major had worked on the Wellington docks and had been what was called a good worker, worth at least three other men. Union through and through. From each according to his ability, he would say, and to each according to his need. There was no nonsense in him. Lift one end of a piano by himself. Veins would stand out on his forehead. Had no need of priests in the union. Relished his time with the battle police.

He had stopped calling the conscientious objector stretcher bearers cowards after seeing what they did under fire but his disgust at their stance remained. You have to fight for what you believe in he would say. Not turn the other fucking cheek. *Jesus* boys what shite is that?

Kicked the handle of the priest's stretcher. Sniffed. He is no fucking Father Kennedy this one.

The priest, Father Hickey, insisted he was not mad but had had instead a prophetic vision. A revelation no less, my children.

All four of the stretcher bearers had replied yes father yes and kept moving across the open ground to the rear, crouched over, ducking their helmeted heads, arms out to the side as counter-balance and wishing that he would stop moving about. Hating the open ground. The communication trenches were still being cleared.

Every now and again one of them would laugh and say by the balls or do you have anything to confess. The other stretcher bearers would join in the laughter. Once they were all laughing so much they fell to their knees and dropped the stretcher. David couldn't remember the last time, or if ever, they had laughed when carrying somebody.

I am not, Father Hickey said, a deviant or fallen. I just wanted the killing to stop. I thought he would laugh. Laughing people don't kill others do they? Is this a bad thing? Please do not confuse the message with the messenger. There is no laughter in Heaven you see, he said. There is no need. It is here we need it.

Well you are fallen father, one of the bearers said. We just dropped you. And again they all laughed as if they had just heard the most hilarious of things.

Prophetic vision father? Prophetic is it? Dennis McCarthy the Irish-born bearer said. Ah it's not that bad now. Winked. Would you ever stop laughing lads. The priest too was laughing. Tears were streaming down his cheeks. Can you make it with potatoes?

News later reached them that the Father Hickey had been sent to Goa. They said such things were accepted there more easily. After all they had a god that had an elephant's head, four arms and sat with one foot on its thigh. The bottom of the foot facing heavenwards. For goodness sake. Ah he'll be fine now Dennis McCarthy said and took to referring to him as old Ganesh.

Another called him the holy comedian.

It is raining. It is cold and he is alone in an ancient valley. It is 1922. There is nothing but this for him.

And in his left shirt pocket the letter from Aisha.

It was addressed to Mohammed ibn Monroe.
   Care of General Store Papango Valley
   North Island
   New Zealand
   South Pacific Region

Was that your nickname then David? Mrs Lawrence asked again. Mohammed?

He had read it when he got back to his musterer's hut. He had sat on his single bed. It was late afternoon and he had been unable to move until it became dark. And then he fell sideways and watched the clouds passing the half moon until he slept.

Our dearest Mohammad
   Assalamu alaiküm. Peace be upon you Brother and Friend.
   I write this to you in a desolate time.
   Mahmoud was murdered last week. He was hanged by the jailers of the man who calls himself the Father of the Turks. Mustafa Kemal Ataturk who is also known as The Perfection and The Chosen One.
   Mahmoud asked me to write to you, and to ask you not to grieve. He said to remember the stories that you summoned in the time by the sea on the island.

The laughter you shared. Of donkeys.

That he loved you and knew that you loved him.

And to tell you that the last words on his lips would have been: It is you Friend I have come home.

It is raining here as I write this. Water is running in the gutters and across the ground. The leaves of the apricot trees are yellow and falling away with the rain.

He asked me to tell you to be joyful for him and to remember that the colour of ripe apricots in summer is the colour of sunrise on Lemnos.

As the jailers placed the rope around his neck I am told he repeated the words of Al Hallaj, the cotton carder from Basra.

Uqtuluni ya thiqati innafi quatli hayati.

Kill me oh trustworthy friends for in me being killed is my very life.

With love and respect

Aisha

He holds out his arms and closes his eyes, lets all thoughts travel out to his hands and fingers. All thoughts fall off his fingers. He shakes them. Everything of who he is begins to disappear.

The right hand turns upward, the left downward. He begins to turn. Smiling now, his head tilted to one side as if listening, watching his left hand. A humming sound comes from his throat.

He cries out can you see me Mahmoud? Am I doing it as I should? There is no should David. That is the point. Do not hope, do not expect. Do not want. Turn.

Turning faster now, becoming senseless, feet whirling, splashing in the mud.

Heavier clouds come in from the east, covering the man alone, spinning alone, arms akimbo, in the blue mud of the isolated valley floor deep in the North Island of New Zealand. The end of the victorious world. A Kingdom of Ten Thousand Birds. A land of constant white cloud.

He becomes nothing for just this moment. Nothing. A spinning man.

Eventually he slows. Slows his turning; his turning wavering; wavering staggers. Cannot find his balance. Keeps falling over. Stumbles and falls into the mud. Sits, one arm braced to support himself.

The rain has become very heavy.

It is making a hissing noise as it hits the ground. It is soaking him. Steam is rising from him as he sits.

The world whirls before him. He dies again. And again. And then yet again. Hearing always the machine guns and the bell and the whistles.

The come on now boys. Up you go now. Over the top.

The battle police pushing some of the boys up. Yelling at them. Slapping them around the face. Up you go son. Be a hero for the King and the country. A field of fucking medals out there. Up you go my son. Think of your father. What would he say? Eh?

He lifts one muddy hand and holds the side of his head. I am so sorry. He nods and then shakes his head. Only he hears this. He hears it in his chest. The rain is too heavy for anyone else, even if there was anyone else, to hear this confession.

After a time he kneels, sits back on his heels, his hands by his sides, looks up and recites as in prayer.

I tried to give You up and live without the pain of longing
I tried to be empty of all passion for You
I failed

A long time passes.

Then there is, for a moment, a centre to his world.

The kneeling man, mud covered, rises to his feet.

Floss was barking at the old man. He moved his head forward as he heard her.

He was kneeling in the mud. His hat at his side. Eyes closed, face up and the rain was coming down and streaming across his face. His white beard soaked, water dripping off it onto his chest. He was speaking to himself and humming. Smiling.

Floss stepped forward and barked at him again, almost stamping her two front feet, dipping her head, and then stepped back. Watching him. Barked again.

The old man David turned and looked at her.

Blinked and shook his head. He began to get to his feet, turning over to one side. Said, yes girl. I know.

Got to his feet, paused for a moment and then began to examine his clothing. Mud dripped off his knees. The saddlebag was in the grass next to him. He bent over and picked it up. Looked at Floss as he wiped his knees clean with swipes of his hand.

I know, he said. I know.

Floss turned her head and trotted off towards the woolshed. The old man followed her. He could see that the John was watching him from the stall. He had stopped eating.

The rain continued to come in savage squalls throughout the morning as David rode the edges of the kanuka breaks of the lambing flats, his hat leaned forward into the rain. John's head tucked into his chest.

Floss ranged ahead. The heavy ewes would move slowly and the new mothers became aggressive at the first sight of the dog, turning and stamping their feet in warning, shielding the new-born with their own bodies. Floss dutifully ignored them. David walked the horse slowly across the flats; watching the ewes from horseback as he went.

Twice he dismounted and stepped around a ewe that had lambed twins. He stood and watched the mother eat the after-birth and then stand her ground as Floss approached. He thought, the only time sheep become other than what they are. When they are protecting their young. Floss raised her nose and smelled the blood. David growled at her.

Get away Floss.

They followed a creek that ran down to the river, looking for any stock that might have become entangled or stranded by the rising waters.

The ford, normally shallow, was knee-deep on John as he crossed. Floss whined and ran back and forth along the bank until David relented and recrossed the creek to collect her. All right, he said, get up. She wagged her tail once and leapt up onto the horse's withers to perch in front of David as he once again forded the creek. Off, he said to her as they reached the other side.

He walked John down to the edge of the river and they stopped on a high bank and watched the flood waters passing below them.

Masses of debris were being taken down the earth-brown river. Large tree trunks, turning slowly end for end as they moved. The body of a cow; rafts of smaller sticks; fence posts with wire and battens still attached; uprooted tree ferns.

The old man dismounted and stood with the reins looped over his forearm and watched the river for some time. It kept passing in front of him. Everything the same and yet not the same. Floss sat beside him, mouth open, tongue lolling. John bent his front leg, put his head down and tried to graze through the metal bit.

The old man thought once again about the government men coming for him yesterday. Waiting at his hut when he returned from the morning round. Big men and a black car. One of them smoking, flicking open and closed a Zippo lighter as he waited. The metallic snap. They had spoken to Mrs McKenzie the inspector said. Had her permission.

Wild goose chase the inspector said. Forty bloody years. Who next?

The old man stared at the river in front of him. Remembered something Mahmoud said about an ancient Greek philosopher who had lived in Ephesus which was now part of his country, who had said everything changes everything flows. You never step in the same river twice. This is the lesson. Life like the river. The question is therefore what is immutable? What is unchangeable? And then he said aloud forty years. John paused from eating and Floss ignored him. John went back to grazing.

The brown river in front of him moved in a solid body. Almost something to walk across.

The old man cleared his throat. Said, Heraclitus. Floss looked at him and stood up. John lifted his head, a mouth full of grass.

The weeping thinker Mahmoud called him. The weeping man.
A dark lizard.

Come on the old man said and turned his back to the river.
Still holding the reins in his left hand he stilled the stirrup leather
and then reached up to hold a handful of John's mane. Raised his
left foot into the metal stirrup. A change of weight and a small
push off from the ground with his right foot, he lifted up and
swung himself into the saddle. His right hand went down onto
John's neck. Palm open and holding the flex of his throat muscle.

John leaned into his movement and grunted as the old man
settled onto his back. Stepped sideways to regain his balance.
Made a disapproving sound.

David raised his hands and pulled back gently on the near rein
to control the horse. Dug his heels in. Straightened them and
gave a short whistle to Floss. Said, the girl. And then clicked his
tongue to John. Walk on the John. In behind Floss.

They followed the creek lip for another half a mile until it
meandered into the rising country. The rain had stopped and
the sun was overhead shining white through the clouds.

The old man turned John to the north and followed the tree
line for about two hundred yards and then turned him eastwards
to walk back down towards the river. Then turned them south,
again following the contour of the land for around two hundred
yards and then yet again, eastwards.

He followed this rough grid tracery across the lambing flats,
using land shapes, small gullies, rock outcrops and trees as
markers and indicators of distance. It was this detail that he used
every morning and evening and had never missed a cast ewe or
orphaned lamb in over thirty years.

It was still early when he stopped to help a young ewe having difficulty to lamb. Her first time, and she ran heavily away from their approach. The old man gave a short trip whistle.

Floss leapt forward, sprinting to the front of the pregnant ewe and blocked her line of retreat. The ewe stopped and Floss froze, one foot held up and placed carefully down, almost cat-like. Strong eyes locked into the eyes of the bewildered young ewe. Gave the old man short glances to do the rest.

He dismounted slowly, let the reins trail and walked up behind the new mother. Caught hold of her and pulled her over onto her side.

He knelt next to her and reached into his jacket pocket. Extracted a glass bottle and rubbed an antiseptic solution onto his right hand. Then holding the ewe with his knee and left hand, he pulled up his sleeve and reached into her.

Felt and twisted and eased out two small feet.

A bleating cough from the mother and a high grunting noise. Then the old man pulled, and with one sliding wet movement, a mucus-covered slip came splashing out from the ewe. He reached for his knife and then, realising he had left it in the *pikau*, bent forward and bit the cord with his teeth.

He dragged a thick milky shroud off the head of the newly born lamb. Cleaned out its nose and mouth. Then he bent forward and placed his lips over the lamb's nose and mouth, blew two quick breaths. Leaned back and spat.

Stood the lamb up as he knelt there, his knees in the soft earth. Slapped it twice. It collapsed and seemed to think, shook its head. The tiny body stained red and yellow.

The old man wiped the back of his hand across his mouth and leaned back on his heels.

The ewe made a groaning noise and rocked as if to get up. David blew out through his nose and again reached into her. Pulled out the red placenta with spread fingers. Flicked away the slimy tendrils that clung to his hand and then wiped both hands on the wool of the ewe. Stood up. Put the toe of his boot under the lamb, lifting it.

The lamb stood, staggered forward and then made its first tiny noise. Collapsed, then stood again. Shook its head. Bleated. The ewe was on her feet, turning and frantic, a deep belly reply to her new lamb.

The old man watched them. Floss was sitting away, her mouth open, pink tongue long and eyes slowly blinking almost in approval. As if this had been done as it should be.

An easterly wind was blowing, cold but dry and the old man thought at least the wind dries the new born. They won't go wet into the night.

He waited until the lamb began to feed beneath its mother and then he turned away and found John. Called, here to me Floss. The good girl now.

Continued to follow the patterns of his lambing beat. Wiped his right hand across his thigh three or four times as he rode slowly across the land. Once he smelled his hand and then stopped and took the bottle of antiseptic from his coat pocket, poured some of it into his palm, rubbed his hands together.

He rode to where the Ferntree Ridge flared out onto the flat land. This marked the old boundary of Wit Abernethy's soldier settlement block. The allocation. There were some ancient fence posts remaining. They leaned a little drunkenly left and right.

John stretched his head forward and then raised it again quickly in impatience. The old man let the reins loosen. He looked up the ridge and remembered the flats on the other side. The raised piece of ground above the flats where Wit had built a small hut and how he had helped him to roof it with red corrugated iron.

When the work was finished Wit had brought out two glasses and a bottle. Said I have been saving this and held up the bottle of Australian rum.

The old man sat on the horse and looked out at the lambing ground below him. He let his eyes follow the shape of the land. These lines he rode twice a day during the lambing seasons.

He took a pair of binoculars and began to study the edges of the flats. After a while he lowered the binoculars and replaced them in their case. Continued to study the folds and curves of the ground.

Hundreds of lambs and ewes moved across the ground. Pregnant ewes, heavy and preoccupied, instinctively seeking out more sheltered areas. Most of the breeding flock he had helped into the world. New lambs playing and running in to feed from their mothers, bunting at their udders. The thin sounds of the sheep rising above the flat land; bleating lambs calling out, ewes blaring in response; the movement and gathering lines of the flocks. All as it was.

The gelding John lowered his head and began to nose at the grass, chewing around the metal bit and taking the occasional step forward. A sparrowhawk was riding on an air current. It gave a high-pitched whistling call. John lifted his head; paused, the grass sticking out of his mouth. He looked away in the distance for a few moments then blew through his nose and again bent his head forward to graze. Floss was sitting watching where the old man was watching.

He relaxed his hands and let himself be eased along. He still held the loose reins in one hand between the ring and middle fingers. The other hand on his hip, knuckles down.

He looked away from the flats and again up the Ferntree Ridge, how it kept getting steeper until it disappeared in the top of a bush crest.

Wilfred Abernethy had sobbed from up there. Holding on to the body of a tree as if it were the neck of a horse and saying I am so sorry John.

It doesn't matter, the old man thought. Wit couldn't have helped doing that any more than I could have stopped myself falling to my knees this morning. Covered in mud and weeping in the rain like the fool I am.

Mahmoud would have been proud of me. The fool on his knees. With nothing. The old man was biting on his lower lip and nodding as he remembered. He stood in the stirrup irons and then eased back.

Wit drank the glass of Australian overproof rum. Shuddered and wiped his mouth with his hand. I shot fifteen of our horses David.

David said nothing.

One after the other. And each one said thank you.

Wit.

Or perhaps that was just me. Saying that.

David inspected a small cut on his hand from the corrugated iron.

I mostly remember John.

David put the cut in his mouth and sucked it.

And his eye as I said go on down son.

It was at the end Wit, David said, his words coming up from behind his hand. We all did things.

And David.

Wit stopped speaking and rolled the bottom of his glass on the table. Tilting it to one side and watching what he was doing.

And David, he repeated, I shot this wonderful horse. He would smile when I farted. Wit laughed.

David returned the laugh.

And he would turn away from me when I was being impatient. Teaching me. I shot him. And fourteen others.

David cleared his throat and pushed the bottle towards Wit.

They forgave me. Wit picked up the bottle. They did. Each one of them forgave me. He filled his glass.

The only sound in the room was the clinking trembling sound of the bottle on the glass.

Remember the chaplain, Hickey? David said.

Wit looked at him. No. You make an imaginary cross.

The priest?

No. An X between their ears and their eyes.

He was at Gallipoli and then went to France.

That's the best place to shoot them. In the forehead where the lines of the cross meet. Wit stood up and walked to the fireplace. Holding the glass.

The worst, he said, the absolute worst part is when they stop being who you know and just become another dead thing. They become strangers in death.

David looked at Wit. Sometimes mate it doesn't pay to think too much about these things.

You know that part when the edges of the pupil turn a pale blue and glaze and fade into…just nothing. Grains of sand stick to the eyeball? They don't blink anymore.

David was just watching him.

Wit drank. And then John shits and dies. Every night. John shits and shudders and dies. That last breath that went out of him. It was like a sigh. He will no longer recognise your whistle. Head coming up. Ears pricked. He will no longer forgive you. He will no longer teach you who you can be. Because David. You shot him.

Silence.

Wit sniffed. When I say you David. I mean me.

Chaplain Hickey went mad at Polygon Wood. They sent him to India. He…

Who?

David looked again at Wit. There against the window space. A cigarette in his mouth and unsure how he was going to light the cigarette with one hand as if he was unable to put down his glass. He was making a slight humming noise. Moving from one foot to the other.

Is there any clean water? David asked.

Wit had decided and the cigarette was lit. He had put the glass on the floor. Used both hands on the matches.

Wit was making a faint affirmative noise in his chest, nodding slightly.

Wit?

He didn't reply, still puffing on his cigarette and staring at the ground just off to his left.

Wit. David said again, slightly louder.

Wit looked up and seemed startled by David's presence. There was a moment when they looked at each other, then Wit pushed himself forward.

Sorry old man. I didn't go to France. We went to Palestine. I rode to Damascus on John. Drank from the fucking Euphrates. Bethlehem.

Doesn't matter. Father Hickey was with us at the Cove. I thought you might have heard of him. It all just got too much. He was on Chunuk Bair that night. Then later in the Somme Valley.

I was thinking of young Samuel. We lost him on Walker's Ridge. You knew Sam didn't you?

David sighed. I did. I did. We played rugby together. He was a fine centre. You were on the wing weren't you Wit? Played outside Sam in the juniors?

Yes.

David stood up. Well mate he said. I had better…

Not much of a sidestep. Wit looked at the floor and puffed his cigarette.

David looked at him. No he said. He would run it at the opposition. Good tackler though.

Bit hungry too. Wouldn't pass the ball. Dad always said he should pass it more. He was younger than me.

David sat down.

Wit laughed and held up the bottle of rum.

I bought it at the store. From Mrs Lawrence. Upon whose arse the sun never sets.

David smiled. Nodded.

Wit gulped at the rum. Gunfire, he said.

David laughed and said makes you want to fix bayonets doesn't it?

Wit smiled. Fuck that for a game of soldiers.

The old shared jokes, the codes that only the old soldiers would know.

They both looked to the open front door of the hut. The black and white dog lay there on the front porch. His head on his paws, watching them.

Good dog?

No, Wit said. Bloody hopeless really.

Wit poured himself more rum. You?

No.

Wit laughed and drank. That was funny, a mad chaplain. He sat down at the table.

David decided to say nothing. A long time passed.

They stared out past the porch down the hillside which fell away beneath the hut to the road which ran the length of the Papango Valley and there to the river beyond.

Any good timber left? David asked.

Don't think so.

What's the dog's name?

Tom. The black and white dog lying at the front door lifted his head.

Who the boy Tom? Wit said.

The dog's tail thumped twice on the porch. He put his head back down.

They were looking east and watching the shadows grow longer as the sun slowly went down behind them.

They were in Auckland when they got sick.

You lost them both Wit?

Wit nodded and then filled his glass again. His hand had stopped trembling. The bottle was half empty. Lost them both from the Spanish flu. Bugger Spain that's what I say. Drake had the right idea. Hah! Wit drank and kept talking. The old farm was mortgaged, so the bank got most of that. Little bit left over, some stocks Dad bought in the New Zealand Brewery. And I got this place and the MM. A retrospective award they called it. Came with the farm.

I didn't know that.

Load of shit. Only mugs get medals mate. You know that.

Where?

On Walker's bloody Ridge. Where else?

You never said.

Wit drank. Refilled and held the bottle over to David.

David shook his head again.

And, Wit said. I got to shoot fifteen horses who said thank you.

There wasn't much else you blokes could do. Was there.

Better than leaving them there. I got Sammy back to the beach. But we had already lost him on the ridge. So I went back and got a few more.

David nodded.

They sat in silence. Just looking at the dog and the view down to the main north–south road.

I know what happened to you Davie. I know about it.

I know you know.

They were silent again.

It doesn't matter.

Thanks, David said. He was looking at his hands. He had interlaced his fingers to form a bowl and was watching his thumbs as they gently touched. Thanks Wit. He said again.

I am so pleased you are nearby. Up on the Balmoral.

They call it Papanui now.

Papanui?

Yep. Australian owner. Big land holdings in Australia it seems. Lost an arm somewhere in France. He seems all right. Wife not too keen on me though. Bit homesick I think.

I saw them driving past in a car. She had a new-fashioned sort of hat and looked away when I waved, Wit said and lit another cigarette.

Oh well, David said. Bit different here. Must be hard for the wives. Not their fault.

Wit was frowning. What do you mean Dave?

Well he is still in uniform, doesn't want to let go of it I suppose. Medal ribbons and all. Probably still trying to make sense of it.

How can we make sense of that?

There are ways, David said.

That's good. Wit said and filled his glass.

Later, sitting on the pallet of blankets Wit had made for him to sleep on, David asked what is Wit short for? We have always called you that.

It was Samuel, Wit said. When he was a little boy he couldn't say Wilfred. It became Wit. I was his big brother remember. It started as Witfit. Mum and Dad loved it and it stuck, I became Wit. I said it to him on Walker's. It's Witfit Sammy Witfit. I'm here. But it was too late. He didn't hear me.

Ah, David said. Wit. I am so sorry.

Goodnight mate, Wit said.

Goodnight. David lay on his side to sleep. He saw the back of Wit's legs walking towards the table. The movement scissoring the light, the floorboards rising up to block it out. Closed his eyes. Said night again. Heard the glass clinking.

Later Wit returned to the pallet. David felt him pull a blanket over him and whisper. Night David. A better man than me Gunga Din.

Some time after that, David was woken by a laugh. And then Wit's voice. Speaking low, the clear and clever self-amused voice he'd had as a schoolboy. No slurring or hint of drunkenness in it.

Perhaps Tom, he said to his dog, it is also short for Witness. What do you think old son? Witness? Hah.

David heard the thump of the dog's tail on the floor.

Wit continued to drink as David slept.

After Wit sold his farm to Mr McKenzie for thirty English shillings, what he'd asked for, he moved to New Plymouth to become a schoolteacher. On the day before he left he burned the hut with the red corrugated iron roof.

Mr McKenzie asked David to clean up the rubbish left behind. David dug a large hole in what had been the backyard near the water tank and buried mostly empty rum bottles. He stacked the buckled and scorched iron on the split logs, weighted down with rocks. Raked the burnt ground and made a fire from the remaining timbers.

Mr McKenzie had said I hope you don't mind Mr Monroe but I thought it best as you knew him quite well I understand.

It doesn't matter, David had replied. I am happy to clean up.

Would you take down the boundary fence as well please. It runs up the Ferntree Ridge line. It shouldn't be much trouble. I don't think Mr Abernethy did too much work here. I don't know if he ran any stock? He said there was a hundred or so ewes but they were all full wool and had run wild. He kept saying sorry Mr Monroe.

David said, he would have.

~

The rain had stopped. It was late afternoon and would soon be getting dark. David was very cold. He stood and touched the back of his wrist to his mouth. And cheeks and eyes.

He retrieved his hat. The sky was darkening but the white mist had passed on. A small cold wind was coming out of the east

He followed the pathway he had made back along the valley until it ended, narrowing into a gap between two curving ridge-lines. It was wide enough for two horses and a dray to pass. He walked through the gap between the bracketing ridges and stood on the edge of a scarp which fell away to a creek and flatlands to his left and right as far as he could see.

He looked down at the roof of the musterer's hut he had been given by McKenzie. It was on a level piece of ground and had a gathering of rimu trees on the south side as a windbreak. Away to his left he could see the roof and yards of the woolshed. The shearer's quarters. Cookhouse.

He looked back to his hut. A smear of smoke eased out of the chimney from a log he had left in the fireplace that morning. Off to the right the yards and a lean-to for the horses. Layla, the smart one, had seen him and was looking in his direction. The two geldings Majnun and John had their heads inside the lean-to.

From where he stood the land dropped away to the lambing flats, still covered in scrub and second-growth forest. The flats followed the big river in an elongated curving shape, away to his left for about two miles. All the large timber trees had been taken years ago.

To his right was Wit's place, covered in bush. He could see the smoke from Wit's hut and a sliver of the red roof between the green and black of the bush.

Further on past Wit's place, the established small dairy farms of Papango Valley. Green paddocks and neat fences. Jersey cows moving through the high grass. A dog barked. He saw the Lawrence boys walking out to the cows. They each carried a long stick which they swung through the grass. Heard one of them whistling the dog and a shouted word or name, a command. The cows' heads lifted and they began to moan as they turned towards the race that led to the shed for the night milking.

Across the main road and around a towering natural blue-clay bluff there was the Papango Valley General Store, the domain of Mrs Lawrence. David squatted and studied the path he would take when he had to go to the store and survive the interrogations and insistences of Mrs Lawrence.

He rose and walked down towards his hut. The two dogs he

had kept chained this morning saw him coming and began to convulse with expectant joy.

He whistled a greeting said who the boy Sam and sit down Meg. Who the good dogs? They yelped in reply, shaking, quivering with anticipation. Meg gave a nervous yawn and sat down, anxious to do as told.

David smiled, said good girl Meg. Speak up Sam.

Sam began immediately to bark, turning on his chain. A big booming noise. David said that will do now Sam. The dog stopped. Stood looking at him quizzically.

David walked to the veranda of his hut. Stood for a moment and then turned towards the door, took his hat and greatcoat off and hung them on a nail. Next he took off his boots. Scrubbed the mud off them and carried them towards the front door.

Floorboards creaked under his feet as he walked across the veranda. They had been nailed when some of the timber was green. The nails had loosened as the timber dried. He opened the door.

Inside the hut the air was warm. It came over him like a smile, he thought. A warm hand. He glanced at the corrugated iron fireplace that had been built outside the hut and connected with an enclosed space as big as the fireplace itself. The log he had left on that morning was almost burnt to ash. When bricks became available, perhaps he would have a fire inside the hut. An iron stove.

The inside walls of the hut were lined with several layers of newsprint. He had used glue made from flour and water to line the walls and eventually they had all become covered. The newsprint stopped the winter draughts and had proven to be fine insulation for the summer months as well. His mother had said that the English poet Wordsworth lined the walls of his rooms in the Lake District with newsprint. If it was good enough for him, she had said.

Who? he remembered asking.

She had loved to swim in the ocean. Why was she at Pungarehu, he thought, swimming all alone? And: she never grew up, he thought. Only fourteen when I was born. A baby herself Mary O'Connell.

⌒

She told him, my father would say it's you yourself when he met me. She said that was a translation of the Gaelic form of greeting. What it meant was that you belonged to something greater that just you. He had not understood what she meant.

This was just one of the many things she told him. She would instruct him of the birds, their habits and their songs.

The grey warbler or *riroriro*, her favourite. And at night, as the sun was going down the owl *ruru* would call out and she would say to him, there the wise owl *ruru—morepoak* is watching over us. Most of us know it by the sound it makes: *morepoak*.

She showed him the English thrush with its speckled breast. Told him to listen to the song of the blackbird. When the native *tui* called in the big totara trees behind the cottage: listen she said. The knocking musical note of the *tui*. Hollow wood and water.

But it was *te riroriro* that made her face come alive. Listen to that, that long melancholy of the lost soul wandering along a stream. It reminded her of a lost love seeking forever the source of his or her love, like a minstrel following a river to where it began to find the answer to his longing. This is the grey warbler. *Te riroriro.*

But it can mean whatever you want to my darling boy. There are thirty-one rivers that begin on the mountain above Parihaka and they all take different paths to the sea.

It had been seven days since she hadn't returned.

He knew she would never be back when he saw his father coming down from the main road that led to the North Country and into the long straight of the valley road. David watched his far-off father, his movement in the saddle. The grace and fluidity of the rider. The unsmiling, silent man who terrified him.

He was travelling at the trot but standing in the stirrup irons, knees slightly bent, leaning over the neck and ears of the horse, resting it as best he could, looking back. A team of dogs followed him. At least six. Their wet tongues lolling out, lean, sharp eyed, ranging out in a natural hunting pattern.

All ribs and teeth and tongue is how his father would describe a good dog. Keep them hungry they work better. They ran with the muscular presence of wolves.

Easing back slightly in the saddle, he slapped the horse twice across the withers and changed to a slow canter. Right hand on his thigh, left held the reins up and light. Hips moving to the rhythm of the horse. Hat off, down his back, the string around his neck. Beard flattening slightly against his chest. Pale dust rising.

David watched his father as he rode towards him. Becoming larger and larger. He stopped at the gate, looked up to the cottage and bent over the horse's neck to unlatch the chain, holding the mane in his left hand. Even from where he stood, David could see the distending nostrils of the horse. It was breathing hard.

Walking backwards to let the dogs through. Two of them became embroiled in a fight. His father took a whip from the saddle. Spoke the dogs' names, Blue and Swift. Hissed at them. By god Swift. Snapped the whip.

David heard his voice carry. The high yipping noise of the dogs.

He was standing on the veranda of the small cottage holding one of the posts when his father rode up. Coming to a stop, dismounting, one supple motion. The reins still in his hands he walked up to David and stood on the top step. Dust coming over them, almost an afterthought. The horse had been stopped at the bottom of the steps, her neck stretched out as his father pulled the reins, his arm behind him. The dogs seemed to flow up and around them, running everywhere.

You all right boy? He reached out and put his hand on David's shoulder.

Mum, David said and began to shake. Then he sobbed I have been waiting for you.

He had not made a noise since Mr and Mrs Gill came to tell him. He had wondered why his mother had not returned that evening from the trip to Ruatane. And then the next morning he saw the white helmet of the police sergeant at the Gills' house. His big bay gelding tied to the fence. It had been two days.

It is best you know lad, Mr Gill had said. There has been an accident. Your mum won't be coming home Davie. She has been lost in the sea.

Mrs Gill had hugged him to her. She smelled of whey and her stomach was large and soft. There there she had whispered and wept. He could not cry then. He would not believe it then.

He felt his father's hand leave his shoulder. David sat down and continued to cry. Holding his face in both hands. One of the dogs came over and sniffed at him. David felt the dog's wet breath and a lick at his ear.

Get out of it Swift his father said.

He felt his father turn away. Heard him step back, his boots on the veranda. The metallic clump of the bit in the mouth of the horse. His father saying go back Maggie.

He led the horse to a fence and looped the reins twice over the top wire then took a light chain from a saddlebag and whistled the dogs. He passed the chain through the collar rings of the dogs and took them further down the fence. Fastened the chain to the fence with a clip.

He returned to the veranda. Looked at David.

David said nothing. He was quiet, holding his face in his hands. Hiding his eyes as he would do when he was a small boy.

Unsaddle the little mare would you boy? Take off her bridle too. There is a head stall and a small rope in the offside saddle bag. Get her and the dogs a bucket of water.

David didn't move. He just wanted to stay very still.

Come on boy his father said. Up you get.

His father waited a moment and then said come on son, in a soft, firm, encouraging voice he had never used with David before. Don't sook now. You are a man near enough. It was the voice he used when breaking in horses. There was respect and understanding. There was life in the voice. Something resembling love.

David whispered yes Dad. There was nothing else. Stood up and wiped his face with the inside of his elbow.

Mr Gill was walking up the track towards them. He saw Mrs Gill standing at the gate of the house watching. She was drying her hands on her large white apron. David could see her face. The frown and glances in his direction. Nods.

Mr Gill took off his hat as he approached.

His father walked down to meet him. They shook hands. Mr Gill was shaking his head. Looking down. He saw his father asking questions and Mr Gill again shaking his head. They shook hands again and Mr Gill turned and walked back down towards his house. Mrs Gill was waiting for him. She put a hand to her ear, straining to hear what her husband was saying as he walked back towards her.

His father was still standing there. David saw him look at his feet. He was holding his hat in his hands. Then he looked up over to the direction of the sea. He shook his head again and began to walk back towards the house. Wide steps, the walk of horsemen long in the saddle. Looked to where David was unsaddling the mare.

Watch that little mare boy he called out, she might nip you. Doesn't like strangers.

The mare had laid her ears back as David slid the saddle off. He had been watching his father and Mr Gill. He heard the snap of her teeth and felt the tug of the shirt material on his shoulder.

She get you?

David shook his head.

Growl at her boy. And then rub her ears. That's the way you do it. She will learn she has done something wrong, you are in charge and yet you still care for her. Name is Maggie. That's how you teach them. Punch her in the mouth if she does it again.

David said nothing, his lips pressed together.

His father sat on the veranda steps. His hat was still in his hands. His head dipped.

David thought he heard his father say, I don't know Mary. I don't know. He looked at his father, sitting there holding his hat. Curling the rim. He had so many scars on his big hands. Some of the cuts and scratches were fresh. Mostly from dogs and horses and knives. Then he heard his father say, *jesus fucking christ* why her?

They both sat there for some time. David remembered seeing the grass darken as clouds passed before the sun. Three brown hens come stalking along a tree line scratching with both feet, heads up and then searching for something to peck at.

Put a cover on Maggie will you Davie, his father eventually said. He was still looking down at his hat. There is one in the lean-to. March nights can be cold. Remember to cross over the backstraps. And David come here when you have finished. I have something to tell you. Life goes on mate.

On the day of his mother's funeral he kissed her as she lay in the coffin. Held for a moment one of her hands which lay on a posy of cornflowers.

He had never known her hands to be cold. Her cheek was never like that. This was not his mother. His mother was warm and funny and cried a lot. And made silly *Arrangements*. Laughed and sang songs as she worked around the cottage.

He had face powder on his lips, it tasted of lavender. She never used lavender powder. Gardenias. White gardenias in the evening was her favourite powder.

He asked the priest if he would read out his mother's beloved poem. By the Englishman Wordsworth. She had said he must have invented that name. Nobody worthy of such words could have a name like that. He would paste newspapers on his walls as wallpaper. Lived in a room of words.

Like morepoak, he remembered saying. The owl you love. *Ruru*. Named for the noises it makes.

Her laughter like wings.

The Ode to Immortality. The priest said it didn't seem appropriate at this time son. They had sung instead her favourite hymn How Great Thou Art.

On her grave he placed the driftwood and grey stones and shells that was *The Flight across the sky of God who we can see as a Meteor.* He didn't get it quite right, he couldn't remember where all the pieces went. But they were there anyway.

He looked in the direction of Parihaka. And thought here she is.

Then he went to help milk Mr and Mrs Gill's cows.

As he carried two buckets of milk to the dairy for Mrs Gill to put into the separator he thought he heard *te riroriro* crying out for the source of love along the river which ran through the valley.

Mrs Gill said thank you David as she turned the handle. It will be all right. Time is a great healer and routine makes good bandages.

Thank you Mrs Gill.

His father rode back to Te Taurangi the next day.

I've got to get back is what his father said to him. There are ten or so two-year-olds need finishing. I am contracted to finish them. Made the boss Campbell Grey a promise. Shook his hand. That's enough. He smiled, that's what *te taurangi* means boy, the promise, funny eh? He had the bodies of three brown hens tied across the front of his saddle. They had no heads. Their feet trussed with wool bale twine.

David never saw his father again.

He was told when he was in the military prison at Étaples in France that his father had died. A horse had kicked him in the head. And it was a good fucking riddance if he was anything like you, you traitor *cunt* you. English laughter always seemed cruel he thought, a betrayal. He was sick for two weeks before he passed away.

And that night he thought he heard *ruru* comforting him. There were no *rurus* in France. It must have been a dream.

He smiled and thought of his mother's hair. And, for some strange reason, the size and beauty of her fingers and hands. The pale blue of the cornflowers.

It was almost four more months until he could leave the Gills. Mr Gill asked a local shearing contractor, Alan Finer, if they needed a roustabout.

Mrs Gill said I will miss you Davie.

Mr Gill said all the best. And then come on Mother, those slips need milking.

He was surrounded by words and photographs. Recent headlines, advertising slogans. The flour and water paste he had used still smelled fresh. Lumpy to the touch.

Late afternoon light came into the room from the one west-facing window. A bold headline declaring the Armistice and neat rows of newsprint illuminated.

November 11 1918. A day in history.

PEACE.

A lithograph of King George the Fifth and the Queen Consort. A map of Europe.

Influenza Epidemic Sweeps the World. Thousands Dead.

David still stood in the doorway of the hut. He was holding the door with one hand and an old army pack in the other. There was mud on his knees and on the side of his face. He looked around the inside of the hut. Walked in and closed the door.

Morrinsville Bull Sale.

Riots in Palestine 47 Jewish 48 Arab deaths. Ethnic persecution in Turkey continues.

First Miss America Pageant held in Atlantic City.

He carried his boots to the opening in the wall that allowed access to the fireplace. Read the walls.

Warren G. Harding Inaugurated as US President.

For Rent. Two-bedroomed bungalow in Liardet Street.

He knelt and gathered some sheets of newspaper from a box, screwed them into balls and packed them into his damp boots. In the morning he would clean them again and rub mutton fat and Stockholm Tar into the leather uppers.

He stood and gathered some kindling from a wooden apple box and placed it around the glowing, ash-covered log in the fireplace. He took some more newspaper and screwed up another loose ball. Placed that among the sticks and knelt over it. He blew on the burnt log which groaned open. Exposed the glow at the inside of itself. Red sparks flew up and then small flames took hold of the kindling. One or two more quick breaths at the base of the flames and the room was filled with the reassuring crackle of the new fire.

If there could be laughter in the natural world this would be it, he thought. The sound of a new fire; water falling over stones.

Summer rain in an orchard.

He noticed the shadows and flame shapes moving around the interior of the room and glanced at the window. The light was almost gone.

There was a white wax candle stub near the fireplace. Holding it aslant, he lit the stub from a piece of burning kindling he had taken from the fire. Placed more thin pieces of wood on the fire.

He stood up and found the table lamp. Took the glass off and used the candle to light the wick. Blew out the candle and adjusted the lamp wick until a soft yellow glow filled the room. A pale yellow circle. Almost white.

He nodded and stood just beyond the line of light. Put his hand into the light, withdrew it.

His body heat had partially dried his trousers and shirt. He undressed in the dark. Socks, underpants and cotton singlet thrown into a washing pile. Trousers, shirt and woollen sleeveless vest draped over a thin wire nailed along the wall. They would be dry by morning.

He walked naked through the pale yellow light, bent to place more wood on the fire. Squatted, warming his hands and body as the fire flared. Then stood and turned and warmed his back and backside holding his arms across his chest. Changing his weight from foot to foot.

Returned to the dark and rubbed himself down with a towel. Put on a blue woollen singlet and sat. Placing his lower body into the light he lifted his left foot up onto his right knee and inspected between his toes, drying them and looking for infection. Then the right foot onto his left knee.

A habit from the trenches. Dusted both feet with talcum powder, rubbing it between his toes. Then his fingers began to explore the old scar tissue. He closed his eyes and let his fingers touch. They came over his chest and shoulder. For some reason, counted. Touched his neck and cheek as she would. Held his ear.

It was an old enough thing; Sarah said oh my dear Jesus have mercy the first time when she saw, and touched, and then kissed him.

He turned away and said please don't say that.

He checked his groin. Again, the talcum powder, feeling cautious, reassured. There had been weeks when this was impossible. Began to inspect for lice then stopped, reminding himself. No more lice now.

Well. God willing.

A pair of thick, dry woollen socks coming to just below his knees, the bottom of both socks thin, soon to need darning. A baggy pair of shorts and a black polo-neck seaman's jumper.

Holes in both elbows. This was what he wore most evenings when he returned from working on the station.

David carried the lamp to the meat safe. Yellow light thrown from the lamp swayed and moved as he moved. He read the walls as he walked.

Worldwide progress on war memorials has slowed due to the huge demand for marble and a massive shortage of monumental stone masons.

King Faisal of Iraq crowned in Baghdad.

Major riots in Munich due to food shortages and rising prices.

The death of well-known pioneer Mr Frederick Theo Gill as a result of a fall from a swing bridge across the Papango River.

Then he stepped through to the other room of the hut where a single mattress lay on the floor. Next to the mattress there were two rugs. One a small purple black and white rag rug he had been given in Germany by a boy called Joachim.

The other was a prayer rug Mahmoud had posted to him.

David looked at the prayer rug with the light on it. Nodded. Thought I will put it on the wall. Next to the window. Where the light from the setting sun will be near it.

Saw for a moment Mahmoud's laughing face.

Knew the laughter would be at his attempted humility. This was truly worthy of our loving laughter. And then his footless leg. He saw his leg without a foot. A great club of white bandages. Do not try David. Be.

He knelt and placed the lamp by the mattress, took off his jumper and got into bed. He smelled of fern, creosote, blue mud, mutton fat and a sweated horse. Something too of a wet dog. And faint memories of his father.

He washed as often as he could. Water he carried up from the creek in old kerosene tins. Now he knew his bedding needed washing also and hanging in the sunshine.

He reached out and turned down the lamp wick until it went out. The oily smell of kerosene smoke drifting over him in threads.

He lay there and watched the fire in the corrugated iron fire place in the next room of the hut.

Went over what he had to buy the next day.

Sugar, bread, more newspapers, a pen and ink, an exercise book, coal tar soap, cheese, butter, flour, salt. More matches. Seed for cornflowers.

The last thing he heard before he slept was the owl *ruru* calling out *morepoak* and then a long wait as if to say I remain here, then again—*morepoak*.

Thought this is what we call the owl. From the noise it makes.

Before you David, Sarah said. And after Jamie. She laid a hand briefly over her lips. There was this hopelessness which would come over me.

David stroked some hair back behind her ear.

It was like that southerly wind that comes up the valley. So. Just so as it does. The nights seemed as long as I don't know what. That old owl would call *morepoak* and it would be dark. Like all the colour had drained out of the world. It's such an empty sound. As if there is no one else left.

It's not all that bad David said.

She took his hand and kissed the back of it. Held each of his long fingers in turn. Turned his hand over in hers and then kissed his palm. His fingers closed gently around her face.

You know, she said as she lifted her head. I washed all of Jamie's clothes and bedding when he went away. It kept me busy so I wouldn't have to think about him going. That day. The day of his face in the sun and his dogs wagging their tails and running behind them as Gerald drove him to the town. So confused when he called go home at the road gate.

And the last words he yelled were see you Mum. His father did not turn back. I had my hand in my mouth.

So there it is. I washed them all and kept them clean and smelling nice because when he came home they would be lovely for him wouldn't they?

David nodded and said nothing. They were still holding hands.

Anyway, she whispered.

And then the day the card came. The notice came.

They were both quiet. They could hear each other's breathing.

And all I had of him were his clothes and bedding smelling of soap and camphor.

I hunted for something in his room that I would have overlooked. Something that was dirty. Anything so I could smell him again, that was of him. But there was nothing except the smell of soap. And the card from the government that had his name on it.

Pte James Gerald Mitchell.

Wellington Inf. Regt. N.Z.E.F.

The words above his name were something like let those who come after see to it that his name not be forgotten.

I burned the card. And

I don't want to talk anymore for a while.

That's all right David said. Don't talk.

She smiled and reached out her hand to his face. Touched the scars with her fingertips.

Some time later she was standing in the fading light of his hut. A candle burned and she said I want to tell you something else.

Yes Sarah, David said.

She spoke, again looking out the small window and holding her hands around her body. I do not want to be proud of my Jamie. He is not coming back. I would rather him here. I wouldn't even have cared if he was in a wheelchair.

Then she put one hand up and reached out to the prayer mat next to the window. Felt the wool, traced some of the shapes as she continued to speak. I say how proud I am. And smile and look at my feet. I am lying.

David was silent. He let her speak without interruption. He would wait until she finished and came back to him.

He would be teething and...

David nodded. Silent.

I remember him learning to walk. Hands stretched out as if to catch I don't know what. But I clapped so at the smile he gave me whenever he reached something to hang onto. My skirts or

Gerald's hands. Sometimes a dog or a table leg. I dreamed I could feel the tug of his little hands on my skirts.

Sarah paused, sniffed and gave a tearful laugh. I want to be annoyed with him for leaving his boots on. Yell and wave my hands about at the dirt he walked in the house. How could he be so thoughtless? Look at the mud on the floor I just swept it...

She stopped speaking. Looked at David with a question. As if he could answer something.

Oh jesus. David said nothing, looked away out the window.

I do not want to see his name in gold letters, she said, on the wooden memorial thing in the hall.

I want to make the peace between him and his father when they disagree about some new farming idea or such and the young man telling the old man how it should be done because this is a better way and the old man saying that this had worked for his father and his before...

But John Deere has this machine all the way from America. His father saying I do not want to hear this. Sarah, talk to the boy. I am going for a walk.

I want cross words. Disputes over milking methods and bobby calves. I don't want to remember at the damned going down of the sun and in the morning. I do that every day. It is with me from the time I wake until I close my eyes at night. I want to forget how proud I am. Or how proud I should be. I want it to be different.

A long time seemed to pass and they both were silent.

She shrugged and opened her hands, held them open towards him. Tears had run down her face. How can I? she said. How can I not?

You cannot, David said. Want. You are supposed to always remember I think. It is like expecting things to be different. If they were supposed to be different they would be. To remember is the way into purgatory and perhaps too, the way out. Wanting is hope. He put his hand up to his mouth and groaned.

She looked at him. That was a very foolish thing to say.

I know he said. I know you think that.

They were quiet for a while.

Sarah took a deep breath and continued to speak.

I did not know what to do with the Notification of Bereavement they sent me, she said. What would a mother do? I thought perhaps I could surround it in flowers and put it on the mantelpiece.

Sarah stopped speaking and put her hand over her mouth. She turned and looked out the window. David knew he would always remember her thus, framed in afternoon light, darkening blocks of newsprint around her. Advertising images. Headlines in Gothic type.

Mahmoud's prayer rug next to her face. You are the cure within the pain. The loyalty in betrayal.

And, she whispered between her fingers, I burned it and I mixed the ashes with water and I drank it. I don't know why. I somehow wanted him back in me I suppose, in my body again.

And it tasted like what it was. Burnt paper in my mouth. I had to drink a glass of milk to get rid of the taste. It was nothing like I thought it would be. I ate a spoon of jam. She reached out and pushed her fingers into the rug. Turned to face David. Her mouth open.

Am I sick?

No. David leaned up on his elbow.

I do not want to remember my son. I want him here. Am I wrong?

No David said and sat on the edge of bed. You are not.

How can…

It was quiet again for a while.

Anyway. She turned and looked at him. Anyway.

David watched her. Breathed in through his nose. Took her in through his eyes. Felt himself lifting, changing, becoming her. Wanted to cry out as he flew above them.

Whispered, I think it's going to rain Sarah.

She stood, her back to the window of the fading clean daylight. The walls of the room had darkened. Her breasts swayed as she stepped towards him. The candle threw a shining yellow white light across her thighs and stomach and then the shadows of her walking towards him.

He lifted the blanket and smiled at her approach.

David raised John's head and moved his heels. Said come on the John we had better keep moving. Wilfred Abernethy was a good man. Became a headmaster they say and a fine rugby coach. John's ears moved back and forth at the sound of David's voice. Only drank once a year. The anniversary of when the horses forgave him. And that is how you got your name boyo, the John.

It was mid-morning when he came into a small tree-fern hollow and found the dead ewe with the new-born lamb beside her. The lamb was weak and uselessly bunting at the ewe's shoulder looking for milk.

The old man walked John down into the hollow and stopped. He looked at the dead ewe and her lamb. There was some blood, not much afterbirth. She had probably died during the effort of expelling the lamb from her womb. The lamb made a weak bleating noise and Floss sprang forward towards it.

The old man hissed at her. And then slowly eased himself down from the saddle. He let the reins trail. John stood still.

He bent forward into a stalking posture and put his hands out to catch the lamb who sensed his presence and stumbled away from his approach. Floss whined and opened her mouth. Closed it and sat trembling in obedience.

The old man couldn't quite grab hold of the lamb and as it turned instinctively to its left and then right, away from the strange shape bearing down on it, he lost his balance and slipped over.

Catch it Floss he called. Catch him.

Floss leaped forward and seized it in her mouth, growled and knocked it down.

That'll do. The old man said and slowly got to his feet and walked over to where Floss was standing over the lamb, one paw on its belly. The lamb flopped and struggled to get to its feet.

The old man reached down and picked it up under the chest. Said girl, Floss. Then he took it back to the body of its mother and knelt down next to the dead ewe.

He reached between her back legs and found the udder. Felt the temperature with the back of his hand and tried to squeeze some milk from the ewe. He grabbed the lamb by the scruff of its neck and used his thumb and index finger to open its mouth around the teat of the dead mother.

The lamb instinctively bunted and sucked at the udder. The old man sat back and held the back leg of the ewe up as a grotesque support. There wouldn't be much milk for the lamb but even if it got a mouthful it might survive.

After about five minutes he leaned back, rested his elbow into the soft belly of the dead sheep and checked if any milk was coming from the udder. There was nothing, but the lamb's mouth had some milky fluid around it.

He got to his feet and carried the lamb under one arm. Walked back to where John was waiting. Pushed the newborn lamb rump first into the near side of the *pikau*. The lamb's head peering, comical, from between its four soft white hooves. It bleated again.

Then the old man took two coiled lengths of rope and secured them to metal rings on each side of the gelding's breastplate. Threaded each of the rope ends through the stirrup irons and walked them back in turn to the dead ewe. He bent over and took a knife out of the leather pouch at his waist and cut through the skin in each of the ewe's back legs just above the hock. Threaded the rope ends through each of the hocks and tied them off in bowlines.

He returned to where John was standing and picked up the reins. Made a kissing sound with his lips said walk up the John, come on son you have done this before. John walked forward and stopped as he felt the weight of the dead ewe slow him.

Come on, the old man said and walked ahead, turned and put some pressure on the reins, pulling John's head towards him. John leaned against the weight and took it; walked on and came up over the crest of the small hollow dragging the dead ewe.

The ground was soft and the grass cushioned the body of the ewe. The old man knew he wouldn't lose too much wool getting it down to the drafting yards by the river. Next to the yards there was the tree where he had a gambrel and pulley gibbet. There he could pelt her and butcher the carcass for dog food.

They descended to the river, traversing the slope to avoid the body rolling ahead of them. Floss followed sniffing at the drag marks left by the dead sheep.

When they reached the drafting yards the old man took the bridle off John and made a simple hackamore from a length of rope. He untied the ropes from the breastplate, eased the girth strap and led John to a tree away to their right and secured the hackamore to a longer length of rope. Left him to graze with the rope trailing.

He returned to the dead ewe and untied the bowlines. Took the ropes out of her hocks and rolled them up into two neat circles. Finished the rolls with a waist hitch, looped the rope and tied a small piece of baling twine into the upper part of both.

Then he found the gambrel and chain and wire pulley, dragged them out and threaded the hooked ends of the gambrel through the back legs of the ewe. He returned to the chain and hauled up the body.

When it was hanging about six inches off the ground he hooked one of the chain links into a holding cleat hammered into the trunk of the tree.

The ewe's body swayed slightly.

⌒

She said when she arrived that afternoon that it had become what it shouldn't be. You know this David don't you?

He agreed that was so. Then he said perhaps we are missing something.

She looked at him and smiled sadly. I wish you were right, she said, but you aren't. It was wrong and it was mad. I felt I could not live without seeing you. She held a hand under her belly. The longing took me over. And now…

I believe Jamie has come back to me David. Is in me now.

David stared into her eyes for a long time. Then he placed one hand on her belly, felt the rising swell of it and closed his eyes.

I am so happy Sarah. For you.

Beneath his three smallest fingers the child moved and rolled in her mother's womb. Fluttered in awakening.

It is a boy Sarah said. It is Jamie come back. What else could it be? Don't you think so?

He shook his head. Smiled.

And you understand don't you. She walked to the door and turned. You see this don't you David I cannot...

He said nothing.

Watched her until she turned out of sight.

The old man looked up from the knife and the steel in his hands. Continued sharpening the knife.

He could feel the wet swishing of his heart, suspended in his chest. A series of small waves began breaking against the white lines of his ribs and across the shield of his sternum.

A daily heartbreak. He smiled as he whispered to himself. He felt them, the waves, hissing into his left arm and shoulder. Like the love thoughts of a young man. A daily betrayal of who we are. Almost laughed.

The words of Mahmoud.

When we are in love we think our hearts will burst. That we can fly. That flames are coming from our heads. But it is true and not true. Everything is contained in yes and no. The This is our Beloved. The love we feel makes us know our death and everything that could be beyond death. It is the knowing of death that ensures our immortality. Every heartbeat is a promise of now and a betrayal of what will be. The consciousness of time passing.

Perhaps. Mahmoud would laugh with the word perhaps. Said like a question to him.

Of you Europeans I think the Italian language says it best. *Amore*. A-more which means opposed to death. Love is therefore the death of death. Love is the everything. Love is God. Mahmoud smiling at him.

This is what it means when your heart is breaking no? When you see your Beloved.

David saying, I think you are drawing a long bow there mate. I can't speak Italian.

A daily heartbreak, he whispered again. *Amore*.

I cannot speak Italian.

He kept sharpening the knife. His hands moved, as he waited for them to know to stop.

He had seen the inside of chests too many times. He knew what was there. The sparkling pink of lung blood when the sun catches it. Seen enough of it, he whispered to himself. The coughing up of pink blood. Who would think such a thing.

He was still softly speaking. Said, ribcages. And again, separating the two words. Rib cages.

Shook his head at this whispering to himself. Been doing more and more of this lately. Who is whispering and who is being whispered to, that is the question. These government men like a bomb in a trench. Shook his head again. He was still sharpening the knife.

⌐

When they first ran, David always thought this about the young officers, they ran like it was a fierce schoolboy game. Calling out come on boys. Mouths wide open.

Winning the race, until the machine-gun shot punched them back with such an unimagined savagery that their bodies exploded in front of their eyes. It was then that he often saw the immensity of the gulf between what they had imagined at school and the books they had read, and what was occurring now. It was so grotesquely tender. This disbelief that it wasn't a game of rugby or something fathers and other old boys would admire.

Young sir, David would say gently, because he knew they had become used to being called sir, look at me. Look at me son. I am here. Look into my eyes. The head would often shake, side to side. A refusal of what had happened. It wasn't supposed to be like…

Yes. You have been shot but…no it is. Sir here. Here is my finger. Hold my finger. And look into my eyes. Look. Don't say that. Stop saying no and look into my eyes. Hold my finger, squeeze. Yes, you are bleeding. Oh yes it is. Look at me. Squeeze.

The young men had gripped his finger with a fierceness and absolute trust that only the newborn display.

It was something Mahmoud had taught him. This comfort. Our first touch often is to grip the finger of our mother. The first noise we hear is *sssh*. As if to comfort us after being rudely expelled into the world. Slapped into life.

David would whisper bless you as the grip slackened and their neck arched back in death. Please, he would say, don't. Don't go. Not yet. But, of course, they most often did.

He breathed heavily through his nose, cleared his throat and hummed. It was tuneless, just a noise, an agreement with something or somebody.

He stopped sharpening the knife and tested the edge with his thumb. Said good and placed the knife on top of his jacket. Replaced the steel in the knife pouch around his waist.

He found the bucket he kept at the yards and followed a narrow track down to the edge of the river. The river was in flood and much higher than usual. By hanging onto a branch and leaning out over the water he managed to fill the bucket with brown water and sticks. He carried it back to where the ewe was hanging. Placed the bucket to one side. Scooped the sticks out with his hand.

He took the knife and cut the ewe's throat. Pulled back her head and stepped to his right. Let the blackening blood out of her. Waited a moment and then cut the tag out of her left ear. Rinsed his hands, put the tag in his pocket. Next he cut off her head and dropped it next to the bucket. Opened her and cleaned out the innards. The familiar gut smell rose around him. He breathed through his mouth and started to hum a tune in the back of his throat as he cleaned the intestines of the ewe. Threw the kidneys and heart to Floss.

On the wings of a snow white dove.

This was the tune he always hummed when butchering and dressing animals. He didn't know why.

He pressed the contents of the grass-bag and bowel and bladder out onto the grass. Cut away the lungs and liver and stomach. Inspected the liver for fluke. Said no you don't to Floss who had eaten the kidneys and heart and was eyeing the liver in his hand. The eels will get this.

He carried the liver, the head, feet and the remaining offal to the river and threw them in.

He sends his pure sweet love.

~

The closest hospital to the front line was located in what had once been the wine cellars of an ancient chateau known as the House of the Three Swallows. La Maison des Trois-Hirondelles. There was barely anything left of the old chateau above the ground but underground it had become extensive. The brigade engineers had taken out walls and excavated the cellars until it was five times larger than before the war.

The roof of the cellars had had extra iron support beams put under the oak floor joists. These iron beams were held up by adjustable steel screw-pillars.

The chalk walls were lined with corrugated iron painted white. Large black letters and numbers were written along the walls. Lengths of four-by-two timber secured, through the corrugated iron, into the chalk. Support for rows of the beds and operating tables.

The underground hospital was reached by descending a set of stone steps widened to allow two teams of stretcher bearers to pass each other in opposite directions.

In the triage clearing station there was an orderly clerk seated at a desk signposted as A&D. Next to him there was another station for anti-tetanus serum. Then blood and gum infusions. Hung along the walls there were splints made from wood and wire.

One long trestle table contained packets of dressings. Hot blankets came next and oxygen bottles, ether bottles and a set of examination and operating tables. The floor was a series of raised duckboards. Not the ordinary trench duckboards, the slats were more closely nailed together. A central drain ran the length of the cellar.

The interior of the hospital was lit with a set of naked electric bulbs that pulsed with the workings of the mechanical generator operating in what had been the chateau's music room.

The noise coming out of the underground hospital was, from a distance, the sound of a swarm of bees.

David heard the noise of the bees increasing as they approached. The chaplain's eyes opened. He looked at David. He knew his name.

David he whispered are we coming into Hell?

David laughed. They were all walking upright now, away from the sniping and mortars. They passed plane trees in bud. A field of self-sown red poppies beneath the trees.

Have you not heard that the Messiah fell and formed a heaven from what he discovered in the abyss? A madman called William Blake wrote that. Another madman called Mahmoud ibn Afghani told me of this Englishman. Isn't that the strangest of things? He called him the Sufi Blake.

The chaplain looked up at him and said no, I haven't heard that about Afghani and I don't think they were mad David. Have you seen the poppies?

I have.

They passed through groups of soldiers standing and smoking, their packs and equipment in untidy piles at their feet. Haunted glances in their direction. More soldiers were unloading lorries and stacking boxes. Three field kitchens were being wheeled into position.

Teams of mules in harness, ammunition canisters strapped to their sides, were being pulled and whipped along the sunken road. The sounds of the whips and metal linkage, the grunts and braying of the mules. Helmeted men hissing and calling to the animals, round steel helmets, raised arms and black whip shapes silhouetted against the pearl sky. Walk up Jenny girl. Naming them in urgency and cursing them. Get up you *cunt* mule you I will *fucking* cut you open. Good boy Billy walk on son. That's the good mules. Come on good mule.

A line of black soldiers, stripped to the waist with tribal facial scars and red caps, were splitting wood and stacking it alongside the field kitchens.

A leader was calling out the invitational lines of an ancient chant, asking high-pitched, searching for affirmation. *Who, answer me this, are you?* The work crew seemed to rise up in reply. Answering the invitation. Sang back *We are here. This is what we are. What we are doing. Look at us as we do this.*

In a field to their left there was another line of soldiers. These were gas blind, their eyes bandaged. They were walking each with his left hand on the shoulder of the man in front. Leading them was a French nun, holding the right hand of the front man. His head was held up and slightly to one side as if he could see through his bandages. He had a cigarette in his mouth and his left arm was in a sling. There were sergeant's chevrons on his arms. The other men all held their heads down. They formed a ragged line, stumbling as they walked amidst a grove of pear trees in white blossom. Long meadow grass at their feet. The crowns of white clover, red anemones and poppies.

David and the stretcher bearers carried Father Hickey down the stone steps past the triage sign. They passed the next regimental aid post and the next field ambulance and the arrow next to the entrance sign and stopped behind three other stretcher parties lined up. They rested the top handles of the stretcher on the uppermost steps. The two men holding his feet still held their handles. One of the bearers below them turned and passed back two ammunition boxes.

Here you are cobber he said with an Australian accent. Winked and smiled. They rested the lower end of the stretcher on the boxes, managing to keep the stretcher somewhat level.

Thanks mate. David smiled at him.

Here he is Georgie boy, the Australian turned and spoke to the medic who waved them into the entrance. He turned back to them and said see you fellas, behave yourselves now. Smiled then laughed, fuck this for a game of soldiers, as he picked up the handles of the stretcher and disappeared into the underground hospital. Fix bayonets. Laughed again.

The smell came up of blood and bowel and ether and raw spirit. Gangrene and rotted feet. Carbolic soap and Jeyes fluid. The noise coming out of the clearing station had become individualised and yet still held the collective shrill clamour of trauma. There were cries and orders. Commands.

Nothing extreme or hysterical. Raised voices and yells. Pain and blood and numbing loss and hope and love. Death. Here there was mostly death and loss and a deep compassion that David could only think of as enduring. Something he would never forget.

Someone was saying: just lifting you now mate. Ah that's the boy. Someone humming Jerusalem the hymn.

Another, orderly.

Orderly! The scream stifled with a hand. Morphine and saline please.

Gone sir.

Sir.

Gone to his maker. God bless him. Ah.

Fuck you you droopy eyed *prick* you.

Now you I will not have that language. Please stay calm man.

My wife said I should wear a white shirt once a week and keep my feet clean. On Sundays.

Clamp. Steady. Walk. Do not run in this theatre. Is that clear medic? No running.

Singing. Me mother's name is Lily she's the whore of Piccadilly.

Corporal, keep that man quiet.

A triage medic stepped up out of the entrance and stopped. David. How are you mate?

George, said David. Good. George was wearing a white tunic buttoned to the neck and a large white apron. There were spots and smears of blood. A large red hand-print smudged on his chest.

He nodded. What have we got here Dave, a chaplain? You blokes have got him tied down. Is he?

We have George. Yes, he is. David looked away at the wall so the chaplain could not see what he was doing, made a ticking motion with his finger pointing at his ear.

All right, George said and nodded. Looked at the chaplain. Due for a rest father. Eh?

The chaplain was weeping. I am so sorry, he said. So sorry.

Don't be father, George said, it's all right. Wrote S/S on a tag and threaded the string through the chaplain's epaulet. Patted his shoulder. Left his hand resting on the chaplain's chest.

The chaplain tried to kiss his hand.

Get out of it, George said and snatched his hand away.

One of the bearers started laughing. Said, don't ask him to hear your confession.

All the bearers were laughing now, bent over.

George was smiling. Been a handful? Yes?

The bearers all howled. Handful all right.

George frowned.

David straightened. Yes mate. George I'll tell you about it when you have a minute. Unbelievable.

Nothing is unbelievable now. George said, and ran a hand through his hair. He wiped his hand on his apron. Bloody butcher shop, he said. Nothing is bloody believable any more. Let alone unbelievable. The whole world is on its arse.

George, David said. I know.

Take him over there Dave. Being a chaplain they'll whisk him off pretty smartly.

Hold on, George said and winked at David. He leaned over the chaplain and took a large black crayon out of his pocket and wrote a large M on the forehead of Father Hickey.

What are doing my son?

I just wrote M on your forehead Father. It stands for Mary. As he said this, George was holding Father Hickey's forearm and pushing a hypodermic needle into a fat vein. There you are.

A nearby battery of Australian artillery began to lay down a barrage of gunfire. The lights went out briefly and then back on again.

The light from her navel blinded me, Father Hickey yelled above the din. Blinded all humanity with her compassion.

Can't agree with you there father, George yelled back. Then he turned away. Put him over there Dave, next to that stretcher.

The chaplain had closed his eyes and had begun to recite *Our Father which art in Heaven hallowed be Thy name.*

He stopped and looked at the shape next to him. He raised his hand and tried to make the sign of the cross. Because his arms were still tied at the elbow, his hand only came up halfway and it looked like he was waving.

He began the recital of the extreme unction. The shape he was looking at was a stretcher with a black-stained khaki blanket pulled over the face of a dead soldier. His boots were still muddy. One puttee had unravelled. A mud-encrusted hand hung over the side of the stretcher, the fingernails long uncut.

Father Hickey began to weep and shake, said Oh my dear God. Ungentle purpose. Ungentle purpose.

George was speaking at the top of his voice to David. You

had better get back by the look of it there will be more needing you. He lifted his chin in the direction of the gunfire. There's a push on.

David looked to where two orderlies were struggling to keep a man down on a table. A doctor bending over him glanced up briefly; the light caught the lens of his glasses and flashed.

Mahmoud, David whispered. He began to tremble.

A spray of blood arced up and across the white corrugated iron wall in the shape of a fern. David felt George grip his biceps. The blood ran down the corrugated wall in wavy lines.

Are you all right mate?

A muddy hand from another stretcher reached out and grabbed George's hand. Cobber. A whisper.

Yes George, David said. I am all right. Look after this bloke. He nodded at the shape on the stretcher. A steel helmet covered this face. They all knew what that meant.

George took the mud-covered hand and felt automatically for a pulse. Said, move him in you blokes. His heartbeat. But he is good.

He lifted the helmet and looked at what was there. He is just fine boys. Gently replaced the helmet. Going to keep his good looks.

Looked back at David, his lips pressed in a line. And then he was hurrying the next stretcher into the clearing station.

Come on Davie boy, Dennis McCarthy said. Stop dilly-dallying. The push is on. They'll be needing us. They will be waiting out there. He tried to smile. All alone and cryin' for their mammy.

Dennis's mouth was open and he blinked. He looked away to his right, tears in his eyes. They all knew how he was, his courage and compassion for the wounded. He would be down on his knees and weeping, working like a fury to save the boys.

Stop tryin' to be the tough one Dennis, David said. Be your dear self. All right boys. Let's go.

When he returned to the carcass Floss was tentatively lapping at the half-digested grass he had cleaned out of the ewe. Get, he hissed. Put his hands into the bucket of water and began to wash the blood off his forearms.

He sends his pure sweet love…On the wings of a dove…

Floss looked away in the direction he had thrown the liver.

He dried his hands against his trousers and walked to the pulley. Took the weight from the chain and then, leaning his body back, hauled on it. Raised the carcass up until its backside was at shoulder height and began to remove the skin from the body of the ewe.

He was punching the pelt away from the carcass around the ribs when he stopped. The lamb, he said and left the skin hanging off the ewe and walked to where he had tethered John.

The lamb was still in the *pikau*. It had closed its eyes and appeared be asleep. The old man lifted it by the loose skin around the back of its neck. The lamb opened its eyes and bleated.

Hah, the old man said. Still alive. He put it down on the ground where it collapsed onto its chest. He touched it with his foot and rolled it over. Felt the bones of its tiny body sliding beneath his foot. The lamb righted itself but didn't stand up.

Good, he said and picked it up and replaced it into the *pikau*, but this time with its two front feet out and its back legs under itself. He returned to the carcass and completed skinning the ewe.

He replaced the knife and steel into the pouch. The wet hair on his arms was flat and each white hair seemed defined. His hands smelled of mutton fat. They felt smooth and greasy. He bent and picked up a handful of grass. Scrubbed his hands with the grass then dried them on his trousers.

The old man paused and turned his face into the sun. Birds called along the trees. Cicadas had begun to sing in the grass.

Hey cicadas, you listening? There are one hundred and fourteen, the old man said. There are a hundred and fourteen chapters in the Koran. They are called Surahs. And some say they sing like you. Mahmoud told me that on the morning he told me about his grandfather's apricot trees and I discovered the shape of the universe on my arse. Isn't that right Floss?

Floss opened one eye and her tail wagged once. She closed her eye.

He took the bloody pelt and hung it, wet fleece down, over a top board of the drafting yard next to his jacket. Crossing to the bucket, he rinsed his hands and washed the blood off his forearms.

Turned back to the naked carcass and studied it for a moment. Mottled red and streaked fat-white, hanging there beneath the tea tree. Collected his jacket from the top rail of the yard.

Whistled Floss. Yes he said to her. A hundred and fourteen. Do you like my singing girl? Better than those locusts anyhow.

On the wings of a snow white dove.

236

He picked up the bucket and threw the water onto the patch of grass where he had bled and gutted the ewe. Placed the bucket upside down next to a post on which a gate had been hung. Put a stone on top of the bucket.

Said the John as he walked towards where the gelding was grazing. John didn't raise his head but turned away with his head still in the grass and flattened his ears.

Don't be lazy the old man said. Stand still.

John stopped and raised his head and looked away with something resembling chagrin. The old man held his ear and talked softly to him as he began to put the bridle back on.

The October sun on his back. It was almost forty-seven years since it ended. Spring here, he thought. Almost northern winter.

On the day it all ended he smelled burning gum leaves. He was attached to the 3rd Field Ambulance of the Australian 5th Brigade, and they were bivouacked on the outskirts of a small village known as Courcelles.

Smell that Davie boy, an Australian soldier said. That is the smell of home. And the bloody thing is over. Come over here mate. The huge Australian put his arm around his shoulders. Squeezed him close. There it is. Done with. No more of our boys to carry back no more of them Davie.

What is the date?

Eleventh of November.

They hanged Ned Kelly on this day someone said, shit it's getting cold.

Who?

Ned Kelly.

A group of Australian soldiers were gathered around a steel drum cut down to form a makeshift cooker. They had collected gum leaves that had been sent to them in letters from home and burned them. They would close their eyes and just smell.

There. Some wept and then turned away to hide their tears and others simply smiled.

Bloody bush fires. Would you ever smell that? Would you ever smell that? Lord and summer. Dulcie in the sand dunes.

David could smell the hot resin-filled smoke as it wafted up. Drifted for a moment and disappeared into the air of France.

Ah bugger it another boy said. Do you have any meat?

I have got some Hun sausage. Bratwurst. Some onions. And Belgian beers. Some plonk, calvados.

Well would you bloody believe it you josser Good old Collingwood forever.

Would you stop that man singing.

Who is this Peb? Ah another Royboy from the Oracle.

Laughter and then silence.

One of the soldiers had put pieces of wood in the drum and then a square steel plate across the top of it. Flames emerged from around the edges of the plate. Another soldier stepped forward, brushed it with his hand. Poured on some water from a canteen and used a rag to clean off the plate. The water steamed.

They hanged Ned Kelly on the eleventh of November then? someone asked.

They did.

They reckon he was a tough sort of a rooster.

A murderous bastard my uncle said. A killer. Mad in the head.

A wild colonial boy.

Look at that it's hot enough.

Someone came forward with a bowl and a bayonet. Flicked a bladeful of lard onto the plate. It began to spit. Another bladeful.

Where is the sausage mate?

Get those onions on there.

Have a beer Davie boy. It's all over.

David smiled and took the beer. He looked at the November sky. It was silent. The clouds were building and soon it would rain. He could hear cheering and laughter in the distance. There was no sound of gunfire or artillery or flares or fireworks of any sort. He could hear a bugle playing a dance tune and more laughter. An illumination flare soared high, whistling into the sky. Burst gently and began to float back to earth.

They watched the bright glare of it, dimmed in the daylight.

What now mate? An Australian asked him.

I have to report back to battalion, David said.

Someone turned to him. It will all be forgotten Davo. All of this shit.

You think this will be forgotten? David said.

The Australian looked at him and said, nothing surer mate. Then burst out laughing. What would I know? Have a bloody beer David Monroe and let's think about the tomorrow tomorrow.

Suddenly there was a cheer come up from the group of soldiers. Someone called out bloody Albert Collins. Street you old bastard.

A soldier stood there with a young calf. He was bent over with his arm around the chest of the black and white calf. Look what I have found, he said, and kissed the head of the calf. A German calf.

Steaks, someone said.

Someone else said look at its colours it must barrack for Collingwood.

Laughter. Oh yes. Veal on the day the war ended.

And beers from Belgium.

Cheers and then there was silence. The onions were cooking on the hot plate. The sausage fried.

Here, the soldier who held the calf said, I have a good Green River. He held out a small butcher knife. I got him, someone can cut his throat. Come on now. Steaks boys. Bleed the little bugger and it will be all right in half an hour or so.

Here.

Everyone looked away. How is that sausage going?

Ah now Albert. You do it. You have done enough before.

I don't want to.

Why not?

Not today. Look at the little bastard would you.

I don't want to fucking look at the thing.

Well cut its throat then.

No I won't. I am celebrating the end of the war.

Are ya? You have done yer share of throats.

Who do you think you are to say that to me in that tone of voice you fuckin' Elizabeth man ya?

I am a better man than you or your pox-ridden father.

The man named Albert Collins they all called Street looked to David and threw him the knife. He dragged the calf over to David. Take this mate he said. Hold it will ya, while I sort this *cunt* out.

Street, David said. He held the scruff of the calf's neck as the two soldiers fought, pushing and wrestling each other. The others were laughing and moving aside around the burning drum. They were passing the bottle of apple brandy between them.

The two men rolled and fought and then stood and faced each other. Another man, a sergeant, stepped forward and said that's enough boys. Enough now. Stop it, the war has ended. We are going home soon.

It was becoming dark in the early winter of November 1918. The night was cold and the ice-filled wind was beginning to blow through the fire in the drum. Sparks flew away to the east, towards the old German lines.

David took the chin of the calf in one hand and bent it back. He stepped through its front legs and arched its neck back across his upper thigh. He then wiped the blade of the Green River knife once across his forearm, tested it with his thumb and then pushed it into the calf's throat between its windpipe and spine.

Cut out quickly and then pulled back with his left hand to cleanly snap the calf's neck. Held it quietly as it groaned and then leaned right down and bled the calf into the soil.

There, he said. This little one has a clean liver I am sure. And you boys will have steaks without fighting over nothing.

The Australian soldiers had stopped to watch this man the most compassionate of the stretcher bearers as he began to butcher the carcass of the calf they had found.

What? David said to them. He opened the calf's belly and delved in behind the stomach paunch and coiled intestines. Used his knife.

There it is. The liver. He held it up in one bloody hand. It steamed in the November air.

I can't look at the fuckin' thing Davie.

Jesus man.

Don't be bloody silly

It's a good colour. Cut it thin and fry it with those onions. Just the shot. Bit of salt.

It's still hot, someone else said. Look at it. Steaming.

Here, David said and threw it at him.

He twisted away from the thrown liver. It landed in the dirt.

Would you close its eyes David, the man named Albert said.

Sorry?

The calf, he said. The calf lay on the ground, its tongue protruding, head bent back, throat an open wound. Its entrails lay between its legs. Its eyes blueing in the air.

David stared at Albert. He drank from the bottle of calvados. Close its fuckin' eyes.

Someone began singing sadly in the background *Good old Collingwood forever…*

And everybody laughed except David and Albert.

Then, coming from a distance they heard the sounds of a woman yelling. A middle-aged Frenchwoman dressed in black approached them from the village. The sky darkening behind her. She was holding her hand out towards the butchered calf. *Là*, she screamed *là*.

They stood and looked at her. Drank.

Stop the gash you *cunt*, someone said.

Another man turned on him and said you don't speak to a woman like that young Peter. Let her do her bun. She'll be right in a minute. That calf was probably all she's got left. Until Bert here came along.

Get fucked. What are you?

What are you mate?

Albert stood up and walked over to her. It was me, he said. Sorry mother. Here. He reached into his pocket and took out some promissory notes. What do you want, take it all. He handed her a wad.

She slapped her hand up under his offering hand. The paper notes flew out of his hand. She spat at his feet. Her hand out towards the dead calf.

He nodded and looked at his feet.

She continued to curse him and all of the soldiers standing there. Spat again and sneered. Stepped forward and screamed in Albert's face. Some of the soldiers laughed.

David was watching him. No Street. No. It doesn't matter.

It was too late. The man named Albert Collins lifted his head. His left hand shot out and he grabbed the Frenchwoman by the front of her dress. Lifted her up and cuffed her across the head. And then as her head jerked to one side he cuffed her in the opposite direction. Shut up he said. And then punched her in the face, smashing her nose. He punched her again and then again. She tried to scream, but Albert had pushed her over onto her back and driven his fist into her mouth. I tried he said. I fucking tried. Now I am going to *end* you.

He was pushing his fist further and further down into her mouth. Her teeth were broken off. He was killing her. Her eyes were huge.

David leapt up and was pulling him off the woman.

Street no stop it.

Albert stood up and pulled a pistol out of the holster at his belt.

David got between Albert and the woman, who had turned and was crawling away. She was making mewling noises. David held up his hand. No Street.

Albert was pointing the pistol at the back of the woman. He smiled.

Street, someone else said. Don't mate.

Nobody sent me any fucking gum leaves he said.

The sun was shining and the air was warming as the old man rode up through a bed of rushes to where he had discovered the dead ewe. When they reached the hollow, he stopped John and then looked back to where they had come from. Then he looked up at the sky.

The tune he had been humming was still in his head.

He sends his pure sweet love. On the wings of a dove…

When troubles surround us.

He took a pocket watch out of a leather pouch he carried on his belt and looked at it. Held it at arm's length and turned it into the light to read it more clearly. John walked back two steps as he did this.

The old man said almost midday. And then, I need glasses.

Floss was lying about twenty yards behind where he had stopped. Her belly distended from the offal she had gulped.

He reached forward and put his hand on the lamb's head. Then twisted in the saddle and touched the top of the thermos. Nodded and dismounted. Took the saddlebags off from behind the saddle. Time for me to eat now Floss, he said. Eh fat dog?

He had decided not to go back to his hut for lunch today. It seemed the government men had finished with him but it would do no harm to make himself scarce anyway.

He had placed his oilskin coat on the ground and was sitting on it. He had dug his heels into the earth and was sipping tea and looking back the gentle slope towards the Papango River. It was shining in the sun. He had taken the lamb out of the *pikau* and it was lying on the grass beside him, legs tucked under itself, eyes closed and tiny head drooping.

John placed his head over the old man's left shoulder and was smelling him. His top lip mobile and gentle, nuzzling at David's ear.

You want some bread? David said and broke a piece off the rough sandwich he had made that morning and held it up towards John. The gelding took the bread and lifted his head.

The old man continued to stare back down towards the drafting yards and the river. He could just see the carcass hanging under the shade of the kanuka trees. He looked at the pale lines of the single vehicle track which came up from the woolshed to the drafting yards. The track followed the river in a long arc and ended at the yards in a loop. Raised and hardened with carted shell rock the pale wheel ruts were visible for miles.

Further downriver he could see the rusting roof of the storage shed of Rangiwai landing. The old jetty piles sticking up out the water like broken teeth. Dark green smudges of the pine trees tall now around the landing. Planted to hold the clay banks from eroding. Further north was the te Patu house and small farm where Sarah's daughter was raised. He used to watch her when she was little from up and away on that high east ridge. She would have been about ten years old.

Papanui Station 1935

The highest ridge of Papanui was at the north east boundary of the station.

The shepherd David Monroe sat on the grey mare, the Layla with the white tail which blew now across her off flank from the wind coming up the gully on the other side of the tree-lined ridge. The mare moved under him and stepped, cold, sideways away from the wind.

He held a pair of binoculars to his eyes with both hands and moved as the horse moved. Turning his body to keep watching. His beard, flecked with white now, also blew away from the wind.

There at least half a mile below him on the front lawn of a small red-roofed white house, the girl in the bright red and yellow dress and swinging pigtails was turning in a wide slow circle.

Then she was spinning with her arms out.

He shook his head. How does she know to do this?

Mahmoud had said this is a natural thing. Children do this because they want to. And that is the answer.

He watched as she spun and turned on the lawn. Up on her toes, dancing as a ballerina might. He had seen photographs in the newspapers, the *New Zealand Herald*.

Closed his eyes, felt the shift under his ribs and the ghost of a finger along his scarred flank.

And then she slowed and stopped, staggered and ran to one side of the lawn. She was off balance and falling over. She sat on the lawn near a bean trellis and moved her head in small circles.

Back and forth. Waiting for the world to right itself.

He saw the woman Mem te Patu dressed as always in black come out off the front porch of the small house and hurry to her. She was still holding something in her hand. It looked like part of a flax weaving.

He could see Mem bending over the girl and then standing up, waving a hand and scolding her.

None of the words she was saying came to him, but it was in the way she stood and moved her hands and feet that he knew she was chiding the girl. Mem turned and walked back towards the small white house.

The horse moved under him. Impatient at his stillness on the cold and exposed ridge. Blew out through her nose.

He said stand still the girl and made an *artart* sound in his mouth. Stand still, he said again and took one hand off the binoculars to pull back on the reins. Stop it.

He watched the girl, Sarah's daughter, stand up and follow Mem who, after a few more steps, slowed, paused and then, without looking back, put her arm out to hold the girl around the shoulders as they both walked back to the house. The girl slid her arm around Mem's waist in an unthinking reflex. Thus tenderly joined, they disappeared into the house.

The man smiled and thought about the rag doll with the porcelain face that he had in the hut. It was the girl's birthday next week.

Wary of the curiosity of Mrs Lawrence, he had ridden into Ruatane and asked the young Chung Moon to order it for him. The old Chung Moon was dying and spoke only pidgin English. He had been a gold digger on the Otago fields. Saved enough to bring his wife and son out from China and purchase the store in Ruatane.

Young Chung said what you want that for? Then laughed at his silence. All right Mr Monroe. Two week maybe three?

Thank you Mr Moon.

The doll had a red spot on each cheek. And Sarah's daughter was about to turn ten. Her name he knew was Catherine.

The te Patu house was on a sharp bend in the Papango River and just north of the old Rangiwai landing where the paddle steamers would come up the river in the old days.

A horse track left the te Patu house and ran north into the bush towards the village called *Koroniti* which translated as Corinth and then further north to *Atene* Athens, and finally to *Hiruharama*, Jerusalem.

A place of cherry trees and nuns and a prophet poet whose father he had seen in the Étaples prison yard.

Many years later David had stood behind the son at the Ruatane store. The poet, barefoot and weary after walking up from the river, buying Park Drive tobacco from Chung Moon. His hair was matted and dirty. There were lice in his beard and he smelled of sour sweat and shit.

They had both nodded as if they had recognised each other. David wanting to say I knew your father over there but realising he didn't, he just knew of him, a brave and difficult man who had also suffered the Field Punishment Number One.

The poet opened his mouth and then raised a nicotine-stained finger. Almost spoke. Smiled and raised a hand in farewell as he turned away to walk back down to Jerusalem.

David thought you are of *Jesus* and Mahmoud would kiss you

and tell you that you have come home. That is a stony road and you have no shoes.

Some in the Brotherhoods use pain and suffering to get closer to God, Mahmoud had said once as David carried him along a stony beach on Lemnos. Blood on the stones behind them. Rangi te Patu said that the poet had told him his name was *Hemi* which meant James but perhaps it also meant half a whole, as in hemisphere. Rangi shrugged. Said Ruatane translates as two men so who knows what that means.

Carazy. Chung Moon said.

David turned to him. What?

Chung Moon nodded towards the departing poet, pointed to his head and made a face of distaste. Carazy. No wash. Smell very bad. He waved a hand in front of his face.

David nodded and said like me. Just like me Mr Moon.

Chung Moon looked at him and then said no and laughed, high pitched, no no you not carazy. They both knew he was lying.

How much for the doll?

Ten shilling.

David put the binoculars down and sat and studied the small house. It was neatly kept with vegetable gardens and fruit trees. A pig sty and poultry run on the east side of the house. The fences painted white like the house.

He saw a rider come out of the bush from the direction of Jerusalem at a steady canter. He was following the well-used horse track. A young rider who sat, easy and balanced, above the neck of a striking tall bay horse. It could have been a colt or young gelding. A white blaze between its eyes. A front and rear fetlock also white.

One white foot try 'im, two buy 'im. His father's words.

The horse and rider came out into the wide clearing and paddocks, slowed to a trot and then eased down to a walk. Stopped, walked in a circle, stopped again. The rider was still, watching the house and the path that ran past the house.

Then David saw him as he suddenly dug his heels into the flanks of his horse and threw his hands forward. The horse reared slightly, both front feet coming off the ground and then sprang forward.

A flash of the white feet. The rider leaning along the horse's neck as they broke into a gallop. His hand came round in an arc and whipped at the backside of the bay, sods of wet grass flew up behind them.

They came past the front gate of the house; he turned in the saddle and held a hand up in greeting. Called out.

Pulled the horse up hard a hundred yards past the house. The powerful young bay colt, it must be, almost standing, coming back on its hocks and then David watched as the rider turned the colt around, dug his heels in again and slapped the reins cross both withers. The whip held in his teeth. Galloped past the front gate, sods of earth again flying up behind them. This time the rider waved his hat and whip. Called out *whoop whoop whoop* and riders of the purple sage my dears riders of the purple sage.

Mem came running out of the house with a straw broom, shaking it at the young rider.

The old man heard the faint noise of the *whoop whoop* come drifting up to him and smiled. Layla had lifted her nose as she heard the rhythm of the horse's gallop. Ears pricked forward. She moved her head back and forth as if nodding. Lifted her chin and, nostrils flared, set herself to whinny out but David pulled her mouth and head down with the reins. Hushed her.

He watched the rider performing his circus in front of the house. It was young Drew McKenzie, the owner's son. Run wild with no mother.

He lifted the binoculars to his eyes again and saw that the girl in the red and yellow dress had come out of the back door of the house and was watching the rider from the side of the house where Mem couldn't see her. She was laughing and waving to him. Jumping up and down on the spot, clapping her hands close to her chest.

Young Drew McKenzie was riding away, southward along the track that led to the river road and the homestead Wharekaka. Standing high in the stirrup irons and twisting in the saddle to look back at the girl. One hand on the rump of the bay. He waved and called out something. *See you Cat.* The old man could see the white of his teeth.

Mem was standing at the front gate. Chin up, her hands on her black gabardine hips. One hand still held the broom. Watched until the rider had disappeared. And then she turned and looked up to where he was. Inclined her head.

David took the binoculars from his eyes, backed the horse into the trees. She must have seen the sun flash from the lens.

The next day he was preparing the soil in the small vegetable garden behind his hut. It was late morning and he had finished mustering for the day.

Doing a good job there David. *Kia-ora e-hoa.*

David looked up from the garden bed. The dark clay soil freshly dug over and dusted with sweetening white lime.

G'day Rangi. He hadn't heard him walk up from the river.

Rangi smiled. He was carrying a flax bag, a *kete.*

Was that you yesterday up on the high ridge boy? Mem said you were up there again. Saw something flashing in the sunlight. Got sharp eyes. *Whatukaahu* hawkeyes, that old woman.

David slapped his hands together, brushing off the dirt and white lime powder. His boots were splashed white. The mark of burial parties and latrine duty, white lime on your boots.

Yes, he said. That was me.

Rangi leaned on the top rail of the garden fence and laughed. I dunno, he said. Mem told me to tell you to come down and talk. Have a cup of tea. *Korero* with us, boy.

David shook his head. He stared at the earth of the garden bed that he had prepared. Waited for a while.

I've got something inside for her, he said. For the girl. A doll for her birthday. Would you? David turned and looked into Rangi's eyes. Please?

Rangi was nodding and smiling. Don't I always David?

He straightened and lifted up the flax *kete*. Mem sent this bread for you. She still thinks you are a mad bugger. *Porangi* all right she said. Rangi laughed.

After a while Rangi said, you better get that doll for our Hine's gift.

Ah David said. Yes, and disappeared into the hut.

He emerged a few minutes later holding a doll wrapped in brown paper and tied with string. Its head and feet were sticking out at each end. Rangi nodded as he took it.

Is that what you call her? David asked. Sarah's daughter. You call her Hine?

Mem doesn't like Catherine.

David nodded.

ॐ

The sun continued to shine and dry the earth. And then as the
air stilled, the strumming of cicadas coming once again as a
chorus from the long grass. He dug his heels into the earth and
smelled the soil and crushed grass. Early spring. The bleating of
milk-hungry lambs.

Floss was sleeping on her side.

He ate the unleavened bread and mutton, some dried eel. Spat
out a piece of skin. Picked a thin bone from between his teeth
and drank his tea.

He was facing east. Where the sun came up. Shut his eyes for
a moment, resting them.

When the old man opened his eyes he saw the green Land Rover.
Saw it before he heard it. For a few moments he stared at the
silent moving vehicle as it passed the woolshed and came along
the track from the river. Then the sound of a gear shift and the
motor floated up to him. It had come from the direction of the
station homestead Wharekaka.

The Land Rover stopped and a woman got out. She put one
hand on her hip and another up to her forehead, shading her eyes.
She was looking straight up at him. She waved and called. Her
voice rose to where he was sitting.

Mr Monroe she called. Is that you?

He stood up and raised his hand.

It was Mrs Catherine McKenzie the owner. She must be over forty now, he thought. Sarah's daughter. Please no, he heard the words in his head.

Mr Monroe.

He raised his hand at her. Here, he called.

Would you come down? he heard her call out. Please.

The word please seemed to hang in the air and come up and over him like the hand of a blind man reaching out to greet him. Her please was a physical thing. He remembered how her mother had asked about her first born. She too had said please like that. Jamie. And how Jamie had loved plum jam.

He looked down at Catherine McKenzie, her daughter.

She still had one hand held up to her face and the other was suspended now in the act of waving.

She could be all the way from London he thought. Both his mother and her mother had always wanted to go to London and for the same reason. They said it was where all this began. The centre of the world. He had not understood what they meant. He had passed through that place but it was in the back of a prison lorry. The ship had arrived at night.

I'll be right down, he called out and with a flick of his wrist threw the tea out of the cup.

As the old man began to walk down the hill he thought of the Memorial Hall and the first time he had seen Catherine's mother. Sarah.

He stopped and looked down at her, still standing in the same attitude. Her mouth was open and she was smiling up at him. It was still a long way down.

He continued his descent, following sheep paths; walking diagonally to the slope and then zagging back to enable both himself and John to keep their balance. Watched carefully where he placed his feet.

⌇

Ruatane 1925

David had stopped at the clean marble statue of the young soldier outside the hall. The gleaming memorial seemed impossibly white and already as still as he could not imagine. It had been unveiled and spoken about that morning in a ceremony he had not attended. Somebody it was reported said it was a Giobanni and made of Carrara marble shipped from Italy and nobody except Colonel McKenzie, who had paid for it, knew what that meant.

The soldier had the smooth, pale face of the weeping boy David had seen in prison. The translucent lips of a silent angel. *Amore*. His perfect rifle in reverse arms. Left hand over right. Nails trimmed. The buttons of his marble tunic fastened. Stone ammunition pouches, water bottle, sheathed bayonet. The detail exact. Neatly wound puttees and hobnailed boots. White on white over bruised stone. *Amore*. An immense shimmering purity.

The soldier's eyes were open, shadowed, staring with infinite sadness at the ground. Unblinking. And he would never sing. Or smile or look up.

Beneath him the dead. Listed.

The words their name liveth for evermore.

David turned away. Walked into the Memorial Hall.

The women of the Papango Valley District had brought in their preserves and bottled fruit to help the charities for the returned men.

There were lines and lines of shining Agee jars. Regiments. Jars of peaches, yellow and clinging to the glass. White pears. Stewed apples with small clove knuckles. Two tables of beetroot and tomatoes.

A polished wooden board had been erected at one end of the hall. There were wooden scrolls and swags and miniature Ionic columns framing the list of names.

Dedicated to the Memory in gold-painted lettering.

To the men of the Papango Valley and Districts
who made the Ultimate Sacrifice
1914–1918
The Great War

The hall was decorated with fern fronds and flowers and coloured ribbons just like the dances before the war. A table of marmalade and jams.

David was standing next to the jams. He felt a hand on his forearm and looked down. A white-gloved hand gripped him.

The plum was his favourite, she said. Our Jamie did you know him? He was with the 7th Reinforcements. Wellington Regiment into France April 1918. Jamie Mitchell? He was seventeen. He had begged me you see and I could refuse him nothing. His father had said not to.

David said sorry. No. Tried to smile. Could not look at her.

Saw only the pearl earring on her left ear. An old fashioned pale grey hat. A black hatband. Hated the look in the mothers' eyes. Crazed, like the look of the mares when the foals were separated for branding, a white-eyed rolling desperate look, capable of anything. Or the mad ewes at docking, frantic, tongues blaring for their lost lambs. You couldn't...

It didn't bear thinking about.

He liked it on the plain scones, she said. With whipped cream. Wild blackberry too. Pikelets he was particularly fond of. Would you like some? I have both.

He shook his head at a place above her head. Looked towards a back door. No thank you. I'm all right, he said.

Scalded cream too of course. We all enjoyed that with the blackberry jelly. Jamie...She stopped herself.

You must be so pleased to be home David?

Yes missus. I am. Thank you.

I'm sorry I haven't...My name is Sarah. Sarah Mitchell. He was our only son you see. Our only child. She held out her gloved hand.

Pleased to meet you Mrs Mitchell. David made a noise of politeness, cleared his throat and held the end of her cotton-covered fingers, shook them gently once. Could not meet her eye. David Monroe, he said.

She smiled and nodded. I know you David she said. You worked for the Gill family. Their farm is next to ours. Jamie was about seven years younger than you. It was so sad about your mother. I am very sorry. And your father too of course.

Thank you Mrs Mitchell. It was a while ago now.

You were wounded weren't you? At Gallipoli? Served in France too.

He looked at the honour board and nodded. People here didn't know. About the court martial, the time in prison and the rest.

He held a pot of plum jam in his hand with a cloth top of blue and white checks. Tied with a blue ribbon. There was a label with a date on the side. *Plum Jam 1919 (Damson)*. He hadn't noticed her giving it to him.

He looked back at the honour board.

She was watching him. Frowned again. Touched her top lip with a finger.

Abernethy Samuel 1915

Brady Peter 1915

Sorry, she said. It is just…we miss him so. We will have to sell, more than likely. Getting too much. Jamie's father is older and we were waiting for him to take over. To come back. Her hand had returned to his arm. Rubbed his forearm and squeezed. She was looking at the honour board.

He looked away.

Brennan Joseph 1915

Brennan Liam 1915

Burns John 1915

He remembered John Johnny Burns, everybody called him that, John Johnny, drunk in Cairo. Laughing and trying to tell him a joke. Saying drink this Davie boy. And would you guess? I did it. She showed me her kish and I did it.

The Brennan boys, cousins he thought. Lost one on Chunuk Bair the other of wounds at sea was it? Not sure. But they had such kind faces those boys. Good with horses if he recalled. Joseph played the mouth accordion. Sang badly. Liam the fiddle.

She was speaking to him. It was something about trying to see a travelling clairvoyant Madame Kerensky at the Winter

Show but she had a cold and there is quite an industry in wooden limbs these days. Can't keep up. Do you believe in these things David?

I suppose not, he said and looked at her. Looked directly into her face. And then, immediately, back at the board.

Curruthers Paul 1918

Daly George 1915

Daly William 1917

She was looking where he was looking.

Mr and Mrs Daly, she said. They sold the farm and moved to Auckland. He started to drink. Found work in a boot factory. A good farmer that man. And poor Mrs Daly went to work in a seminary. Both of them, her sons, you see and then there was nothing left really. Sold out to Balmoral, well the old Balmoral. It's called Papanui now. All of the smaller places in the valley are selling to Balmoral it seems. An Australian fellow owns it, a gentleman. Lost an arm by the look of it.

David was turning the pot of jam in his hands.

Washing and cleaning for the priests seem somehow most fitting for Mrs Daly don't you think? I mean there is none other to do it for, not to be unkind. Much comfort in their kind words, Mass and the candles before Our Lady isn't it?

David found Jamie. His name on the board.

She had been talking as if it was what she had to do. As if it was the clothing she wore. Most of it meant nothing. And he knew she also knew this, like putting food into your mouth and not knowing what you were eating, just chewing. Because that is what you did. She didn't remember what she had just said. She didn't remember what she had eaten that morning or what clothes she wore.

He felt her read her son's name. She moved her feet and gripped his arm tighter. Relaxed and then kept talking.

The weather has been good for a while now hasn't it? Good for the bobby calves to put on condition, the slips are milking well too. Jamie was such a bright boy. Especially with mechanical things. I remember him fixing the separator once. There are too many of those Californian thistles along the river paddocks. Gerald said the seed will blow for miles. Did you know Peter Whiting? Had a stutter, poor man but a very good shearer. Shore some, I forget what on our place.

Two-tooth wethers, David said. They were both looking at the board.

Mitchell James 1918
Whiting Peter 1918

Yes it was, Sarah said. Two-tooth wethers. She looked at him, how did…You…

The green and earthy smell of the cut tree ferns was strong in the hall. Tobacco smoke was drifting in from outside where the men had gone to smoke.

He was staring into her face now. She had stopped talking and was frowning just so and staring back at him. Her open wet mouth. Her teeth shining in the uncertain smile she was giving him. A tremor passing across her lips. Her skin. Her eyes looking into his eyes. For a moment there was nothing else.

He said, *jesus*.

She stepped back as if he had insulted her.

He had been able to smell her well before he had the courage to look at her face. From the moment she placed her hand upon his arm he had felt the blood surge up into his balls and cock. It was no use, he couldn't stop it. Felt her fingers curl around the edge of his forearm. Each finger and thumb. The shape of each one. The bones underneath, the skin and nails, the tendons. The quiet strength as they pressed into him. Moved back and forth with such comfortable familiarity.

He wanted to open his mouth and call out.

Did you know, she whispered. How...

Smelled her. That vanilla smell of a washed woman gently sweating. White gardenia talcum powder.

He stepped back too then. Said I. Nothing.

Turned to escape.

She saw his desire. Looked down at him. The clear, large shape of his cock in his trousers. Straining at the material, unmistakable. She changed feet and blushed. Imagined what was there. Knew. Looked away and then, to save him embarrassment, took two quick steps forward, leaned closer on tiptoes and kissed him on the cheek, holding again his forearm. Another hand on his biceps. Her skirts brushing his trousers. Hiding him. Caressing him.

David, she said, bless you. It's all right. It's all right.

He felt tears come into his eyes. His throat closed. The crown of his head burning, it was as if it had begun to catch fire.

Thought the words, it's not all right. You are so tender. I want you to hold me. I want to be able to. Please. Thank you for just... for your hand on my arm. I feel as if I should not.

Made a choking noise as if to speak. Could not say anything, shook his head. Said oh my. Tried to say dear me, his throat closing with emotion. Pressed a thumb into his forehead, between his eyes. Shook his head. Said nothing more.

He turned and walked quickly from the hall. Leaving by the back door.

She stood, bewildered, almost panting in her sudden need of him. To take him in her arms. That ache that sounds like yes. That wet coiling arch between her legs; the opening of herself that has as much to do with taking as giving and the urgency making no sense at all. Wanting, inexplicably, to sit and then stand. To swim. That's it, to swim in the sea with hard wet nipples. Urgent to the thumb. Knowing as she felt this how shocking it was. That this thing, this cold stone of loss she had been holding into herself, had just for this moment gone. As if somebody had lifted her off the ground, shaken her free and said just be alive now. You, Sarah Jane Williams. You. Who I was.

She had last swum in the sea when she was eighteen. At Pungarehu, and she thought Oh god that was where David lost his mother.

She was slightly crouched over. She blinked and straightened. Touched a hand to her face and hair and then her ear. Tugged an earring and wet her bottom lip with her tongue.

Glanced at the back door where David had left. He had not closed it properly in his rush. It was moving, gently, still slightly ajar.

Her throat constricted in a want to go through that door. As if a part of her, invisible, lifted and flew there.

The band was playing the Donegal Reel. They were playing it badly. Liam Brennan the best fiddle player in the district was dead. Buried in the Aegean Sea.

She would never go through the door.

Smiling women were asking the returned soldiers to dance. Some of the women old enough to be their mothers and grandmothers. They were bringing them home. Back here from where they had left to go off to war. She smiled and looked around to see who was looking. There was no one.

Except of course as usual her darling husband Gerald. He nodded to her. His eyes holding so much kindness. It was only in his mouth that she saw still the rawness, the loss that was their Jamie. Gerald had such a tender mouth. And the way he bit his bottom lip beneath his moustache. His hand raised to her from his knee. A small nod.

But then, again, she suddenly thought, the rawness in him is my grief. He has already brought Jamie home. Now he is waiting for me. She smiled at her husband, his shining eyes.

And she knew then that she would accept, and go on from here. And it would be all right.

This was what she told David when she came to visit him, to bring him the bottled fruit he had forgotten. Peaches, stewed apple and of course Jamie's plum jam. A tea cake.

But not the first time.

It would be the third visit, she would talk to him. Tell him things she could tell no other. Touch the scars the shrapnel had left across his face, neck and shoulders. Across his lower back, hips and buttocks.

Would feel her feet leave the ground when he said I wish I were a shining trout, and I would swim into you. All the way into you and know where to find your heart. And I would eat it whole.

Could not believe this simple damaged man could know to

say such things. Would come to believe that God had sent him to her.

Hold him. Shudder with an unknown and unimagined sensuality as he first entered her.

He hadn't looked at Sarah's daughter Catherine again until he reached her. He had led John down and Floss had followed.

He came to the pale, shell-rock roadway about fifty yards from her. He turned and walked up to her and stopped. Looked at her and nodded.

Ah, she said. Mr Monroe. She had been watching him. Stretched out her hand. He took it and held it. She shook his hand. And said twice in two days.

The old man looked into her eyes and then quickly above her head. Mrs McKenzie, he said and then cleared his throat. His voice broke slightly as he spoke. They let go each other's hand.

Oh look a lambkin. She almost smiled, her lips pressed down on themselves. A small muscle in her jaw flexed. She reached out to touch the lamb in the *pikau*.

Her jaw, it was like her mother's. The same cleft in her chin.

Mr Monroe, she said again, turned to him. Reached up and patted John on the neck, kept her hand on the gelding, fingers in the mane.

Mrs McKenzie. His reply cautious.

She spoke while still holding the horse. I wanted to ask if you have a moment.

The old man said nothing, stared at her and then turned and gestured behind himself. The lambing. The early ewes.

Ah yes she said, I know you are busy. But there are a couple of things. Is everything all right?

Yes Mrs McKenzie.

She paused. I mean in regard to the men from the government? They called me yesterday morning. I had no way of letting you know before they came.

Oh yes. The old man nodded. Bit of a wild goose chase they said.

Ah good.

Was there something else? He turned and gave a short whistle to Floss who was wandering over a rise to inspect something. Here to me girl. He cleared his throat. Sorry.

Well yes there was Catherine said. She stopped and looked away and then at her feet.

The old man fiddled with the reins in his hands, undid the buckle and did it up again. Yes Mrs McKenzie?

I have been wanting…For some time now I have been wanting to ask you about my mother.

Your mother? He frowned.

Yes, she said, you did know her? You mentioned her yesterday. The hair.

He cleared his throat. Nodded and took a nub of skin on the inside of his mouth between his teeth. Held his beard with his left hand. Yes, he said, I knew your mother.

I didn't you see. Particularly well, she said. At all really. I was very young when she was, when she died. And my dad.

The old man looked over her head and away to the north east and the bush-covered high ridges. He nodded. Looked up at the sky and clouds. Turned his head to watch the rain-full clouds easing over them. Noting the direction of the wind.

Have you been to London? She wanted to go to London, he said, still looking at the clouds.

Pardon me?

Your mother did. And mine for that matter. He looked back at her.

Catherine stepped slightly to her left and shaded her eyes again as if to see the old man from another perspective. Paused and then said, no. No, I haven't been to London.

I passed through London, he said. A big city, but I didn't see any of it really. The noise of it went on for a long time. He shook his head. No, he said. But another man told me that he had arrived with a pocket full of dried currants.

She was staring at him, unsure what to say.

Sorry, he said. He watched her. She was quite beautiful. Her mouth slightly open. Her mouth was his mother's mouth. He wanted to kiss her mouth. Kiss himself, mirrored. Her nose was his mother's nose. Her eyes and hair her mother's. He looked at her and thought there is no seaweed there. No sand beneath her tongue. My mother had I believe sand beneath her tongue when they found her. Seaweed in her hair. How could I know such a thing?

This woman could not be just this woman. She could not be. She would always be something else.

No, she said, it's quite all right. Everyone says you don't. That you are. She paused and then said, different.

He smiled and looked back up the rise. Said, different. Laughed. Yes. Crazy old man. *Koro porangi.*

After some time she said, I saw you once when I was a girl, turning in a circle. You were all alone in one of the small clearings above the Abernethy Flats. And you had your arms out and you were spinning. Your eyes were closed. It looked like you were dancing.

The old man was staring straight ahead. He nodded. She sensed him tense and then relax. I never told anyone. Not even Auntie Mem, she said.

He looked at her. So you know then that it is true?

What?

What they say. I am really crazy. An old fool.

I don't know. When I rode back I tried it. But I just got dizzy. I told Drew to do it when he came over. He was always coming over from Wharekaka. Just about lived at our place. Auntie Mem used to call him *te kahuiti*, the little hawk. He whooped and yelled out look at me Cat with his eyes rolling back in his head and fell into Auntie's bean trellis. He used to call me Cat.

Catherine sniffed and laughed. She went crook at him.

She was fierce all right.

Catherine looked at him. You didn't ask me what I was doing there. To see you. To see you like that. You fell over and curled up in a ball. It wasn't the only time I saw you dancing by yourself like that.

He shook his head. That doesn't matter. A man called Mahmoud taught me this thing. He said…The old man stopped, pressed his lips together and then continued to speak. He was a Sufi. They are mad, crazed with the love for God.

God? Catherine frowned at him.

The Beloved Allah. He said it was how we align ourselves with the universe and therefore heal our damaged selves. By

270

remembering our divine self. Something like that. But that is not even close to what I am meaning.

What do you mean? Catherine asked. She was fondling the lamb's head. Mr Monroe?

He shrugged. The words are not right. I don't know. The old man laughed then. That is the point Mahmoud said. To stop knowing anything in order to remember everything.

Catherine frowned again, studied him for a moment. Those government men said you could clear up some matters. That is what they said, matters in relation to your time in the first war.

The old man shook his head. It was after Gallipoli, he said. This man Mahmoud and I, we were wounded together trying to save an Australian boy. Then in hospital together. And. Well. We sort of stayed together for a while.

Catherine moved to the nose of the gelding. Rubbed his nose. The muscle in her jaw flexed. This is not really my business Mr Monroe but I wanted to ask you.

This is your business Mrs McKenzie, the old man said.

She looked into his face. An old man with a long white beard. Calm eyes and white hair cropped short under his hat. Tufts and patches. It was like he had done it himself with old fashioned sheep shears. She had a vision suddenly of him standing in front of a mirror trying to cut his own hair. The reputation of an eccentric hermit. Irritable and strange. Thought, we have the same colour eyes.

The old man was speaking to her.

Mahmoud said once that when we turn, when it's done properly, it is only the beautiful music that is being played that keeps the dancer from disappearing into the sky. Into Heaven.

Catherine was watching him. That is quite lovely, she said.

He would hum when he showed me and he recited verses from Jalal al-Din in Persian. Or, I should say, try to show me. He had lost a foot you see. Forget yourself. Take your head off and put on a pumpkin. The old man smiled.

She was watching him.

He looked back into her eyes, swallowed. I am sorry, he said.

No. Don't.

They were quiet again.

That's what the government men really wanted to ask me about yesterday. That time. And Mahmoud. He was a prisoner and I helped him escape. We didn't get far. I was court martialled and found guilty. In prison for a time. And then I was a stretcher bearer in France.

Catherine was looking at him. Holding her arms across her body.

The old man shrugged as if somehow to bring their meeting to a close.

Did you know my mother well Mr Monroe?

He waited.

You see I have nothing, she said. Of her. Catherine was staring at him, as if trying to see something that wasn't there.

Nothing?

There is an old bible with some notes in the fly leaf. And a pressed flower.

A flower. The old man's head was shaking slightly.

A cornflower I think. Did you know my brother James? He was killed in the First World War. In France I think. 1918.

A cornflower the old man said. My. Your name is Catherine isn't it?

They stared at each other. The old man with the white beard holding a horse. The handsome middle-aged woman looking as if she wanted to weep.

Please, she said. Did you? Did you know them?

No, he said. No. Put his hand on the lamb's head.

Yes. He looked up at her. Said you have your mother's voice Catherine. It is as if I can hear her yet.

Tell me.

He stared at her. Nodded.

⌒

She was sitting on a pony she called Dinny outside his musterer's hut.

David, she said, I have missed you so.

She lifted her right leg up, crossed it over in front of herself and slid off the pony. She was holding a basket draped with a black and white cloth.

Took a pace towards him. Stepped onto the bottom step of his hut. Arranged her skirts.

He held the door open. He had seen her ride up from the river crossing.

There was a memorial parade yesterday, she said. I wanted to come and tell you about it.

They both knew this was a formality, an excuse.

She tied the reins of the pony to the rail outside his hut. Touched her hair, smiled and walked up the steps.

These are for you Sarah. He held out three cornflowers.

She looked at them. Put down the basket. Her hands closed over his hand. Thank you, she whispered. The blue is so pretty. Did you grow them?

He nodded. My mother liked cornflowers. Mrs Lawrence got the seed for me.

She held the flowers and put her left hand on his biceps, stood up on her toes, leaned forward and kissed his cheek.

Thank you David. She stepped back and smiled. May I come in?

Of course. Please.

She picked up the basket and walked through the door.

He closed the door of his hut and turned to her. A parade?

They are calling it Anzac Day, she said. It was the day our boys and the Australians landed at Gallipoli. I still don't know why we even went there. Do you? She turned to him.

Her poise almost gave way. She made a noise in her throat as she looked at him. Blinked once and then again as if to focus. Smiled and said…You. You are so. Stared and smiled.

David smiled back at her. No, he said. I don't really.

Sarah shook her head. Taking a breath. Talking. As if it was the most normal of things. Looking away.

We travelled into town the day before, she paused for another breath, before yesterday and stayed in the Dominion Hotel.

Did she know how beautiful she was? How she glowed?

Gerald drove the little mare Velvet. She is just new to the harness but behaved herself admirably. Fine girl.

He was holding an apple, a Cox's orange pippin. Dappled and striped red yellow and green. Yes, he said. I know that little mare.

274

She is neat. Nice feet. Then he said, have you seen this apple? It has such...

Smiled. Tears in his eyes.

Sarah was sitting at the table and cutting through a tea cake she had taken from the basket. She looked at him and began to stand.

No, he said, don't. It's all right. He held up a hand, go on Sarah. He looked at the tea cake with the bread knife sticking out of it on an angle.

She sat and began to speak quietly. An old school chum of Gerald's she said, John Corbett, he let us paddock her with them. He lost his son Ken in France with the Signal Corps. Ken's sister Louisa was just married last week. Beautiful looking girl. Expecting by the shape of her walk, springing, Gerald said. Don't run for the train love. We used to laugh about such gossip. Now it doesn't matter.

No David said, no matter.

She looked at him. David you look so sad.

He nodded.

Here, she said and passed him a slice of the cake.

The wind moved through the trees outside the hut. A team of dogs barked somewhere and further away the sound of sheep bawling as they were mustered down through gullies from the hill country.

She held his hand in both of hers.

After a while he asked, and how was it, the parade?

She smiled. It was drizzling a bit, she said. She let go of his hand and pressed the tip of finger on a yellow crumb. Brought it to her mouth. But it didn't matter. Colonel McKenzie was in charge. He let the men in wheelchairs lead the parade. Behind them the one-legged and one-armed men. Then the main body. I saw some of the men so drunk they could barely walk. One of them collapsed and vomited. His friends took him off.

The main body, David said.

Yes, Sarah said. That's what they called it.

They are still getting used to being home. He stood up and walked away from the table.

Were you all right Sarah?

She glanced at him. They had the Salvation Army band playing It's a Long Way to Tipperary. Then God Save the King.

Ah, David smiled and moved his head. King George the Fifth.

Then we listened to the speeches. A Member of Parliament telling us of pride and sacrifice and the nation. The British Empire. It almost all felt worth it for a minute then.

Sarah?

They looked at each other.

You know why I am not there don't you?

She nodded. You told me. Yes I know.

I was a criminal. A traitor.

She stared at him and went on speaking. We sang the Old Rugged Cross and Abide With Me. There were so many other women dressed in black, some of them quite young. Their faces seemed so very white. But then it was raining and the concrete was quite wet.

He shook his head. Look at me he said and listen to me.

Yes, she said. She looked up.

Your words, he said they are like the rain. Or leaves in the wind, they are just falling off you.

Sarah nodded. Yes.

They mean nothing to your heart.

She shook her head. What?

You are preoccupied with your own feeling of what should be. You have become…encased in the prison of your grief. Just another white face reflected in the wet concrete. It is becoming a lie.

She stood up, the chair scraping was loud on the floorboards.

What, she cried. What are you saying?

David was staring at her. Yes you are mad with loss but it is not hatred we must remember but the truth. Your grief is a veil on the known. It is only a possibility. I…

She slapped the cake to one side. It fell onto the floor, the plate smashed and the knife clattered away. How could you say that? she shouted at him. Her hands shaking.

Because I love you.

What? Her head moved from side to side as if she could not believe what she had just heard.

I love you.

Where, she gasped, where do you come from to say such things to me? That is so stupid. She was glaring at him. One hand raised and then lowered. So hateful. What would you know?

No, he said. It is not. It the opposite. Remember? He placed his hand on his chest. I come from here Sarah. Where you come from. There is no hope you see. I don't know anything but this, I am a fool.

Her mouth was open, eyes wide. Tears spilling from them.

Please, he whispered. Don't. He stood.

She stared back, a hand over her mouth. Feet apart, braced.

He took her outstretched hand in his. I am a fool.

You give me...she whispered and paused. Life, she said. And then you take it away. Don't touch me. Let go.

David nodded, he still held her hand.

She said, the night I met you I wanted to swim in the sea. At Pungarehu.

They both waited. He looked at her. Nodded yes, a question.

It is true she said. And I don't have any idea why.

Then he reached out once again and with his thumb pushed open the neck of her dress. Her shoulder was naked.

Your dress. His voice was soft. Take it off.

Then the sound in her throat coming up could have been Jamie and it also could have been Jesus, or Yes.

‮❦‬

No. The old man frowned. Said no again.

He walked past her outstretched hand. He led John by the reins. They crossed the track and made their way down a slope that fell away towards the Papango River. The black and white dog followed. You can come with me if you want he said without looking back.

Mr Monroe, she said. But he and the rump of the horse had already gone past her.

I don't want to talk about the past Catherine.

Catherine stood staring into the space where he had been. Then she became aware of herself standing there. One hand had reached out to him, her heart beating as if for a secret lover. She hesitated for a moment, dropped her arm.

Turned and began to walk after the old man and the horse and the dog.

They had walked for about a hundred yards when he pointed and said, over that rise there is natural shelter. A lot of the ewes go there to lamb.

She was breathing hard. Had to hurry to catch up to him. They stopped on the lip, below them a dish-shaped hollow, fringed on the east side with inward-leaning kanuka trees. The grass greened wet where the sun had touched it but on the south side of the hollow it was still in shadow and frozen white. Under the trees it was dry.

He let the reins trail and walked into the hollow. Floss trotted alongside him. He was carrying his knife in his right hand.

He turned back to Catherine, pointed with the knife. There.

A ewe was nosing at her dead lamb, anxious and almost oblivious of the intruders. Floss ran over to her and the ewe put her head down and charged.

In behind, the old man said. Floss. He walked over to the dead lamb. Knelt and tested the knife edge with his thumb. Turned and smiled at Catherine. His voice gentle. Go and get that newborn in the *pikau* would you please Catherine?

The ewe stood off a few feet and blared, mouth open.

The old man picked up the dead lamb. Made several quick cuts around the neck and hocks. Stood, holding the back legs under his boots and started to peel the skin off the lamb. When it stuck, he bent and used his knife to free it.

He was holding the dripping pelt. Nodded to Catherine as Floss crept in and sniffed the naked carcass.

Catherine walked over and put the mewling lamb down on the ground. The old man placed the wet pelt on its back and tied the loose, bloody ends around its body. The lamb bleated and the ewe made a deep belly reply. He used some baling twine to secure the pelt onto the live lamb.

There, he said again. Gently urged the lamb towards the ewe and stepped back.

The ewe came over to the lamb and sniffed at the pelt. The lamb bleated again and began to nose along the ewe's flank. Then it was down on its knees and seeking out her teats. She stepped over it. Turned again, smelled the skin of her stillborn. Touching her nose along the back of the lamb. Tongue out, blared again. Then she stopped still and allowed the new lamb to feed.

The old man walked over to the carcass and picked it up. That's it, he said. This one for the eels Catherine.

She nodded at him. The old man standing there with the torn body of the freshly skinned lamb in his hand.

He turned away. Gasped in pain and held his side just above the left hip.

Are you all right? She stepped towards him with anxious eyes, reaching.

Fine, he said. Bit sore. Moved away from her hands. Pulled a muscle I think. He was quiet, limping back towards the horse.

She noticed he had dropped the carcass. His bloodied hands had marked the jacket below the breast pocket. Mr Monroe?

I feel fine Mrs McKenzie. He was standing next to John holding the stirrup iron. Just a twinge.

But, she said and scooped up the carcass. Wondered why he had gone back to the more formal name. No longer Catherine.

The eels, he said and pointed with a look in the direction of the river. Smiled. Whispered sorry.

She stared at him and then, after a moment, nodded. He watched as she carried the body of the lamb down the slope towards the river's fringe of scrub and flax and rangiora.

Then he saw the ewe walk up and out of the hollow followed by the lamb with the pelt tied around its body. The skin would fall away in a day or two and that would be enough. The ewe paused to graze and the lamb tried to feed again, but the ewe kept walking. It was content.

And then he looks up and watches the rain-filled clouds passing. Murmurs oh, my. Raises his hand and falls.

The old man sees his hand as it takes his fall and the soft, wet ground curling up under his hand. Mud and grass. His head striking the ground. Sarah's daughter moving over him. Feels her hand under his arm. His face against the wet ground. This powerful smell of grass.

Catherine's voice calling to him. It is high and frightened.

It is his smell as she reaches him and kneels. Strangely, Stockholm Tar she thinks. Or that he washes with coal tar soap, Wrights or Pears.

This is not the smell of shellshock. Not the smell of mad old man. He is clean and strange and beautiful.

And he is, the old man, calling her Sarah, her mother's name saying I am all right Sarah. My head's on fire. I can fly, Sarah. If I wave my arms up and down I can fly. Look at me I have my clothes on back to front and inside out. I am a pelican.

He is trying to smile and she has never heard such silly things.

Mr Monroe she keeps saying and holding him as she kneels next to him. Her knee wet and sinking into the soft ground. Floss is barking. Walking backwards and barking.

She gets him onto his hands and knees. Can you stand? She says and then, let go of the reins Mr Monroe.

John is looming over them. Catherine takes the reins out of his fingers and lets them fall. John turns away.

The old man is too heavy for her to lift and he seems unable to move. She lifts one hand and moves it forward and then the other. Does the same to his knees. Moving them one by one like loading a reluctant yearling onto a float for the first time. Hears him groan. Knows of his bad hip from a fall, that white pony with the hairy ears when she was a girl.

Old man Monroe had that young horse he was breaking come back on him. He is on crutches up there all by himself. Doctor said it was to have split open his pelvis.

Auntie Mem took some bread and smoked eel up to him. She sitting on her pony outside his hut while Auntie knocked on the door. Remembered his white beard in the black gap of his opened door. His glance at her.

Floss runs in and nips at her arm. Growls as she does it.

Catherine growls back at her. Hisses get out of it.

She got him to the Land Rover and rolled him over onto his back. He lifted his knees and pushed himself upwards. Then, with Catherine pulling, and his pushing with his feet, he managed to sit up and lean against the wheel. He raised his right hand and placed it in the middle of his chest.

His eyes were closed and he was breathing, open mouthed, in small panting motions. A blue tinge around his lips. Oh god.

Catherine, still kneeling, leaned back on her heels. Can you stand do you think Mr Monroe?

The old man tried to speak, closed his mouth and wet his lips. His hand raised slightly. Just give me a minute.

She nodded, murmured all right and stood up.

Much later the sensations of being undressed and Catherine's voice saying look at these doctor.

Shrapnel wounding more than likely from a blast. Looks like he's been through a cheese grater no? I have seen this before. Soldiers usually. Lucky not to have suffered major tissue loss. These are very old wounds. Something may still be in there.

Fingers palpating along his hip and ribs.

He tried to say Orion's belt across my arse. Was unable to speak. Wanting strangely to laugh and say they gave us such lessons in astronomy the British Navy.

Her voice. Coming from a long way above him. She must be speaking to him, he thought. Although it could be that she is speaking to herself.

Mr Monroe I don't know if you can hear me.

He felt her place her hand on his chest. Felt the rise and fall of it.

A woman's hand on the centre of his chest.

Her beautiful fingers.

After a while she said well. It doesn't matter.

You knew my mother and my father and I think my brother who was dead seven years before I was born.

She waited then said, I was told she never got over the loss.

So it was what it was for almost an hour. The woman sitting next to the old man on the bed. Her bending forward, seated, leaning out with a hand placed on the old man's chest. It began with memories and pain.

She began, after a while, speaking to him.

I went back to the place where the house was once but there was nothing there. Just the stones from the windfallen fruit in the grass. They were sharp under my feet.

She waited. It was very quiet in the room for a long time. The wind sighed outside. The house creaked. Creaked again and settled.

It is, she said, no matter. It is nothing worth...

Stopped and then said, no I think I would like to tell you who I am. She was quiet again. Silent.

Isn't that the strangest of things?

She listened to her breathing and watched the old man. Her breathing began to coincide with his. She lifted her left hand from his chest, reached out, hesitated; her hand above his face. Then reached further to smooth back his white hair.

There it is she whispered.

When I was born, she smiled and tears spilled from her eyes, my mother went mad and became invisible.

She took her hand away from the rough cropped hair of the old man. Let the back of her fingers touch his cheek, rest on his beard. Almost touched his mouth, the ragged ear. She sat back. Her hands in her lap.

A boy at school yelled that she was a mad slut. Where is she? Your mother, where?

Catherine sniffed and cleared her throat. Well. I never told Auntie Mem about that. Drew found out and got so angry that he gave him a hiding.

Anyway. She waited. Anyway Mr Monroe.

She watched him. The hair across his chest like white grass in a hayfield. The pale shapes of scars. She leaned and took hold of the top blanket, drew it over his chest.

After a while she said I had instead a woman whose name meant memory and sweet leaf but I always knew her as Auntie or Auntie Mem. And there was her man Rangi. He was so big he would block out the sun. I still think of him whenever I eat mussels or dried eel. He would carry Drew on his shoulders. Auntie said he was of a common tribe and she was *ngati porou* much superior. But, he would say, he had the best *horepara* though. The best silver bellied eels eh *ngati porou* woman? Look Hine she is laughing on the inside but all fierce on the face. Typical of those *ngati porou* girls. So *meke*. So you know. Sexy.

Catherine laughed softly to herself. They were beautiful.

The old man's eyes were closed and still. His right hand twitched.

My father had gone too but then he was here. There is a grave, a headstone. He died the year I was born 1925. Everyone said he was a good man. There was nothing for my mother.

Catherine was holding the old man's hand. It was heavy between her own. Squeezed two large fingers.

Auntie Mem gave me her bible. She said old Expectations had given it to her. Old Expectations that was what she called Drew's dad. Mr McKenzie.

Catherine opened the bible. My mother, she said, has written in the fly leaf. I want to read this to you.

Beloved.

I see you laughing among the red flowers of France.

In prayer and then at peace somehow in lanes calling to me. The dogs Mother. Look to the dogs.

All ways forgiving my mistakes. Your laughter washed me and made me laugh. You know this my darling.

You remain with me. Eternal.

He saw you ascending. I do believe he came from the house of the Lord. 13:2. Hebrews.

But you will be who you will be. Romans 10:20. Uninvited, you found me. Known I did not ask for you.

She placed the bible down and turned back to him. She was staring at the old man and then she shook her head. You gave me things on my birthday.

I am sorry that little pup you left for me drowned in Mimi Creek. The book of poems by Lewis Carroll and the kitten. I asked who you were but Auntie said you were just *porangi*. Rangi would scold Mem and say to leave you alone, you were shy. I still have the doll.

Why didn't you say anything old man?

There was nothing. He slept and breathed. His lips almost translucent.

Catherine stood up from her seat. Walked backwards looking at him. Turned away as the choking anger came over her.

You knew she said. And then as she heard her voice said it

again. You knew what happened. Why wouldn't you tell me?

Waited.

She screamed then.

It was a sound as unlike her as she had ever known. You fucking bastard she screamed at the old man lying on the bed. You stupid uncaring fucking bastard man you. I had no mother. No father. There was just some great thing that no one spoke about. It was empty. Just empty. I had no one who... would.

Catherine was crouching in the room, reaching, her hands imploring the sleeping old man. You knew, she screamed again. You knew. All those years. Her voice hurting her throat. Why didn't you? You knew.

Then she half turned and grabbed onto her shoulders. Sobbed, held herself tightly hunched and nodded.

Then straightened. Said yes yes. Yes all right. I'm sorry.

I know you came to Drew's funeral. And I thank you for that. She breathed through her mouth. Big angry breaths. Mem told me you sent a crystal vase as a wedding gift. And a mirror. That you were not invited I am sorry.

Catherine walked then the length of the room. Stood leaning against the door. Both hands once more holding her shoulders, her chin tucked into her chest.

After a while she whispered but you knew nothing of my life.

All right, she said. The last thing she my mother wrote in the back of the bible was this.

The world is 1925 and not as it should be.

And underneath,

Beloved

The evening is long and blue and the old owl will call by and by. We will rest together all together soon enough.

The psalms tell us such. Scripture holds the comfort.

My mother was a woman of deep faith I am sure. Her love of God.

Catherine looked at him for a long time. Then she stopped looking. The old man was still asleep. He stirred, eyelids fluttered and then stilled again.

There was the glow of a small lamp on the table beside the bed. It made a white circle around her hands as she placed the bible on the table next to it.

His breathing rattled as if something had caught in his throat. He gave a gentle snoring sound.

Please, she said to the old man lying on the bed. Not yet.

The white hair on his wide moving chest. There were so many scars. His big hands with black blood under the nails. The short, badly cropped hair on his head. His spreading white beard.

Ssssh she whispered as he groaned. Sarah.

The old man almost woke then. It is…he said softly, it's raining…the lambs need to be…has John a cover?

She squeezed his shoulder.

Remember to cross over the backstraps. Mumbled again, Mahmoud. Then Sarah oh she is, and smiled, so very fine. Swift you are a good dog. They both can't ride a bicycle.

She comforted him again. One hand on his hand. One hand on his chest. It rose and fell.

He slept for some time then.

Catherine sat with him. Once she wept. Wiped her eyes on the inside elbow of her shirt. Continued to hold his hand. Slept.

She was woken as the old man arched on the bed and his throat gave a slight choking noise. His chest rose up and then eased back. He seemed to become smaller as the air went out of him.

Catherine stood and walked backwards towards the open window. Her hand to her mouth as the thin white curtains blew around her.

This is our earth it is God and sees you as you see God. What is looking when you see? I say to you it is the mind of God. Hear what I say. Hear what I say with your entire being. Many believe this is a pronouncement of death, this blasphemy.

Mahmoud's eyes had become eyes never seen. They became moving oceans and clouds streaming across the land at dawn. A huge sun rising from the desert. Grasslands, mountains and moons appearing through mist. Lakes reflecting the sky. They became a hundred suns and a hundred colours of suns. The moving sea and his mother's hair blowing in the wind. Her smile at his walking towards her. He could see the stars beginning to race over him in the shape of men's faces; mountains rising out of clouds; the life season of a plant in the space of ten breaths. The lighted faces of prophets streaming upon him from out of the darkness.

Mahmoud is sitting on a white block of stone in the shadow of the wall. Behind him, in bright sun, there is an arch covered with a grape vine. The leaves turning orange and red in the autumn.

Assalamu alaiküm, brother. He is smiling in welcome. Peace be upon you. You are coming home. Come.

And upon you peace, David is saying.

Wa alaiküm assalaam.

291

Acknowledgments

The poems, aphorisms and some detail of Rumi's life and Sufi teachings and philosophy have come from:

thinking like the universe: the sufi path of awakening by Pir Vilayat Inayat Khan. Thorsons—HarperCollins Publishers 1999.

Rumi Past and Present East and West: The Life Teachings and Poetry of Jalal al Din Rumi by Franklin D. Lewis. Oneworld Publications, 2000.

Details of the Number One Field Punishment have been represented from a letter by Archibald Baxter (father of the poet James K. Baxter) as published in: *New Zealanders at War* by Michael King. Heinemann Publishers 1981.

Some of the locations on the Western Front in World War One have come from: *Spring Offensive* by Glyn Harper. HarperCollins Publishers 2003.

Many thanks to Mandy Brett, senior editor at Text Publishing, who did such a wonderful job.

Also thanks to Maryvonne Bestel of UWA who lent me an umbrella and generous advice on some points of French translation, and to Samina Yasmeen, also of UWA, for some points of Arabic translation.